THE BACKUP PRINCESS

A Royal Romcom

Royally Kissed
Book 1

KATE O'KEEFFE

Wild Lime Books

Wild Lime
Books

About This Book

When a Texas gal punches a prince instead of curtsying, you know this isn't your grandmother's fairy tale.

Taking the bull by the horns is child's play compared to ruling Malveaux. Yet here I am, a Texas girl turned princess, swapping tacos for a tiara. Then I meet Europe's most eligible bachelor, the irritatingly handsome Prince Alexander, and accidentally deck him instead of curtsying.

Oops.

I'd feel bad if he wasn't such a self-satisfied jerk.

Now, I'm racing against a royal clock that ticks with the urgency of a preening peacock, trying not to let down my newfound country or my own wild heart. Alexander? He's a walking contradiction, with a smirk that heats my blood and eyes that tell tales of a depth I didn't expect.

Decisions aren't exactly my rodeo, but this time, my choice could cost me my new crown—or lead to a love story that rewrites my happily ever after. Will this Texas girl rise to the royal challenge, or is this one fairytale destined to end with the slipper never found?

Introduction

 Prince Alexander the Great, as you know I so love to call our Prince of Royal Hotness, is nothing short of a runaway success in America. Are you surprised? Of course you're not. He's Prince Alexander Archibald George Canossa of Ledonia., aka Prince McHottie. Everyone adores him! And if they don't, well they clearly don't know him.

Americans are certainly not immune to his charms.

Much like when European Royals have visited their fair shores in the past, our Prince has been whisked from glamorous function to glamorous function, always representing Ledonia with the flair and charismatic presence we have learned to expect from Prince McHottie, the future heir to the Ledonian throne.

Which is more than I can say for our neighbor these days. Poor Malveaux, losing its heir when Prince Nicolas decided the job wasn't for him. With no obvious backup option, this reporter wonders whatever will the Malveauxian royal family do?

We've got no such problems in our fair country, thanks to the delectable Alexander and his fine siblings. It is true we are blessed, and we're counting the hours until you're back home with us, Prince Alexander. God speed!

#PrinceMcHottie
#TimetoGiveHimBack
#MalveauxInAPickle

Your ever devoted royal correspondent,

Fabiana Fontaine xx

Chapter 1

Maddie

I know it's weird, but I've never really felt like I fit into my own life. Like something went wrong in the planning a life part of my creation and I'm here by some kind of freak cosmic accident, when I was in fact meant to have an entirely different life.

Although I've got no clue what that other life might be, what I do know is being a sales assistant for a glazing company in an industrial area of Houston, Texas, doesn't feel like the life I was meant to have.

Told you it was weird.

I search the database, blinking at the screen with its serial numbers and product descriptions until I land on that line item I'm searching for. "We do have that item in stock, sir," I say into my headset. "How many were you looking for?"

I feel an elbow hit my ribs in rapid succession and look up from my spreadsheet at my best friend, Chloe. Her brown eyes are wide, her not so naturally pink hair pulled into a top knot, as she gestures in the least subtle way I think I've ever seen as someone breezes past my desk.

I open my mouth to say "What?" but if I'm honest, I already know what. Or rather who.

Eric Camden.

Office flirt, contender for most handsome salesman in the whole state of Texas, and my crush for one year, three months, and about four and a half days, aka the day Eric started working here.

He's tall and broad, with dark blond hair and dreamy blue eyes. He told us he's descended from Vikings, and I'll admit, sometimes I lie in bed at night and imagine him dressed as a Viking, all manly and strong.

But let's not go there.

At the sight of him, my heart rate picks up and I swallow, my throat suddenly dry.

His eyes flash to mine as he saunters past with his long-legged stride, and I can only imagine the way his firm muscles must ripple with each and every step.

"Like a gazelle," I murmur to myself.

"Good morning, Maddie. You're looking particularly fine in your—" his eyes sweep over me and every part of me tingles, "—cardigan." A smirk teases the edges of his mouth, and even though I know he's toying with me, I do not care.

When it comes to Eric Camden, I'll take anything he wants to throw my way.

"Thanks," I mumble, enough heat to scramble eggs blooming in my cheeks. "You look good in your…everything."

Good grief.

"My everything?" he questions. "Thanks." His eyes shift to Chloe, but all he does is throw her a scowl before he pushes through the door.

As it swings closed behind him, I let out a sigh.

Eric Camden, my favorite Viking.

"Hello? Are you still there?" the voice on the end of the telephone asks.

The customer. Right.

I clear my throat. "Oh, sorry. Yes. Still here, sir. I think this is a bad line or something? Anyway, what was it that you wanted again?"

He has a distinct tone as he tells me what he wants and I promise to place the order for him before I hang up.

"Girl, you need to either make a move on that guy or move on," Chloe tells me. "And you know which one I would recommend." She makes a neck slitting movement with her thumb.

"I'm not moving on, but the idea of making a move?" I let out a laugh, the very idea making my belly tie up in a tight knot even a fisherman would be proud of. "There is no way I'm ever doing that."

"Why not? That's better than sitting here all day dreaming of becoming Mrs. Madeline Camden when you haven't even kissed the guy."

Kissing Eric Camden.

That fisherman's knot turns to warm jelly.

Chloe shakes her head at me. "You're thinking about kissing him now, aren't you?"

"No," I reply indignantly, but we both know I was. "I was thinking about how much work I have to do."

"Sure you were. And I'm salivating over stock levels."

We share a smile. Chloe may not agree with my choice of crush, but we've been work buddies and besties since we met when I started working here almost two years ago. Where I can be awkward and shy, she's confident and sassy.

The perfect opposites attract friendship.

I always tell myself Chloe's the way she is because she's happy in her life. She fits. She's who she is and she fully accepts herself.

Me? I'm more of a work in progress thanks to that whole *not belonging in my own life* thing I've got going on.

One day, everything will click into place for me and I'll be happy.

Chloe gestures at her screen. "Your crush isn't anywhere near as hot as this guy."

"Who?" I push my chair over to her desk to look at her screen. I'm met with a dark-haired man with a close-cropped beard that looks too perfect to be real, with dark, smoldering eyes, and a self-satisfied smile that fits with his classic tux and air of privilege.

"Hot?" I question. "He looks to me like he thinks the sun comes up just to hear him crow."

Chloe bats me on the arm. "You'd be vain if you looked like *that*. He is dreamy."

"Seriously, Chlo, the guy looks so self-satisfied he probably broke his arm patting himself on the back."

Chloe giggles. "You are such a Texas gal, Mads."

"Born and raised. Who is this Mr. Smooth?"

"My future husband," Chloe replies on a sigh.

"I thought that was Patrick Dempsey, or whoever the sexiest man alive is this year."

"No, Patrick is still number one on my list, but this guy? A close second."

"Well, congratulations on your upcoming nuptials." I roll back to my desk.

"If I married him, I would be a princess. You know, I always thought I'd make a great princess."

I chortle. "He's some kind of prince?"

"Are you seriously telling me you don't know who Prince Alexander of Ledonia is?"

I return my attention to my spreadsheet. "Nope."

"Girl, you're missing out. He's the total royal smoke-show from Europe."

I shrug and Chloe rolls her eyes.

"You know he's here in the States?"

"That's great news!"

She narrows her eyes at me. "Why?"

"He can pop into the office and propose to you."

"He's in DC, so first, I'd have to wrangle myself an invite to the White House."

Chloe could probably pull that off.

"Can you imagine? Prince Alexander, the President, the First Lady. All that glamor."

I give an involuntary shudder. "Give me a bubble bath and a good book any day of the week."

"You would say that."

"We can't all be extroverts like you, Chlo. I prefer quieter things."

She arches an eyebrow. "Like soaking in your tub on your own, dreaming about so-called Vikings?"

She's nailed it. But I'm not about to tell her that.

"All those people is a lot of…pressure."

"Makes you anxious, huh?"

I downplay it. "A little."

"You'd be with me, so you'd be fine." She grins and I

don't doubt her. With Chloe's confidence, I bet I could do anything—even if it involved attending a lavish party at the White House to meet some prince.

My phone rings and I glance down to see a picture of my dad's smiling face.

"Hey, Dad." My dad and I have always been close, particularly since Mom passed away when I was only nine years old. He's a good man and he's always looking out for me, his only child.

"Hi, princess. I need to talk to you about something."

"I'm at work. Can it wait?" It might be just me and Chloe here right now, but our boss, Deidre, is never far away.

"Can we meet for dinner tonight? Manuel's at say six?"

"You had me at Manuel's."

Dad and I have a tradition of going to our favorite taco place about once a week. We know the owner, Mateo, and his very pregnant wife, Sierra. They welcome us with big smiles and lots of free chips and guacamole, and free chips and guac is never a bad thing in my books.

"Good, good, good. I'll see you there tonight," Dad says, and I pick up on a tension in his tone.

"Everything okay, Dad?"

"Of course, princess. I just need to talk to you about something."

"Something good?" I lead.

"It's...news. Good or bad. Probably good. I don't know."

I smile. I can guess what this is. Dad is getting all nervous about telling me that he's met someone. I helped set up a profile for him on a dating app a couple weeks back, not that he was exactly into the idea. The truth is, if he has met someone, I couldn't be happier for him. For the longest time I've wanted Dad to find someone. It's been 15 years since my mom passed away, and he's barely even been on a date since. It's time he put himself first and found someone.

Eric breezes back into the room, accompanied by one of the other salesmen, Terrence.

"Dad, I gotta go. See you tonight," I say into the phone.

"Love you, princess."

"Love you, too." I quickly hang up as Eric approaches my desk.

"Ladies," he says.

"Twice in one morning," I reply, smiling up at him.

"Yeah. We were thinking of going to grab Starbucks," he says in that deep, velvety voice of his that does things to my belly. "Want anything?"

"You're...offering to get me a...a coffee?" I stammer, not quite believing my ears.

Eric Camden wants to buy me a cup of coffee? This is a major new development in our relationship.

His eyes flash. "Sure thing."

"That would be great," I reply with a smile. "Thank you, Eric." I pull my purse from my bottom drawer and fumble around for some cash when I feel a warm hand fold over mine. Startled, I look up into Eric's eyes.

"My treat," he says.

For a moment, I allow myself to get lost in the fantasy that somehow, despite the fact he's never done anything other than flirt with me since the day we met, he's suddenly overwhelmed with passion for me and can help but scoop me up in the most breathtaking and wonderful kiss of my life.

Of course, in my fantasy this doesn't happen at my desk, and not with Chloe and Terrence watching. (It happens at sunset in Memorial Park, with us sitting on a picnic blanket and him telling me how he's always loved me but has never had the confidence to tell me, before he sweeps me up in a kiss, murmuring that one day, he intends to make me his wife.)

"That's so sweet of you," I say, and as he pulls his hand from mine, I miss it. I actually miss it.

He straightens. "Wait. I just remembered. We've got that thing. Right, Terrence?"

Terrence nods. "We sure do."

Eric tsks. "I cannot believe we forgot that. How stupid." He turns to me. "Maddie, you wouldn't…? Nah. Forget it. That would be me taking advantage of you."

"I wouldn't what?" I ask, my voice breathless, because as terrible as it sounds, Eric Camden could take advantage of me in any way he wants.

"You wouldn't go grab the coffees for us this time and I'll get the next one for you?" he asks.

Wait. Did this just get turned around on me?

I just know Chloe is rolling her eyes like they're a planet orbiting the sun.

"Oh, sure. Yes. Of course," I say brightly.

"Thanks, babe," he replies with a wink, and my stupid heart squeezes.

He pats his thighs. "Dang it. I forgot my wallet and I need to get to that thing. Right, Terrence?"

Terrence nods again. "Right."

"Maddie, I don't suppose you could get them and I'll pay you back later?"

"Sure," I breathe.

I do not look at Chloe.

The door opens and in walk two men dressed in black suits, sunglasses hiding their eyes. They look every inch the CIA cliché you see in movies, only bigger and scarier, their collective bulk filling the space.

I blink at them, wondering whether we're about to be infiltrated for some highly secretive ops—or worse—when Eric steps over to them and puffs out his Viking chest. "How can I help you gentlemen?"

One of the men removes his sunglasses, revealing a face with the squarest jaw I've seen outside of a cartoon, and a heavy brow that more than hints at Neanderthal origins.

He looks Eric up and down before he says, "I'm looking for Madeline Josephine Turner. I understand she works here."

Wait, *what*?!

Why the heck are these two guys looking for me?

Eric regards the two men—who, in a sinister turn of events, I've decided look a lot more like undertakers than CIA operatives—in obvious disbelief before he turns to me and says, "I didn't know your middle name was Josephine?"

"Good one, Eric. Now you've gone and outed her," Chloe snarls, which is a good point.

Eric looks shamefaced, but of course I forgive him. He was taken unawares, that's all. Easy mistake to make.

"Lucy's clearly failing at her job if she let you guys just waltz in here," Chloe says, naming the office's receptionist. "What do you want with my girl, Maddie?"

Undertaker #1 turns his attention to me, and it's clear I'm not what he expected. "Are you Madeline Josephine Turner?" he asks in a clipped British sounding accent. But it's not quite British. It's almost as though it's *pretend* British, if that makes any sense. Although there is something familiar about the way he sounds.

In fact, if I really think about, his accent reminds me of my mom's.

"What did you do, Maddie?" Eric asks, his eyes bright. "Break some federal law?"

"What? Of course she didn't," Chloe snaps. "You're an idiot, Eric."

"No, I'm not. You are," Eric replies. Not exactly mature.

Tentatively, I rise to my feet, my eyes on the Undertakers. "I am she," I announce, my voice shaky.

I wonder about my sanity. These guys might be hired killers, or worse! Not that I can think of what could be worse than hired killers right now, but still.

Undertaker #1 and #2 size me up.

I tug at my cardigan, wrapping it around myself, and cross my arms. "What's this all about?"

"I ask that you come with us, ma'am," Undertaker #1 says.

He wants me to go with him and the other guy? I might not be street smart. I might not have graduated anywhere near the top of my class. But I know one thing from watching cop shows on TV: you never go anywhere with someone who looks as threatening as these guys.

And what's more, he's calling me ma'am? How old do I look? I take a mental note to review my skincare regime.

"Oh, I…no thank you. I'm good," I reply weakly.

"What's going on, Mads?" Chloe asks. "Who are these guys?"

Eric steps forward. "I'm not happy about all this. What do y'all want with Maddie?"

Oh my, if I don't swoon a little, right here in the office. Eric is coming to my rescue, like a knight in shining armor. Or a Viking in…braids?

It's a lot sexier in my head.

"That's between us and Ms. Turner," Undertaker #1 replies curtly.

"Can I ask what it's about? I mean, I'm more than happy to talk to you guys but, to be honest, you're making me a little nervous," I say.

Or a lot nervous.

Definitely a lot.

"There's nothing to be nervous about, ma'am. We're here on official duty. Is there somewhere we can talk?" Undertaker #1 asks.

Chloe brandishes a finger at them. "You're not taking my friend anywhere, scary suit dudes. If you have anything to say, you can say it right here, right now." She hooks her arm through mine and straightens her shoulders. "Right, Maddie?"

I press my lips together. "Right?"

The undertakers share a look.

"Is this—" Undertaker #1 gestures at Chloe, "—*person* your designated chaperone?"

I snort laugh at the thought of Chloe being anybody's chaperone, let alone mine. She's the one who's always trying to get me to go dancing and drink shots. She'd be a horrible, horrible chaperone.

Chloe nudges me.

"She is my…err, chaperone," I tell the men.

"We'll have to clear the area. Everyone but her goes," Undertaker #2 says.

"But I want to stay and see what happens," Eric protests, and his knight armor loses some of its gleam.

Eric and Terrence are ushered from the room, and as the door swings shut behind them, Chloe folds her arms and glares at the undertakers. "Okay, scary looking dudes. Spill."

Undertaker #1 pulls his brows together in confusion.

"She means explain," I clarify, certain, despite their proficiency, that English is their second language.

He clears his throat and shoots me a meaningful look. "It is my responsibility as a representative of the Crown of Malveaux—" he begins.

"Crown of Mal-what-now?" Chloe interrupts.

But it all begins to fall into place for me.

Malveaux. The country of my mother's birth. The country she left to marry my dad.

The country where she was a princess.

"—to inform you that your presence is required at the Royal Court with immediate effect."

"The Royal Court?" Chloe chortles. "Mads, this is hilarious."

"Why?" I ask, my heart doing double time.

"With the expected abdication of Prince Nicolas, you have become the next heir to the Kingdom of Malveaux by right of your royal birth."

The ground beneath my feet turns to quicksand.

I'm now the heir to the Malveauxian throne?

Chloe barks out a laugh. "These guys are good!" She flicks her eyes to mine, only for her expression to drop. "Mads?"

"I'm kind of a...princess. Kind of. Not official or anything," I say with the reluctance of a cat taking a bath.

"Wait, what?"

"My mom was a princess before she left Malveaux to marry my dad. But there was no way I was going to ever actually *be* a princess, let alone the heir to the throne." I glance at the Undertakers, who I now realize are in fact royal security. "This is...unexpected."

My parents chose to raise me as a regular American girl, away from all things royal back in Europe. I might know I'm a princess on paper, but it's never meant anything.

Until right now.

Chloe pulls back from me, her eyes the size of soccer balls. "No. Freaking. Way. You're a real-life princess?"

I shrug, although I know it to be true.

"Wait. Does this mean you're Prince Alexander's sister?"

"Prince Alexander?" I ask, feeling like I'm not quite in my body anymore. Why is she talking about him?

Undertaker #1 ignores Chloe. "I'm sorry to tell you, ma'am, but time is of the essence."

"Is it because she needs to get to the White House to hang with her brother?" Chloe asks. "'Cause I'm totally free to go there with her. I am her official chaperone, as you know."

"Prince Alexander is no relation whatsoever to Princess Madeline as he is a member of the royal family of Ledonia and not *Malveaux*. Two entirely different countries," Undertaker #1 says as though speaking to a toddler.

"Whatever you say, dude," Chloe replies. She winks at me. "You're going to have to introduce me to Prince McHottie for sure."

My thoughts bounce around in my head. Prince McHottie. Ledonia. Malveaux. Prince Nicolas abdicating.

My mom.

Panic slices through my belly like ice, my heart thudding, my breaths short and shallow, my head tight enough to explode.

Is this…really…happening?

Suddenly, I feel myself falling forward as though in a dream. *Falling, falling, falling.* And as everything turns black, the last thing I see is the gleam in Undertaker #1's shiny polished shoes.

Chapter 2

Alexander

❝ He wouldn't be our Lord of Lusciousness if Prince Alexander wasn't seen out with a veritable bevy of American beauties at his beck and call. Last night's soiree at the White House saw him stepping out with a senator's beautiful daughter. They looked happy and relaxed, but this royal correspondent wonders what happened to one Carlita Perez, the beautiful supermodel our Prince of Perfection was spotted enjoying a drink with only a few nights ago at New

York's Plaza Hotel. Poor Carlita. It looks like you've already been replaced. Such is life as a love interest of the future King of Ledonia.

#CrownAndSwoon
#OutWithTheOldAndInWithTheNew
#NotYourAveragePrinceCharming

Your favorite royal correspondent,

Fabiana Fontaine xx

I think I love America. Seriously. Although I can't quite be fully anonymous here, what with journalists following me from Ledonia on my official visit, it's still a far cry from my life as Crown Prince back home.

What's more, here in Washington DC, I can go sight-seeing along with every Tom, Dick, and Harriet without being trailed by the entire freaking royal guard.

Of course Antony and Hans, my ever-protective, ever-present bodyguards, are watching my every move, but they're doing it at enough of a distance that I can chat with the pretty girl who asked me out when I met her at the White House last night without feeling like I'm on display.

"So, you're telling me that you're not only a prince but you're the first-born son, so that means you'll become king someday?" Freya, aka the pretty girl, asks me as we walk up an expansive set of steps.

"Yes, although personally, I think it should be the first-born regardless of gender. It's very old fashioned that Ledonia still insists on the male line ruling. Malveaux changed their law back in 1983 so that the first-born child would become the monarch, regardless of their gender."

"Sure," she replies and I wonder if she's actually listening to me. "I can't believe you're going to be king." She places her hand on my forearm. "I'm touching a future king. That's c-*razy*."

I suppress a sigh. "Crazy indeed."

She giggles. "You're so proper. 'Crazy indeed'," she repeats, putting on the worst imitation of my accent I think I've ever heard. And I've heard a few.

A change of subject is required. Anything to get her to move on from her delight in my royal status, which I'm quite happy to forget about on this sunny afternoon in the American capital.

"Remind me again why you get to go to functions at the White House?" I ask her as we come to a stop in front of a hugely oversized seated statue of a former president.

"I told you last night, silly. My daddy's a senator," she replies in that attractive southern drawl of hers.

Really, she could say anything and it would sound pretty. Anything but commenting on my status as a prince, that is.

"You don't know what a senator is, do you?"

"Don't they go around wearing white bed sheets, speaking in Latin?" I tease because of course I know what a senator is. My father ensured I studied world politics and history. As the heir to the throne of Ledonia, I need to know who's who when I visit a country, particularly on a PR junket like this one, trying to get more American tourists to my country. When you're a small principality on the large continent of Europe, you've got to do what you've got to do to survive.

Freya lets out a tinkling laugh. "That's *Roman* senators,

like on the movie with that guy who had to fight everyone else at the Colosseum in Rome, Italy."

I arch my eyebrows. "Do you mean *Gladiator*, starring Russell Crowe?"

"You've seen it?"

Hasn't everyone seen it? It's a classic.

"I may have. The thing is, where I'm from we don't have senators. We have Lords and Ladies of the Royal Court, with a parliament that represents the people."

"The Royal Court? It sounds so fancy, Your Royal Highness."

"Alexander, remember?"

"Okay." Freya blushes when she adds, "Alexander."

"That's better." I smile at her, thinking what I always think when I meet a new woman. Most of them, if not all, get goo-goo eyes for the royal part of my title. Even the Americans.

Not that I'm complaining, of course. I'm not a poor little rich boy yearning for a different, simpler life. Heck no. Being a prince is one sweet gig—if you ignore the perpetual media interest, the fact I need to live up to my father's expectations, and women like Freya, blinded by my title.

It's being the heir to the throne that I'm not so keen on.

"Who's this guy?" I ask as I gesture at the imposing statue looming above us.

"Abraham Lincoln, of course!"

"Is that why this place is called the Lincoln Memorial?" I deadpan, because yes, I knew it was Abraham Lincoln.

She nudges me. "You know, it's lucky you're a handsome prince."

"Why is that?"

I already know her reply. *Pretty but dumb.* I've heard it before.

"Because I bet you didn't have to go to college and learn stuff."

I attended Cambridge and graduated with a first-class honors degree in history before I joined the Royal Ledonian Navy as an officer. But I'm not going to bother Freya with that kind of irrelevant detail. She's made her mind up about me already.

Prince equals not having to know stuff.

Oh, and being pretty, too.

I feign a smile. "You're so right."

"I knew it!" She beams. "Did you see that we were talked about on TMZ today?"

"I don't generally follow the media coverage of the events I attend. If there's anything I need to know, my chief of staff will tell me."

"It wasn't the event so much as you and me." She gestures between us. "Here, I'll show you."

"It's fine."

"No, really. I want to."

Before I can stop her, she's pulled her phone from her purse and is showing me an image of us dancing at the White House last night. Her eyes are bright, her smile broad as she gazes at me in her sequined silver dress.

"You look lovely," I tell her, barely glancing at my own image.

"*We* look lovely," she corrects. "Everyone is saying I'm your new girlfriend."

"I imagine they are."

What Freya doesn't know is any woman I'm photographed with—be they a friend or a cousin or someone I've known for less than five minutes—is labeled as my latest girlfriend. At last count I believe I had dated close to 259 women in the last four years alone.

All in all, they've been right a grand total of never.

And yes, I know that makes me sound like some sort of sad sack with no actual relationship experience. But there you have it.

"It's so funny because last night was the first night I met you, and they're already saying we're dating, which we're not."

"Facts should never get in the way of a good story," I reply.

"Right?"

Thankfully, she slips her phone back into her purse.

"Tell me more about what it's like to be an actual prince."

Do I have to?

"Why don't you tell me what *you* think it's like to be a prince."

"I'd love to! I figure you sit in a gilded chair, wearing a crown, and make decrees as peasants line up to give you their suckling pigs and baskets of strawberries for your feasts."

Not even close.

"Then on Sundays you go and inspect the guard at the Trooping of the Color."

That's Britain.

"During the week you'll turn up at charity events and sip tea and cut ribbons."

Far too accurate, although I prefer coffee, not tea.

"And I bet you've got a castle in the mountains some-where where you go and ski and relax."

It's on the Mediterranean, and it's more water skiing than snow skiing.

"Anything else?" I ask.

"Oh, you sleep in a four-poster bed with curtains that you close around you."

"Do I wear a night shirt with matching cap?"

"I bet you do!"

"I think you'll find that's Scrooge from the Charles Dickens novel, *A Christmas Carol*."

"You mean the duck?"

And she thinks *I'm* the one who didn't "learn stuff" at university.

I give her an impassive smile. Why did my father's PR people think it was a good idea for me to go out with this woman today? "The duck. Exactly."

"Oh, you are way cuter than that duck." She nudges me with her shoulder. "Now, where was I? Oh, that's right. I bet I've got it all a hundred percent right."

"Right down to Scrooge McDuck."

She beams. "I bet you get woken up by a chamber-maid every morning instead of an alarm clock like us regular folk, and she curtsies to you before she draws the curtains and says 'good morning, your Royal Highness' and then she hands you tea and crumpets for your breakfast."

She falls into a satisfied silence, and I realize she's finished.

"You have quite the imagination," I reply.

"Oh, I've watched *The Crown*. I know *all* about royal life."

"Ah."

Her eyes widen. "Oh my gosh, do you know William and Kate?"

"Of course. We meet up regularly in our night shirts and matching caps to eat suckling pig and strawberries brought to us by well-meaning but impoverished peasants." I do my best to keep a straight face.

I can tell she's trying to work out whether I'm pulling her leg.

She must decide I am when, after a beat, she lets out a

laugh. "You're so funny. I love that about you. I never would have thought a prince could be funny."

"Fancy that," I reply, suddenly tired.

What I wouldn't do to be sightseeing on my own in blissful, anonymous silence.

The thing is, when you're seen as an exciting European Prince, people want to be with you. *Women* want to be with you. But here's the thing. They don't really want to be with *you*, more the idea of who they think you are.

Looking into Freya's eyes right now, I know she has no interest in *me*.

In fact, it's been a long time since I met a woman who wants to know me. All they see is the fancy title and the fancy clothes, the lavish events and the media coverage. And that's great.

Or it *was* great.

I'll admit, I've had dalliances with my fair share of the women of this world. Probably more than my fair share, if I'm going to be totally honest.

It's been easy. Very easy. It's like I'm some kind of royal rockstar, with women flocking to me wherever I go. Beautiful women. Smart women. But I never feel that real connection that I want. Call me maturing or getting old, but I no longer want flings and ego boosts with models and actresses and It girls.

It was fine for a while, but not anymore.

I want what others have: a loving, committed relationship with someone who actually knows me, someone who loves me. I want the kind of solid permanence of love, a love that lasts more than a few weeks.

I want a love that lasts a lifetime.

I blow out a puff of air. I sound like a romantic sap who's watched too many Hallmark movies and needs to grow a pair. For the first part, I blame my little sister,

Amelia, who makes me watch a seemingly endless list of romantic Christmas movies every year. Well, I say she makes me, but really, I relish the chance I get to spend time with her. We came to a compromise a long time ago: I would watch her movies with her—determined not to enjoy them, of course—and she would tell Father all the things I want him to know about me—not what they say in the media.

And for the other part? I'm safe in my masculinity. I don't need to grow anything.

I'm a man who knows what he wants, and I'm not going to stop until I get it.

Knowing what Freya wants from me and not feeling willing to give it, I walk her to her car, where her father's driver has been patiently waiting. I say goodbye to her with a kiss to the cheek.

"It was just wonderful to spend an afternoon with a prince," she breathes as she takes my hand in hers.

An afternoon with a prince. Just what I thought.

"Safe travels back to your home state."

"Goodbye, Your Royal Highness."

I open my mouth to ask her once more to call me Alexander, but close it. There's no point. To her, as to the rest of the world, I'm nothing more than a prince.

Chapter 3

Maddie

You know when you're at work, going about your business, perhaps flirting a little with the guy you've got a crush on, and then *Wham!* you're hit right between the eyes with the news that you're now first in line to the throne of a small European country?

No one? Just me then?

That was my yesterday. My today involves me being on a private jet, with everything around me covered in royal monograms, from the headrests to the napkins to the staff's lapels, winging my way from my familiar Texas home to Malveaux, a country on the Adriatic Sea that I haven't visited since I was a child.

It's a lot.

Of course Undertaker #1 and Undertaker #2 are here, too, sporting their black ensembles and looking appropriately grim. No change there. Those two—real names Vladimir and Gino as it turns out—have been my constant companions since they sprung the "you're needed in Malveaux as the next heir to the throne" thing on me.

Apparently, one of them picked me up when I fainted, carrying me to the state vehicle parked outside the office block, complete with little gilded flags on either side of the hood and blacked out windows. He was trailed by an outraged Chloe, who insisted on accompanying me to The Houstonian, one of the city's swankiest hotels, where they had the presidential suite waiting for me.

The presidential suite, people!

I lean back in my leather airplane seat and rub my forehead, "How did we not see this coming?" I ask Dad.

"We thought Nicolas would inherit, and his children after him. Your mom was totally out of the picture."

"But Uncle Nicolas didn't have kids."

"That's right. Unfortunately, his marriage fell apart years ago and he hasn't remarried." He reaches across the table and takes my hand in his. "Honey, I know this is a lot to take in right now. It's not how I thought this would go."

"Really? How did you think it would go exactly, Dad?"

"I didn't think Nicolas would abdicate, for starters. Look, your mom left Malveaux because she'd fallen in love with me and she didn't want us to lead a royal life. I sure as heck didn't want one, either. She persuaded her parents—your Grandpapa and Grandmama—that the family didn't need her."

"What's so wrong with living in Malveaux and being royal that neither of you wanted it?"

"I think it was less about what was wrong with that and more about what was right with living with me in Houston."

"Did my grandparents not like you or something? 'That horrible man from Texas'."

"We're fine, even though they did think I took their daughter from her duty."

"Which you did."

"Love is a very powerful thing."

I roll my eyes. "Daughter here, remember?"

"They weren't thrilled your mom left, but they understood. Not everyone is born into the life they're given. Some need to search for that life on their own."

His words ring all too true for me. I might not have felt like I was living the life I was meant to before today, but do I want the life I'm literally flying toward now?

I bite down on my lip as I gaze out the window at the cloudless sky.

"Your mom gave up a lot for us, honey."

I press my lips together as a lump forms in my throat. I have only fuzzy memories of my mom. I was nine years old when she died, so I should remember more, and it saddens me that I don't. I remember her smile, the way the skin around her eyes crinkled, her floral scent. Most of all, I remember her wearing a navy-blue dress with white polka dots that brought out the color of her eyes. Blue, just like mine. It had a lace trim and white piping around the waist. I remember her standing on the patio, laughing at something someone said. I remember how happy she was, how full of life.

"I never thought this day would come, princess," Dad

says in a soft voice. He smiles. "Huh. I guess I need to say that for real now. Princess Maddie."

I shake my head. "It's so surreal, Dad. One day I'm me, and the next day I'm supposed to be this totally different person. And not just any person, a royal person from a country that sounds like it's from a fairy tale."

"You don't remember our vacations there?"

"I remember my grandparents and Uncle Nicolas, of course, and the super ornate gardens with lots of hedges and statues. And I had a room with a canopy that initially I thought looked wonderful, but totally freaked me out at night. I thought a monster was going to jump out and attack me."

"You did have nightmares, and the next time we visited, they took down the canopy for you."

"That was nice."

"The place you're describing is the royal palace in the capital city, Tleurbonne. Do you remember playing in the gardens with a bunch of kids?

"Like relatives?"

"They were the royal family from the neighboring country, a place called Ledonia."

Memories pop into my head of a family of strikingly good-looking people, all with dark hair, the girls enviably pretty. "I do remember some kids."

"You'll probably meet them again."

"One royal family at a time, okay?" I lean back in my cream leather seat, resting my head against the mono-grammed headrest. "I'm super nervous about being an official princess, but I'm also nervous about seeing my grandparents."

"They're your grandparents. There's nothing to be nervous about."

I level him with a look.

"Just imagine them in their underwear."

I snort laugh at the idea. "I don't think I'm going to do that."

"However you do it, you've got this."

"Only if the King likes to walk around in his tighty-whities."

"Excuse me, Your Royal Highness. Excuse me, sir," Jill, the flight attendant says. "The captain has asked me to advise you that we've begun our descent into Malveaux. We expect to be on the ground at Tleurbonne International Airport in approximately 25 minutes."

"Great. Thanks so much," Dad replies.

I lean into him. "I am never going to get used to being called 'Your Royal Highness'."

"I think there are a few changes you're going to have to get used to, honey."

I give him a sardonic smile. "Like my entire life?"

"That, and the fact they may ask you to wear some-thing other than dirty white sneakers."

I lift my foot from under the table and inspect my shoe. "They're not dirty. They're broken in."

"I'm not sure Queen Maria will see it that way."

Exactly 25 minutes since we were told we were due to land, the captain pulls the royal jet to a stop, and I peer out the window at this new country. I can see the bustling activity of the airport, with ground crew members busily working, and other Malveaux Air planes parked at nearby gates. Ground crew are busy moving a set of stairs toward us, and there are a couple of sleek black cars with flags flanking the hood that are waving in the breeze. The surrounding landscape hints at the country's natural beauty, with distant hills peeking out from beyond the airport's perimeter.

I look nervously back at Dad. "How long are you staying again?"

"You know I need to get back to the store. But I'll be here for the next couple of days to help you ease into things."

I offer him a grateful smile.

Jill pulls the door open and instantly the quiet cabin is filled with the sounds and smells of a busy airport.

Vladimir approaches our table. "We are ready to disembark, ma'am."

I've learned over the last 12 or so hours that calling me ma'am is their way of showing respect for royalty. People call me Your Royal Highness first, then drop it down to ma'am after. Although I get that it saves time—saying Your Royal Highness is a mouthful—the ma'am thing makes me feel old.

"I warn you there's some media here, but we have instructions from the palace that we are not to engage with them at this point," Vladimir continues. "Instead, I will assist you in moving directly from the plane into the waiting car." He gestures with his hands as though I need further assistance to understand the plan.

I swallow, my nerves bouncing like ping pong balls against a wall. It's bad enough that I'm about to see my grandparents for the first time in years—grandparents who happen to be royalty—but media? For some reason, it hadn't even occurred to me that anyone else would be interested in what's going on in my world right now.

But of course they are. I've got to be the biggest story of the year in Malveaux: Prince Nicolas tells everyone he's going to abdicate and they drag some random girl out of Texas to plunk her into the position of first-in-line to inherit the throne.

Only I'm not just some random girl out of Texas. I'm a

princess, daughter of Princess Josephine, a member of the Manchois royal family, who have ruled Malveaux for well over 1000 years.

I huff out a breath at the enormity of it all.

Just think, if I had included this part of my family history, I could have blown the socks off Ms. Bayer when we did our family trees in elementary school.

I wonder if I can get a do-over?

"Ready?" Dad asks me, punctuating my thoughts as he unclips his seatbelt and rises to his feet.

"No."

He chuckles. "At least you're honest."

I glance at Vladimir. He's still dressed like Undertaker #1, only I'm getting a little used to having him around. Probably because he's been a permanent fixture in my life since he turned up at my office and turned my life upside down. But also because underneath his undertaker-slash-CIA-operative vibe he seems like a good guy. And he sure as heck knows what he's doing.

Two very important things in my new world.

"When you're ready," he says as he gestures at the door.

It's now or never.

With a deep breath I push myself up from my seat, ready to face my new life, only to come literally crashing straight back down when I find I haven't unbuckled my seatbelt.

"Whoops. My bad," I mumble, heat flaming my cheeks.

Not the start I was looking for.

Dad smiles kindly and Vladimir's face doesn't crack.

Get it together, Maddie.

In one swift move, I unclip the belt, climb out of the seat, and pad across the plush carpet—the plush *mono-*

grammed carpet, of course—to the door, where Gino is looking around as though to ensure there are no snipers or Paparazzi lurking in the shadows.

As I step onto the stairs, blinking in the bright Malveauxian sun, a few people wielding cameras call out my name. As their shutters click, it strikes me for the very first time that I'm a princess now, and my life will never be the same again.

Chapter 4

Alexander

> Ladies, listen up. Our delicious Prince of Gorgeousness is back in Ledonia and oh, my, are we ecstatic about it. He has conquered America, as we never doubted he would, and now that he's back at the Palace, I for one am hoping we'll see much, much more of him.
>
> I wonder what he thinks of this new American princess, spotted arriving at Tleurbonne International

earlier this week. In her jeans and baggy sweatshirt, she's quite the Peasant Princess, wouldn't you all agree?

Some say she's an opportunist, cashing in on her newfound royal status. Others say she's nothing of the sort. Who knows? Time will tell on that front. Let's grab the popcorn and watch this royal soap opera unfold.

#HomecomingHero
#MalveauxInAPickleStill
#OpportunistOrVictim

As ever, your devoted royal correspondent,

Fabiana Fontaine xx

I slip off my blazer and drop it on the back of one of the chairs in my living quarters, loosening my royal mono-grammed tie. Kicking off my shoes, I instruct Carl, the footman who carried my suitcases inside, to leave them. I might be a prince, but I'm more than capable of unpacking a suitcase like a grown man.

Finally alone for the first time since I awoke in my Washington hotel room, I lean back on the sofa, kick off my shoes, and let out a thankful sigh.

Going on these publicity junkets, trying to drum up interest in tourists visiting our fair shores, may be my duty and it might even be fun at times, but there is really nothing like finally getting home.

And, if I'm honest, home isn't exactly a chore. How much of a chore can a palace with 41 bedrooms, 11 state rooms, a private swimming pool, a doctor's surgery, a post office, a bowling alley, a cinema, who knows how many bathrooms, stables, ornate gardens, a 4 km long wine cellar, gaming arcade, sauna, three hot tubs, and a pond that's more the size of a lake be?

I hear it. Poor little rich boy.

But really, it's all designed so we don't need to leave. Got a crick in your neck? We've got an on-call osteopath for that. Fancy a swim? First, you'll need to decide whether it's inside or out, and whether you prefer a pool or a pond. Fancy a midnight feast of baked beans on toast? A visit to the kitchen's walk-in fridge supplies many choices, ready and waiting to be devoured.

In my quarters, I have a living room, dining room, three bathrooms, and two guest bedrooms, as well as my master bedroom. Really, it's more like an apartment, housed within the confines of the palace. My father gave it to me when I turned 21, a kind of "now you're a man you need your own digs" gesture I think, and I've lived here happily ever since.

Well, I say "happily", but sometimes, I'll admit, it is rather lonely.

I may have everything I need at my fingertips, but sometimes this place feels like a luxurious prison from which I can't leave. If I do, I usually have an entourage of bodyguards, my personal secretary, and my publicity officer, to name a few.

So I'm either surrounded by people, putting on a show, or I'm here, in my rooms, alone.

Of course I do have company here sometimes. My sisters barge in at inopportune moments, always with instructions to give (Sofia, my older sister who seems to know better than me on all subjects at all times), or stories to tell (Amelia and Max, my two younger siblings, who are both a whole lot more fun than Sofia, and an antidote to my life as heir to the throne). I have some friends, too, although I see less of them now that they're living their own lives with their partners, out in the world.

And then there are the female visitors, the ones who I meet, have a flirtation with, with whom perhaps things develop into something more for a brief while until they realize I'm not who they think I am and leave.

I didn't get my reputation as a player in the past by sitting on my thumbs all day long, you know.

And, for a while, I enjoyed that lifestyle. Who wouldn't? I was the center of attention, the man women were drawn to simply by virtue of who I am. I didn't even need to try. Any party, any occasion, I would automatically be surrounded by women throwing me flirtatious looks, asking me about my life as a prince. My DMs were so full I had to employ another assistant just to keep up.

But that lifestyle, as fun as it was at the time, got old.

Now, since I made the decision I want to find love, things have been… slower. Maybe it's me and the types of women I attract, but they all seem simply too dazzled by my title to be genuine.

None of them have given me that feeling I've been searching for.

I must have nodded off because the next thing I know my mother and Sofia burst into the room, waking me from a rather pleasant dream in which I'm back at the White House, dancing with Freya, and she asks my opinion on something that has nothing to do with me being a prince.

Clearly a dream.

From my prostrate position, I blink at them, contemplating the very useful benefits of deploying the lock on my door.

Oddly, Sofia is wearing a ball gown, in full flight on one of her rants, as usual. Seriously, my sister rants more than the official Ranter of Ledonia. And yes, we do have an official Ranter, a job carried out by the most annoyed of citizens who love to complain. It was a position created by my great-great grandfather, King Oscar IX, I imagine more as a joke than anything else. But we've had an official Ranter ever since.

"I cannot believe that you actually think an arranged marriage in this century is appropriate, Mummy," Sofia says. Her hands are held in tight fists on her hips and she's glaring at our mother in that oldest child kind of way she does so very well.

"Who's having an arranged marriage?" I question with a yawn from my rather comfortable spot on the sofa.

"All the women of this family if we're not married by the time we're 28," Sofia declares. "It's fine for you. You and Max are both males. You get to do whatever you like, simply by virtue of the fact that you have a—"

"That's quite enough, thank you, Sofia," our mother snaps before my sister begins to label the male appendage.

She's done it before.

Our mother is never happy about it.

"And another thing," Sofia continues, clearly fully committed to her rant. "This whole 'the son gets to inherit the throne' business is a throwback to Medieval times. Medieval! Even though I'm a full 12 months older than him, it's like I don't even exist!"

Drama queen.

Only now that I think about it, that's the only queen Sofia will ever be.

I feel a sting of sorrow for her.

"I don't think anybody could possibly think you don't exist, darling," Mummy replies, darting me a quick wink.

"I'm fairly sure the stable boy can hear you, and he's a half a kilometer away."

Sophia pinches her lips together, not the least impressed.

I rub my eyes and swing my legs into a sitting position. "Although it's wonderful to see you both, as always, why did you bring this conversation in here to my rooms?"

"Your sister has a few opinions she would like to share with you today, and she decided that right in the middle of a dressmaker appointment was an appropriate time," Mummy replies.

"Lucky me," I say without a hint of sarcasm. Honestly.

Sofia isn't listening. "I'm the oldest, you know. I should inherit the throne, not Alex. They changed the laws in Malveaux decades ago to allow women to become rightful queen. They've gone and found one in America, for heaven's sake. Why not us?"

"You want us to find some American to become Queen?" I ask and win a venomous look from my sister.

"Not helping, Alex," she grinds out.

"Darling, I'm not responsible for the Ledonian laws. You know that as well as I do. Not even your father has the ability to change them." Mummy picks up the blazer I'd slung across the chair and pats it down before hanging it carefully on the chair's back.

Sofia pouts. "But he's the King. And you're the Queen."

"Yes, but it needs to be passed by Parliament, darling, a fact of which you are very well aware."

"She's just blowing off steam," I comment.

Of course Sofia knows about the Ledonian laws. She knows that as the first-born son, I inherit the throne. It might be sexist and old fashioned and altogether wrong, but that's the way it is in this country. She also knows that she, just like Amelia, our younger sister, will have an arranged marriage if they're not married by the time they're 28. Again, it's just the way things are.

Pity for Sofia she's just turned 27.

Not that I really understand why she wants to be Queen someday. I've seen what my parents do and it's not all it's cracked up to be. Seriously. Their days are as regimented as a military exercise, each minute accounted for as they move from briefings to ribbon cuttings, to visiting hospitals, to releasing the newest batch of royal pheasants in the wild. Yup, pheasants. It's a whole thing here in Ledonia. Malveaux has their peacocks, and we have our pheasants. In fact, the pheasant is our national bird. Significantly less cool than a bear or a tiger or even a bigger, fiercer version, like an eagle. Sure, pheasants are beautiful creatures, but they squawk and scare so easily, flapping their wings furiously as they try to lumber their large bodies off the ground.

But I digress.

My point is, being a monarch in 21st century Ledonia isn't exactly exciting.

Not that my sister sees it that way.

"I'm not just blowing off steam, thank you *Alexander*," Sofia says with a glare.

"I'm Alexander, am I? I must be in trouble," I quip. Sofia only ever calls me by my proper name when she's angry with me.

And just to be clear, she's angry with me because I possess the relevant male appendage our mother doesn't want named. Not exactly something I can change—the appendage or where I stand in line.

"That neckline is too high on you," our mother

observes, which launches her and Sofia into a discussion on necklines I decide to blank right out.

Our younger sister, Amelia, a far more relaxed and reasonable human being right now, finds her way into the apartment and flops down onto the sofa next to me. She too is in a ball gown, the same Ledonian red as Sofia's. "You're back."

"Very observant of you, Ami," I reply with a grin.

"How was it?"

"The same as usual. Parties, photographers, a lot of smiling."

"How dull." She leans closer to me. "Poor Mummy. Sofe's been going on for the last 15 minutes. It's so boring," she says in hushed tones.

"I'm not going to argue with that." I skim my eyes over her outfit. "Why are you dressed in a silk evening gown and a pair of high tops?"

She straightens her legs and hikes up her dress to reveal both sneaker-clad feet. "I think it's a winning combination. Don't you?"

"No."

She nudges me. "We've all been trying on dresses with the royal dressmaker. You know how much I *love* doing that."

"One thing I've always admired about you is that you have always been and always will be a thoroughly committed tomboy."

"Thank you for noticing."

"You're very welcome. What's this dress for?"

"It's in case we get invited to a ball to welcome the new Princess of Malveaux. Father said it was likely and we should all be prepared. Isn't that brilliant? We'll get to meet her!"

Ledonia and Malveaux have a long history, and not

always an amicable one. In fact, many a war has been waged between our two countries due to some small slight or underhanded land grab. Less so in the last couple of centuries or so, when both of our small countries have worked out that, in a sea of democratic European states, we are both monarchist outliers, both small, and both reliant on tourism and trade to keep afloat. We've become reliant on one another, although still harboring some unspoken resentment, too.

When the royal family of Malveaux does something, we're invited, and vice versa. Not that we've had to resort to dragging an American, kicking and screaming across the Atlantic, to be the new heir to the throne because the actual heir has decided to scarper.

Not that I know whether this new American princess did actually kick and scream, but I do rather like the idea.

"Brilliant isn't the word I'd use," I say as I picture the photo of the bewildered looking woman on the airplane steps that was splashed across the news this morning. Deer in headlights have nothing on this one. She was wearing a pair of jeans, grubby sneakers, and a sweatshirt that said "I prefer my boyfriends in a book."

I made my mind up about her in less than two seconds.

"I'm sure Madeline is just lovely. She wears sneakers, too, you know."

"You already have so much in common," I deadpan. "I'm sure you'll be firm friends by the time the evening's done."

Her features lift. "Do you think?"

I bark out a laugh. "No. I'm certain she's an opportunist and that Malveaux is making a massive mistake. That's what the media's suggesting, anyway."

She punches my arm. "You're so cynical, Alex. I resoundingly disagree."

I arch an eyebrow. "Resoundingly?"

"She looks like a perfectly nice person to me. Not an opportunist. A little scared, maybe."

"What's there to be scared of? She's totally landed on her feet, which, by the way, were clad in extremely grubby trainers."

Amelia smirks. "I adore her already."

"You would."

"Haven't you just been to America, telling them all about how fabulous we are here and how they must visit immediately and spend all their big fat American dollars? I recall seeing photos of you with at least a couple of pretty girls. Was it a terrible, terrible hardship for you?"

"Oh, don't get me wrong. I love the place, and the women are…well, they *are* pretty."

"And?"

"And I had a nice time."

She crinkles her brow. "What does that mean?"

I push the memory of how Freya was only interested in me because I'm a prince from my mind.

"You know, Sofia would like America, too, if she tried hard enough to extract that carrot from out of her bum."

Deflection is such a useful tool.

My little sister giggles and it ends in a snort. "That poor carrot."

Sofia's ears must be burning. She rounds on us. "I do not have a carrot up my bum, thank you very much," she quips.

"Uh-oh. She heard us. Act naturally," I say under my breath to Amelia while keeping a smile frozen on my face.

"I suggest it's time to scarper," she whispers.

"Run for your life while you still can?" I ask.

"More like inch away while we smile sweetly," Amelia replies as she eases herself up off the sofa.

"You lead. I'll follow," I reply.

Sofia watches us and frowns. "Very mature, you two."

"We never professed to be mature," I rebuff.

By now Amelia and I have reached the door.

"Where do you think you're going in that dress?" Mummy asks.

I can only assume she's talking to Amelia.

She turns to face our mother. "I'm done with dress fittings for the day. This is the dress I want to wear to meet the new princess," Amelia announces as she begins to unzip.

"Not in here, darling," Mummy instructs. "Your brother."

Amelia isn't listening. She's already peeled her dress halfway down, revealing the top of her plain white sports bra.

Quickly, I turn to look out of the window.

There are simply some things a brother doesn't need to see, and my sister's bra certainly falls into that camp.

"Alex and I used to have baths together, Mummy. And anyway, I'm pretty sure he knows what the female anatomy looks like, if all the photos of him with a bevy of beauties are anything to go by."

"A 'bevy of beauties'? You sound more and more like an octogenarian every day that passes," I say from my position by the window.

I steal a glance at our mother.

She has a pinched expression. "Hmmm."

I know my parents don't exactly do cartwheels over my dating life. Well, not that I have much of a dating life these days. But, as they say, the sands of time don't erase memory, and the fact I haven't been romantically involved with anyone for well over a year doesn't appear to have had any effect on my parents' view of me—or the tabloid stories.

"You do know that you need to settle down at some point, don't you, Alex?" Mummy asks.

"I do," I reply.

If only she knew how much I want just that.

"Are you decent yet, Ami? I'm getting bored of looking out the window."

"I'm never decent," she replies. "But I am sporting a rather fetching T-shirt."

I turn to see her wearing a T-shirt with the American flag I had thrust at me at one of my engagements in the past week. It's so big on Amelia it could fit three of her.

I eye my open suitcase on the floor. "You went through my suitcase?"

"Don't get all huffy about it. You were never going to wear this shirt. It doesn't go with your smooth prince vibe."

"I might have worn it."

She arches an eyebrow at me.

"You can have it," I concede.

She grins. "Thanks."

"You know you can't just palm me off every time the topic of you finding a wife arises, Alex," Mummy scolds.

Perfect. She's still on *that* topic.

"Your father and I were married with both Sofia and you in nappies by the time we were your age."

You've got to love the guilt angle.

"Didn't you have more to say about Ledonia's sexist laws, Sofe?" I ask, hoping she'll take the bait—and take the heat off me.

Sofia smirks. "Oh, this topic of conversation is much more interesting. When do you intend to find a wife, Alex? I'm sure we're all dying to know."

I narrow my eyes at her, as if to offer her a sarcastic *thanks a lot.*

"When the time's right," is my smooth reply.

Or at least I think it's smooth.

"Alex, that's what you said when we last talked about this. And the time before that," Mummy replies.

"And the time before that, too, Mummy," Sofia adds to be oh-so very helpful. "Perhaps you should arrange a marriage to a suitable young woman for Alex?"

"No!" I scoff at the same time as our mother says, "You know, that's not a bad idea."

I glare at my sister, who winks at me as though this is a great joke. Maybe to her.

"I'll speak with your father about it over dinner tonight. I'm certain we can come up with a few suitable candidates for you, Alex."

I blink at her a few times. "You're not serious. Surely."

"What's good for the goose is good for the gander," Amelia comments with a smirk. "Don't you think?"

"Seriously. Stop hanging out with Grandmother so much, Ami. You sound like you're 90," I say.

"I'm an old soul, you know," she replies. She looks anything but an old soul in that T-shirt she's almost drowning in. She looks like a little kid. Or a hobbit. I smile. Yes, a hobbit. I'll use that.

I open my mouth to speak when my father's personal secretary, Samuel, clears his throat, and we all turn to look at him in his Ledonia red livery, looking imposing in the doorway.

"What is it, Samuel?" Mummy asks.

"Your Majesty, Royal Highnesses," he says with an incline of his head. "We've received official word that you are all invited to a ball in honor of Madeline, the new Princess of Malveaux. His Grace, the King, has asked that you prepare yourselves to travel, leaving first thing tomorrow morning."

My mother claps her hands together in delight. Sofia frowns. Amelia squeals with excitement. And me? I blow out a breath, knowing this new American princess is going to be somewhere between interesting and a total unmitigated disaster.

Chapter 5

Maddie

I gaze out the window as the car drives through the streets of the Tleurbonne, the capital city of Malveaux. We move past the city's Medieval wall, through streets with a blend of old styles I can only guess are Gothic or Baroque. Unlike in Houston, the streets are narrow and often bustling with people, and each and every turn unveils a new vista: charming old buildings with their terracotta roofs, small, picturesque squares lined with trees, and glimpses of the shimmering sea.

I'm stunned by the beauty of this place. How much history there is here. I mean, a city wall? I've never been to a city that's encircled by a Medieval wall, once needed to protect the inhabitants from wannabe conquerors.

"We're not in Texas anymore, Toto," Dad says.

"Isn't it Kansas?" I ask absent-mindedly.

"Oh, look. They're opening the palace gates. We're almost there."

Passing through the large, wrought iron gates, the hum of the city fades. The expansive drive, lined with immaculate gardens and a row of perfectly oval-shaped trees, leads to the grand façade of the palace, an imposing structure with columns and tall windows and even an oversized balcony. I bet the royal family waves to the crowd from it, like they do from England's Buckingham Palace.

Dad nudges me as he looks out at a row of guards, dressed in royal blue uniforms saluting us as we pass.

"They're doing that for you, you know," Dad says.

"I've never had anyone salute me in my life."

"By the looks of this bunch, you may have to get used to that, honey."

I clamp my teeth down on my bottom lip and give it a squeeze. How am I ever going to get used to this? People calling me 'Your Royal Highness', people bowing to me, people saluting. What next? Full body prostration to show their deference?

At this stage, I wouldn't put it past them.

We drive through a grand arch and the car comes to a stop in front of large, open doors. There's a red carpet that stretches from inside, down the stone steps, all the way to the vehicle, and before I have the chance to grab the door handle, a man in a black uniform with white gloves pulls the door open and bows his head.

"Hey," I say, feeling like something the cat dragged in.

He simply bows once more, his features impassive.

Tough crowd.

I do my best to climb out of the car with regal elegance, but I'm not sure I achieve it, mainly because I have no clue how to climb out of a car with regal elegance. It's sure as heck not something I learned at public school, and I can't say I've ever even thought about how I look when I get out of a car before. I just simply *get out*. One second, I'm in the car, the next I'm on the sidewalk or the driveway or whatever.

But right now, I feel like I've forgotten how to do anything, and as I put one foot down on the red carpet, I whack my head against the top of the vehicle.

"Ouch!" I cup my forehead in my hand and give it a rub.

"Your Royal Highness?" the man in the black suit says.

"I guess I found where the top of the car is now, just in case you were wondering," I reply with a self-deprecating laugh.

He pulls his lips into a line. I bet I know what he's thinking. *This new princess is a total idiot.* And I wouldn't blame him. I feel like an idiot. An idiot fish-out-of-water, thrown into a world where I don't know the rules, or what's expected of me—or even how to get out of a dang car.

I try again. This time I manage to get out without banging into anything—yay for the small successes in life— and I walk up the steps and inside the palace without doing any further damage to my cerebral cortex. Or to my dignity.

"Your head okay?" Dad asks under his breath and I nod, despite the throbbing.

There's a group of similarly dressed men and women inside, who all bow their heads or curtsy.

"These are members of the household staff, ma'am,"

Vladimir explains, appearing at my side as though out of nowhere.

"All of them?" I gawk at the crowd. There's got to be at least 30 people, maybe more. But then this is a pretty big place. My Google search on the plane—hello, royal jet Wi-Fi—told me the palace has 42 bedrooms, 47 bathrooms, a bunch of state rooms, along with a pool, a lake, a movie theatre, and even an in-house spa where, apparently, I can get a massage or roast myself in a sauna anytime I like.

"All of them, ma'am," Vladimir confirms.

"How's it going?" I say to the group with a wave of my hand. I catch the eye of a young woman about my age with sandy blonde hair and I smile at her.

"It's…err…going very nicely, thank you, Your Royal Highness," she says before she averts her eyes to study her shoes, which I notice are black patent leather and a whole lot cleaner looking than my own shoes.

"Good. Great. I'm Maddie. I'm new here, but I guess you knew that." My laugh pierces the air, taking even me by surprise.

Way to be dignified, Maddie.

I clear my throat and take another shot. "I'm delighted to make your acquaintance and I look forward to you…err, serving me."

Did I really just say that?

I flick my eyes to my dad. He's offers me a sympathetic smile, which only makes me feel even more awkward and out of place. If that's even possible.

"Shall we go to your rooms, ma'am?" Vladimir asks, giving me the exit I so desperately need, and I could hug the guy, with his deep voice and big burly-ness.

Of course I don't. He's my bodyguard. And anyway, I've got my dad here if I need to hug anyone, and right now I could really use one of his warm, reassuring fatherly hugs.

"Okay, well, great to meet you. I guess I'll see y'all later," I say to the waiting staff.

Dad, Vladimir, and I make our way down the imposing hallway lined with oil paintings, the high, fancy ceiling stretching way above our heads. We're trailed by the poor woman who felt the need to reply to me just before, and a couple of men with white gloves. 'Cause you know, you always need a couple of dudes in white gloves.

I miss my anonymous Texas life with a sudden ache in my chest.

"I didn't catch your name," I say to the pretty blond woman.

"It's Alice, Your Royal Highness," she says with a curtsy. "I'm your lady's maid."

"Cool," I reply. "You'll have to explain to me what that means. I've never had a lady's maid before, or any maid, come to think of it."

"I'd be happy to."

We walk for what feels like at least a mile before we turn a corner and arrive at a set of large white doors with brass double handles, and the words Debreu Suite written on a brass plaque overhead.

"Your rooms, ma'am," Vladimir announces as he pulls both doors open in a theatrical gesture worthy of a princess arriving in a palace for the first time.

I stand and gawk. The doors open onto a marble tiled floor with a circular table covered in an oversized floral display, stretching almost up to the domed ceiling above. The entry hall leads down a wide passageway to the living room, which is filled with ornate furniture and a huge fire-place, over which hangs a really quite ugly painting of an angry looking group of cows.

Weird.

"Your living room, Princess," Vladimir announces unnecessarily.

"It's gorgeous," I breathe. "And way bigger than my apartment back in Houston."

"Way bigger," Dad agrees.

I spy an ornament on a side table that catches my attention. It looks like a ball, but it's made of multi colored marble. I pick it up to inspect it and it begins to play a song. I slap it back down on the table and offer everyone a weak smile. "I thought it was just a marble ball," I explain sheepishly.

"That is a music ball, a Malveauxian traditional ornament. It plays music much like a music box might. That one has clearly been wound and ready to be listened to," Vladimir explains.

"You had a ballerina jewelry box that played music when you were a kid. Remember?" Dad says, clearly trying to help me out here.

"Sure. I remember. What's through here?"

"The formal dining room," Vladimir says as I take in the large mahogany table and chairs, with a matching sideboard.

"Well, I do a lot of formal dining," I say with a smile.

Vladimir works hard at not smiling himself. "You may find you do more now that you are a member of the royal family, ma'am."

"Considering I did a total of none before, even one would be a step up."

"I imagine so, yes. Through here are the guest rooms followed by your master suite."

Guest rooms, I mouth to Dad, who raises his eyebrows at me.

As Vladimir takes us from room to room, I nod and

smile as though having three guest rooms with three adjoining bathrooms is entirely normal for me, when in fact I lived in a one-bedroom apartment back in Houston that could easily fit into the living room of this place.

Finally, he opens the double doors—because why have only a simple single door when you can have two?—to the master suite. It's a huge, light-filled room, with tall windows, trimmed with ivory silk curtains, a four-poster bed covered with enough throw pillows to make even Chloe happy (she's always been into throw pillows. It's weird), ornate furniture and plush flooring that makes me want to pull my sneakers off to enjoy the softness between my toes.

Vladimir opens another door and I swear I hear angels sing. It's a closet, only it's not like any closet I've ever been in before. It's a room the size of my dad's living room, lined with hanging rails and drawers and a glass cabinet for shoes. A cabinet for shoes, people! In the middle of the room is a long pale-pink sofa that Vladimir calls a chaise lounge, and a floor-to-ceiling gold trimmed mirror for me to inspect myself in each day.

"This is insane," I say.

"It's also all yours," Vladimir says. "These rooms were decorated for your late mother, and she lived here before she made the decision to leave royal life for America."

My heart clenches. "This was my mom's?" My eyes flick to Dad's and I can see he's struggling to hold it together.

"It was," he says.

Picking up on the mood in the room, Vladimir says, "We'll leave you now. Alice will be back in approximately an hour to ready you to meet with your grandparents."

Not waiting for an answer, he ushers Alice from the

closet, closing the doors behind him, leaving Dad and me and the ghost of my mom.

"This was mom's," I repeat, my throat tightening.

Dad collects me in a hug. "I know, honey."

I pull back from him. "You do?"

"We used to stay here when we visited. You might not remember. The last time you were here you were only eight."

I look around the room at all its luxurious plushness and privilege. "I don't remember. I wish I did. I wish—" My voice catches.

"I know. Me too," Dad replies softly. "I miss her just as much as you do."

"Being here must feel so weird to you."

"It's bringing back a bunch of memories, that's for sure. But they're good memories."

"She must have loved you so much to give this all up."

"She did. And I loved her with all my heart, just as we both love you."

Tears prick my eyes. "Dad, this is a lot."

"You've got this, honey. It might not feel like you do right now, but I have faith in you."

I think of the way I climbed out of the car and hit my head, how I had no idea what to say to the staff, how these rooms feel way too good for me in an almost overwhelming way.

"Remember, you don't have to do this if you don't want to."

I snap my attention back to him. "What do you mean? The way Vladimir put it, I don't have a choice. Uncle Nicolas has taken off and I'm the next in line."

He sits down on the pink chaise lounge and pats the seat beside him. I sink down into the pink velvet.

"That's what the royal family wants. But it doesn't need

to be that way. You have a choice in this matter, too, just the way Nicolas did. Just the way your mom did all those years ago. You're a princess no matter what, but that doesn't mean you don't have a choice of how you want to live the rest of your life."

Tears prick my eyes. "But I'm the heir to the throne now."

"That doesn't mean you have to do this if it doesn't feel right." He pushes some hair from my face and tucks it behind my ear. "The only thing your mom and I ever wanted was for you to be happy. If it turns out being here is the thing that makes you happy, then I'll support you a hundred percent. If it's living back in Houston, working at the glazing place, hanging out with Chloe? I'll support you a hundred percent in that, too."

My throat heats and the tears that threatened my eyes before spill over. "I love you, Dad," I tell him as I bury my face in his shirt.

He rubs my back. "I'm just trying to do my best, princess. This is all new for me, too."

I squeeze him knowing his best is way more than enough. I've been totally blessed with the parents I've had, and although Mom has been gone for many years now, she gave me so much in the short time we had together, and her love lives on in me.

But now I have this new life up for grabs, a royal life in a beautiful land, and I can't help but wonder whether this is the life I was always meant to have.

Chapter 6

Maddie

Vladimir returns to advise that I'm due to meet my grand-parents, aka King Harald and Queen Maria of Malveaux.

Me? Nervous?

That would be a big fat *heck, yes*.

I have enough time to splash some water on my face, run a comb through my hair, and give my teeth a quick brush before there's a knock on my door and some of the guys in the black suits and white gloves arrive.

I smooth my hands over my sweatshirt. Next to them I

look like a field mouse who snuck into the palace in search of a wedge of cheese.

I'm expecting one of the men to tell me it's time to leave for the big meet and greet. Instead, they simply stand back like perfectly poised statues as an elegantly dressed older couple sweep gracefully into the room.

"Their Majesties King Harald and Queen Maria of Malveaux!" one of the men announces.

Seriously, all we need is a couple of trumpets with crested flags and this would feel like a scene from *Shrek*.

I blink at the couple. There are no crowns, no over-sized, sparkling jewels. They're a perfectly ordinary looking couple in their early 70s, but for the fact that they're wearing what even I can see are expensive clothes. My grandmama's attractive face is made-up, her hair brushed back into a simple and chic French twist. My grandpapa's hair, on the other hand, is virtually non-existent, and what he does have is closely clipped around his ears, giving him more than a passing resemblance to Captain Jean-Luc Picard of the USS Enterprise.

Both sets of eyes are trained on me, and instantly I wonder how I'm supposed to greet them. I mean, I've watched *The Crown*. I know everybody still bows or curtsies to the monarch, even if they're related. But these are my grandparents.

I should curtsy. For sure.

I grab where a skirt should be, hook one foot behind the other, and dip down into the deepest curtsy I can manage without falling over, muttering the words, "Your Majesties."

I hope I'm reading the room right.

"Aren't you adorable?" my grandmama exclaims. "Isn't she adorable, Harald?"

"Quite adorable, my dear," he agrees, and I rise from

my curtsy, relieved that at least I've done something right today.

"It's been too long since we've seen you, my dear. Far too long. And you, too, Douglas." She smiles, and not only do some distant, murky memories of her come washing over me, but I'm struck by just how much she looks like my mom. She has the same face shape, the same blue eyes, and her smile lights up her face, just the way Mom's always did. "Come and give your old grand-mama a hug, dear," she instructs, her arms held open wide.

Without a second thought, I step into the hug and she wraps her arms around me.

"Welcome to Malveaux, my dear Madeline. I cannot tell you how wonderful it is to have you here," she says as I breathe in her floral perfume.

"Thanks. It's cool to be here."

"Cool?" she questions. "That won't do at all. Alice, have some wood brought up to make a fire for Princess Madeline," she instructs my lady's maid, who is currently hovering at the door.

"Of course, Your Majesty," she replies before she turns to leave.

"No! Wait!" I call out, and she turns back. "It's just an expression. It means great, awesome, I'm happy to be here." I punch the air to emphasize the positivity behind the word, and every set of eyes in the room regards me questioningly.

Note to self: they don't use the word "cool" here for anything other than a way to describe the temperature.

Second note to self: maybe don't use the word "lit" either. They might call the fire brigade.

"Well, that all sounds really quite wonderful," Grand-mama replies. "We think it's 'cool' that you're here, too."

And now she's trying to relate to me? Definite points for trying.

"Your grandmama is right. We are absolutely thrilled that you have taken the opportunity to become my heir to the throne," my grandpapa says in a surprisingly sonorous voice for a man of his age and stature.

"Oh, I—" I shoot Dad a concerned look.

"Let's not get ahead of ourselves here. Maddie's come to meet with y'all and look into the options for her future, but she's free to leave if she decides against it," Dad says firmly.

I watch my grandparents for their reaction. Both of them look aghast.

"But she's here. In Malveaux. She must take the role. She simply must," Grandpapa says, his bushy brows pulled together. "If she doesn't, the Crown will pass to my brother. Edgar has made it clear that he'll abolish the monarchy altogether. That'll be the end of us. The end!"

My grandmama pats his arm. "Why don't we give our granddaughter a chance to settle in before we plan the rest of her life, my darling, hmm? For starters, she might need some refreshments. Tea, Madeline?"

"Sure. Sounds great," I reply. *And a whole lot better than deciding whether I'm going to become the next Queen of a country I haven't visited since I was a kid.*

The Queen turns to Alice, who disappears from the room, presumably to get tea rather than piles of wood to make me a fire on an 80° day.

Although I suppose I need to think in Celsius now that I'm in Europe.

"Shall we sit and talk?" Grandmama gestures at the sofas and chairs.

"Sure thing." I sit down, kick off my tennis shoes, and tuck one leg under the other.

Vladimir shakes his head almost imperceptibly at me, and I look up to see my grandparents watching me in disbelief.

I jump to my feet. "Oops. Sorry. Protocol, right? Do you guys have to sit first or something?"

I've watched *Bridgerton* and *The Crown* and *Downton Abbey*. This might not be England, but it's at least Europe.

"That's the usual way of things," Grandpapa replies.

Thank you, Netflix.

I wait for them to sit and then cautiously return to my seat.

There's so much to learn. In the movies it's always things like how to know which fork to use while dining, but right now I get the feeling fork usage is only scratching the surface of this whole princess gig.

"Do I get princess lessons?" I ask as I do my best to sit up straight and look demure.

"When you say princess lessons, I assume you mean royal etiquette training?" Grandmama asks.

"Yes. That. Is that something you...offer?" I ask, as though princess lessons are as common a service at the royal palace of Malveaux as tacos are at a Mexican restaurant.

"A newcomer to royalty could certainly benefit from royal etiquette training," Grandpapa says.

"I have absolute faith that she will," Grandmama agrees. "I'll have Vladimir arrange it for you."

Vladimir bows. "It would be my pleasure, ma'am."

"You're new at this. You'll get up to speed in no time," says Dad, my ever-present cheerleader.

Me? I'm not so sure. This whole princess thing feels totally overwhelming right now. I mean, if I don't even know when or how to sit, I have a learning curve as steep as a San Francisco street ahead of me.

You know, if I decide to stay and take on the role full-time.

"You'll need to be brought up to speed fairly promptly, what with your formal welcome ball coming up in a few days' time," Grandpapa says.

"My what now?" No one said anything about a welcome ball.

"We're throwing a ball in your honor, Madeline. A way to say welcome and to introduce you to courtiers, members of parliament, and our great neighbors and friends, the royal family of Ledonia," he replies. "Although we won't mention anything about you becoming heir, or anything along those lines. Regardless of your decision on that front, you are and will always be a Malveauxian Princess."

I swallow, nervous. "How many people will be there?"

"It will be a reasonable size. Approximately 700 guests, I imagine," Grandmama replies.

700 guests passes for a reasonable size in this country? Yup, I'm definitely not in Kansas anymore. Or Texas.

"That's a big party," I reply with a tense laugh. A ball in my honor sounds like a *lot* of pressure.

"We encourage you to form friendships with the Ledonian royal family, my dear," she adds. "There are four children, and they're all delightful."

Ledonian royal family. *Huh.* The name tugs at my memory. An image of a self-satisfied—but I'll begrudgingly admit, handsome—prince flashes before my eyes. "Is Ledonia where Prince Alexander is from? You know, the prince who just visited America?"

The Queen looks pleased. "You know Alexander?" she asks hopefully.

I snort laugh. "Sure. I ran into him down at Taco Bell last Thursday."

Her mouth forms a perfect oh.

"I'm joking. He's famous, that's all. His image gets splashed around all over the place. My friend, Chloe, has a huge crush on him."

"I understand many young women find Prince Alexander appealing," Grandpapa says.

Most of all himself. I don't say it out loud, but that doesn't mean it's not true.

"You'll have the opportunity to meet him and his delightful sisters, Sofia and Amelia, and his brother, Maximilien. As a family, we spend quite a lot of time with them. Our two countries having what we deem a 'special relationship' that stretches through the centuries. We often say Malveaux and Ledonia are what ebony is to ivory on a piano," Grandmama says.

I plaster on a smile, feeling more than a little daunted. I'm going to hang out with Prince Alexander of Ledonia at this ball? And my family has a special relationship with his? Chloe will die on the spot, right before she demands to meet him.

"So, I guess we're cousins?"

"Very, very distant. There have been surprisingly few marriages between our two families throughout time," she explains.

"Right. Not cousins."

"You sound disappointed."

"I guess. It's been just me and Dad for so long, and I kind of like the idea of having a bigger family."

She reaches out and places a warm hand on mine. "I hope your grandpapa and I can help fill that void for you in some small way."

Her unexpected sincerity and kindness make my heart squeeze. I may be here to fulfill a role, but it means more than that to them. They're not just the King and Queen. They're my grandparents. They're family.

I lift my lips in a smile. "Way more."

"I'm glad. Your presentation ball will be a wonderful evening. I promise you."

"It sounds…fun."

"Would you say it sounds cool?" she asks.

"Totally cool," I confirm, wishing she wasn't trying so hard to relate to me, but also quietly happy that she is. It's endearing and it's sweet and it shows she genuinely wants to create a rapport between us.

"It will be a cool ball for a cool princess," Grandpapa adds with a satisfied smile.

Now the King's getting in on the act? I try not to cringe.

"When's this ball?" Dad asks.

"It's scheduled for Friday evening," Grandmama replies. "Will you still be here, Douglas?"

"I will."

I open my mouth to remind him that he told me he has to get back to the hardware store in a couple of days.

"I'll change my plans, honey. I want to make sure I'm here for your big night," he says when I shoot him a questioning glance.

"But, Dad—"

"You're more important than the hardware store."

I beam at him, my heart squeezing. My dad, the hero.

"Thanks, Daddy."

"You don't need to do that, Douglas. Our grand-daughter is in good hands here," Grandpapa reassures.

"I don't doubt it. I just want to be here for Maddie if she needs me, and y'all might think a ball is no big deal, but it's not an everyday thing where we're from."

The two men regard one another, and I'm sure there are so many unspoken things that hang in the air. For starters, there's the fact Grandpapa expects me to become his heir, whereas Dad will support me whether I decide to or not. Not to mention the fact Mom deserted her role to follow her heart to America and my dad. On some level Doug Turner is King Harald's enemy.

But I'm not going to dwell on that. It's just regular family stuff—only with a whole lot more at stake.

Grandmama's eyes rove over my jeans, sneakers, and sweatshirt combo. "We will need to get you some new clothes, dear. A few things befitting your station."

"I guess."

"I'll have the royal dressmaker visit you tomorrow morning. Gustav is a miracle worker," she says and I wonder if she's implying that I *need* a miracle.

"That would be great. Thanks."

"No need to thank me, dear. Every princess needs a helping hand to look her best, even the new ones. Especially the new ones." She throws me a wink and a smile. "I imagine it will be a lot of fun."

Getting primped and measured doesn't sound like fun to me, but I smile at her anyway. She's doing her best, and the least I can do is be open to it.

As Dad makes awkward small talk with Grandpapa, I lean a little closer to Grandmama and ask, "So, this ball. Is it, like, super formal?"

"Of course. What ball isn't?"

I chew on my lip. "Does that mean I'll need to wear high heels and a floor-length fancy dress?"

She pats me on the hand. "As fancy as you want it to be, my dear."

"I haven't been to a ball before, and the only time I wore a floor-length dress was to a Halloween party in 7th grade when I went as Morticia Adams and my best friend at the time went as Wednesday."

"Your friend dressed as a day of the week? How unusual."

"No. She was Wednesday Addams."

"Oh, I see. Tell me, are these Addams ladies friends of yours?"

I let out a giggle. "Morticia is the mom of the Addams family, and Wednesday is her daughter. They're famous."

"Oh. I don't think I know an Addams family. Unless you mean Herbert Adams, the famous Ledonian ski champion from the 1970s? Although I'm not aware that he had a family. More of a confirmed bachelor, is my understanding."

I decide to drop the whole thing.

"My point is, I don't have a lot of experience in the whole long dress-slash-high heels combo. Can Vladimir cover long-dress-slash-high heels in the etiquette training, as well?"

Grandmama suppresses a smile. "Between you and I, I'm not sure Vladimir has a whole lot of experience in the long-dress-slash-high heels combo, as you put it."

I flick my gaze to Vladimir. He's looking straight ahead with his habitual grim expression on his face. Part of me wants to get up and tickle him to see what will happen. But I imagine princesses don't tickle their bodyguards a whole lot. And if they do, I bet they don't do it in front of their sovereigns-slash-grandparents, anyway.

"I'll ask your lady's maid to help you with how to move in a long dress and heels. I'm certain she'll be able to. Now, Madeline dear, tell us all about your cool life back in America."

"There's not much to tell, really," I reply with a shrug. "I live in an apartment a lot smaller than this, and I work as a sales assistant for a glazing company in an industrial park in Houston."

A hush falls over the room and both my grandparents look at me as though I'm speaking an entirely foreign language. Which, of course, I know I am because we're all speaking English and not Malveauxian—another thing I'm going to need to learn—but it's like they've never heard these particular words in this particular combination before.

"Is that glazing cakes, Madeline?" Grandmama asks.

"Windows, glass doors, pool fences. That kind of thing," I explain.

"Well, all of those things are very useful, I'm sure," Grandpapa pronounces and Grandmama agrees with a bright smile.

"I help out at Dad's hardware store sometimes, too," I offer, as though sharing that little nugget of information will sway them to see just how amazing my life back in Texas is.

"Oh. Hardware is another very useful thing," Grandpapa says.

This is not going well.

"How about you two? What do you do? You know, other than...ruling...your...Kingdom," I ask.

What do you do other than rule your kingdom? Shoot me now.

"Well, we do find that ruling the Kingdom takes up most of our time. Doesn't it, darling," Grandpapa says.

"It does, although we do manage to fit in watching polo matches and maybe some television from time to time, not to mention we do so love spending time with the peafowl. Peacocks are the national bird, Madeline. They feature heavily in our history and on the royal crest," Grandmama explains.

"On that note," Grandpapa says as he rises to his feet. "We shall leave you to settle in. My dear?" He offers his hand to his wife.

I turn to Vladimir for my cue and he gestures for me to stand.

"Thank you so much for visiting. It's great to see y'all again," I say.

"Y'all?" Grandpapa questions.

I grin at my grandparents, King Harald and Queen Maria, glad that this first meeting has gone well enough, and actually excited for what lies ahead. "I may need to take princess lessons, but you're definitely going to have to learn how to speak Texan."

Chapter 7

Maddie

"Good morning, your Royal Highness," a bright, now familiar voice says as I hear the scrape of the heavy silk curtains being pulled open from my oh so comfortable bed. And when I say comfortable, I mean *insanely* comfortable. The mattress is soft, yet supportive, my head sinks into the pillow at just the right height, and the comforter is just that; deeply, deeply comforting.

I always suspected that a princess would get to sleep in

total luxury, and now that I am a princess, I'm glad to report I was one hundred percent right.

I pull the covers over my head and try to form words, but they come out more as a grunt. Houston is a full seven hours behind Malveaux, and I should still be floating through the land of slumber without a single thought about having to get up and face the day.

But sadly for me, it hasn't worked out that way.

"I've brought your American pancakes and bacon for your breakfast, as you requested," Alice says briskly.

I pull the covers from my face enough to open one eye and peer up at her. She looks like she's been up for hours. Totally put together in her black and white uniform, her blonde hair in an elegant bun. She's holding a gold tray on which sits my breakfast, waiting for me to drag myself up into a less horizontal position.

I can't complain. I've never been woken up with breakfast delivered on a gold tray by a person singularly devoted to serving me, even if my body clock is telling me it's something like midnight.

I push myself up into a sitting position and lean back against the velvet headrest as Alice places my breakfast across my lap.

"Thanks, Alice. I'll try to be more awake tomorrow when you come in. Jetlag, you know?"

"No mind, ma'am. Your days are so full. Of course you need your sleep," she says brightly.

"Alice, we've been over this. Call me Maddie."

"Maddie. Of course, ma'am."

It's a work in progress.

I lift the fine China teacup and take a sip. It's Malveaux's specialty tea, made with a certain blend of spices. I should like it. Scratch that. I should love it. Everyone else seems to.

But to me it tastes like cough syrup mixed with something super bitter and unpleasant. I add three sugar cubes and the stuff still makes me feel like barfing.

I miss coffee, nice, yummy coffee, my daily Starbucks Grande Mint Frappuccino in particular.

Maybe if I decide to become Queen, I should look into getting them to open a branch here, right around the corner from the palace? Or *in* the palace! Now we're talking.

For the last two mornings I've been waiting for Alice to leave the bedroom to pull out today's outfit choices, when I've jumped out of bed and poured the tea into the potted plant over by the chest of drawers. That way, she thinks I've drunk it. I don't have the heart to tell Alice I don't like her country's national drink. Or rather *my* country's national drink.

Another work in progress.

Vladimir and Alice have been giving me daily princess lessons, and I've been learning everything from how to greet people of varying ranks, to how to wave, to how to get in and out of a car without showing the world my underpants. All-important life skills for new princesses, apparently.

But today is a big one. The biggest. It's the day of the ball to introduce me to Malveaux as a princess.

"What are the royal family of Ledonia like?"

"They're wonderful, and so very important to Malveaux," Alice replies.

"And the real version?" I lead.

She glances around, as though someone may hear.

"It's just us, Alice. You can tell me what you think."

"The princesses are lovely, particularly Princess Amelia, the younger sister. She is so very friendly and sweet. Everyone says so. Princess Sofia is the oldest. She's quieter than Princess Amelia, but also kind. People say she takes her role very seriously and wishes that she herself could be queen."

"But if she's the oldest then she will be queen, right?"

"The laws of Ledonia are not as progressive as they are here in Malveaux. As such, her younger brother, Prince Alexander, will be king."

Prince Alexander.

"What's he like?" I ask casually, even though I already know the answer. Arrogant, self-satisfied, and altogether rather too pleased with himself.

Alice gets a goofy look on her face. "He's so handsome and charming."

"And a total player," I lead.

"A player?"

"You know, likes the ladies."

"Oh, absolutely. He's very popular with the ladies."

"Hmm."

I know his type. Although Chloe has made it clear how incredibly jealous she is that I get to meet her crush tonight, I'm not exactly looking forward to it.

I pick up my silverware—which is actually *gold*ware—and cut off a slice of what looks more like a French crêpe than an American pancake and take a bite. It's melt-in-your-mouth good because the Malveauxian approach to maple syrup is to drench the pancake in so much caramel sauce you could slip into a diabetic coma after one meal.

"This is delicious," I tell Alice through my mouthful. "You've absolutely got to try this."

"No, no. That's your breakfast, ma'am," she says, gesturing at the tray as though I'm some kind of simpleton. "Err, Maddie."

"I know, but it's so good I really want you to try it."

Alice glances at my breakfast before she looks back at me. "It does look delicious."

"It is. Trust me. Here." I cut off a slice, loaded up with enough caramel sauce to drown a goldfish, and thrust it at her.

Uncertainly, she leans down and takes the fork in her mouth. Her eyes widen, and I know she's now Malveauxian pancake's second biggest fan after me.

"Good, huh? Tomorrow, get the chef to make two plates of this and we can eat together."

"Oh, no. That won't be necessary."

"Of course it's not necessary, but it's fun."

I can tell she's rethinking this.

"If you're worried that the chef won't make it for you or something, then tell him that I'm a huge glutton and I want a stack yay high tomorrow." I gesture with my hands to show just how many pancakes I require. "Oh, and two forks."

"With two forks he might suspect."

"Tell him that I dropped my fork today so you need the other one as a backup. If he was there to see me hit my head on the car when I first arrived, he'll believe you."

She grins at me. "As long as you're happy to do that?"

"That's settled then," I reply with a shrug. "We'll be pancake best buds." Absentmindedly, I pick up my cup and take another sip. "Ugh!" I follow it up with a pancake and caramel sauce chaser.

"Do you not like the tea?" Alice asks.

"Oh, it's great, I'm just not used to it," I lie. "I'm sure I'll learn to love it over time."

"Would you like me to bring you something else in the mornings?"

"Like what?" I hold my breath. If she says a Starbucks

Grande mint Frappuccino, I think I would faint on the spot.

"Whatever you like. Just tell me and I'll get it for you."

"Is there a Starbucks anywhere nearby?"

"A star...bucks?" she questions and I get my answer right there.

"Forget that. Coffee. Do you do coffee here?"

"Of course. Espresso?"

"Sure. Espresso with like a whole bunch of milk."

"Ah. A cafe latte." She glances at the potted plant by the chest of drawers, which I notice is sagging and beginning to turn yellow. Oops. "Perhaps the greenery will benefit from coffee, as well?"

"How did you—"

"It's my job to care for you and your belongings," she explains.

Feeling shamefaced I offer her a reconciliatory smile. "No harm, no foul?"

"Your secret is safe with me. But perhaps flush anything you don't want to drink down the toilet next time?"

The toilet. Why didn't I think of that?

"I'll be back soon with your coffee, and then we must prepare you for the day. Your first appointment is with Gustav, the royal dressmaker."

Caramel pancakes in bed, coffee on its way, *and* a royal makeover? Life is pretty dang good for the world's newest princess.

THIRTY-FIVE MINUTES LATER, I'm caffeinated by some surprisingly decent coffee, showered and dressed, and ready to meet the famous Gustav and his glam squad, who

I am assured by Alice will weave his magic and transform me from an ugly duckling into a beautiful swan.

I'm not exactly thrilled to be referred to as an ugly duckling, but in my comfortable "boyfriend" jeans, sneakers, and monogrammed sweatshirt telling the world about my hobbies, even I know I'm not exactly princess material.

"Grandmama!" I exclaim with genuine delight when I see her sitting in one of the reception rooms. She has her ankles crossed and a cup and saucer in her hands—her little pinkies at just the right angle, I'm sure.

There is a collective gasp among those present: Vladimir, Alice, some guy who looks like he should be in a 90s boy band, and a couple of women in elegant dresses and pearls.

"What? What did I do?"

Vladimir leans in. "Even though she is your grandmother you must greet her with a small curtsy and address her as Your Majesty. You may call her 'Grandmama' after the initial greeting."

"Good to know." I turn to the group and give them a wave that even feels dorky to me. "Hey. Sorry to get it wrong. I'm new at this," I explain to everyone before I hook one foot behind the other and dip down, my head lowered, just the way Alice showed me on my first day here.

Man, am I lucky to have Vlad and Alice in my court.

"Good morning, Your Majesty," I say before I straighten, saying a little prayer that I got it all right.

My grandmama smiles at me as she places her cup and saucer on a side table. "It's very nice to see you again, Madeline. Please, take a seat." She indicates a chair opposite her. "How have you found your last couple of days, my dear?"

"It's been good. I'm getting to know the place and

Alice and Vlad have been helping me with stuff. It's been fun."

"I'm very glad to hear it. Do we meet with your approval?"

"My approval?" I laugh and it ends in a deeply unlady-like snort. I throw my hand over my mouth in embarrassment as the pearl-clutching ladies regard me in surprise.

I don't look at Vladimir.

"Apologies for that… sound."

"It's quite all right, dear. I've been known to snort when I laugh, occasionally," Grandmama says kindly, and I remember why I like her.

"What I was going to say is what's not to like about this place? It's beautiful, my rooms are incredible, everyone is super nice, and I live in an actual palace. Chloe, my best friend back in Texas, would kill to live in this place."

"Would she indeed?" Grandmama's lips quirk. "Perhaps you should invite Chloe for a visit once your investiture as Princess takes place. But tell her she needn't kill anyone beforehand."

I laugh. "I'll do that."

"But how rude of me. I haven't introduced you to my ladies-in-waiting. This is Lady Foster," she says as one of the pearl-wearing women nods at me. Or is it a bow? It's unclear. "And this is Lady Chesterton." The second woman does exactly as the first, and I nod and smile at both of them.

"Great to meet you, ladies. Although you're actual Ladies as well as being ladies, so that's cute."

Why am I talking?

"Both Lady Foster and Lady Chesterton have been meeting with me about some other business, but it will be just you and I for the fitting with Gustav," she explains.

"Gotcha."

"Thank you, ladies," Grandmama says and they curtsy before they leave the room.

"I'm sure you will be talked about around the city very shortly following that," Grandmama says.

"A couple of gossips, huh?"

"They do enjoy circulating information."

That's a euphemism if ever I've heard one.

"Would you like a cup of tea before we invite Gustav in?"

There is no way on this sweet earth I am drinking Malveauxian tea. Not now, not ever again. "No, thank you. I'm good. I just had some coffee so I'm fully caffeinated."

"I'm glad to hear it." She gestures at Vladimir, who disappears from the room.

"Before Gustav gets here, I just wanted to thank you for the awesome welcome I've had here, Grandmama. You've been so welcoming, and my rooms are amazing. No cap."

"I'm glad you think so. We are so very happy to have you here, Madeline. But why do you say you have no cap? And why would you want a cap, anyway? Are you going to the races?"

"The races?" I question. Then it dawns on me. "'No cap' means honestly. But you don't need to go using it or anything." I'm thinking of the whole "cool" debacle from the day I arrived. "I'll try to stick with less slang terms from now on to make things easier."

"That would be helpful, Madeline dear. Thank you."

"You know, my friends call me Maddie."

"Would you like *me* to call you Maddie?"

"Definitely. Dad only ever called me Madeline when I was naughty, and you're my grandmama. It feels right."

"And you haven't been naughty lately?" she asks with a twinkle in her eye.

"Not for at least three months, promise," I deadpan,

and Grandmama looks shocked. "I'm kidding, Grandmama. It's a joke."

"Oh, I see." She laughs. "It seems I'm going to have to get used to your language as well as learn to know when you are joking."

"Grandmama, can I ask you a question?"

"Of course you can, my dear."

"What was it like when my mom left?"

She pinches her lips together and I can tell I've raised a difficult topic for her. It's been playing on my mind since we arrived here. It's been impossible not to think about her.

Grandmama picks up her cup and saucer and takes a sip of tea. "It was a very difficult time, but your mother made her decision and, ultimately, we had to support her."

"Had to?"

"It was either that or lose her completely."

This doesn't make sense. If my grandparents supported her, why didn't we see them? And why didn't I know I was connected to them? That I was their granddaughter?

"But we didn't see you much when Mom was alive. I only have vague memories of coming here once, and that was when I was little, and I sure don't remember you visiting Houston."

"Things weren't…straightforward," she replies allusively.

"Straightforward?"

"We're not like other families, my dear. We're royal. Your mother was born into her role. When she gave up her official duties, things were never going to be the same again."

"But that doesn't mean you stopped loving her."

"Of course not. We always loved your mother, and it was so very hard when she passed away so young."

I lower my gaze, my throat tightening.

"Your parents wanted you to lead a normal life. Your grandpapa and I respected that." She gives me a soft smile. "Personally, I think they did a splendid job with you."

I lift my eyes to hers and smile back. "Thanks, Grandmama."

There's a knock at the door and Vladimir returns. "The royal dressmaker, Gustav."

In walks a tall man who screams *Look at me!* He's wearing a bold, floral patterned blazer Barbie would be envious of, a crisp black shirt teamed with pale pink slim-fit trousers, and red patent leather loafers. The look's topped off with a pair of thick rimmed red glasses and not a hair out of place. He's everything I imagined a personal stylist to royalty would be, a veritable caricature from a movie where the hot mess of a girl gets her makeover.

I sure am living the fairy tale.

"Your Majesty," he says in a deep baritone voice before he launches into an elaborate bow, complete with sweeping hand gestures. "It is my very deepest honor to be here."

"Gustav, how lovely to see you again," Grandmama says. "Allow me to introduce you to my granddaughter, Princess Madeline."

Gustav turns his attention to me, and instantly his features drop. "Princess Madeline," he says in a strained voice and I know just what he's thinking. He's got his work cut out for him, transforming this American girl into royalty.

He's doing nothing for my self-confidence.

"Hey," I say with another of my dorky hand waves. I can't help it. My hand seems to have a life of its own in this place. Maybe I should try tying it to my side?

"I shall relish the challenge," he states with a sweep of his arms.

I'm a challenge. *Awesome.*

Ten minutes later, a stream of assistants have entered the room where I've been poked, prodded, and measured, and turned from one direction to the other with the hair stylist and makeup artist and Gustav himself assessing me in my pitiful jean-clad state.

After much discussion, I'm dispensed to a bathroom where my hair is scrubbed clean, color is applied in Grandmama-approved highlights, and I return to the reception room to try on an endless array of outfits, from evening wear to day suits to elegant dresses and heels, my hair in foils the whole time.

By the end of the afternoon, I've had what little moustache I possessed ripped from my face, my eyebrows shaped, my hair highlighted and styled, and received what the esthetician called a "soft glow" tan from head to toe.

"You must see yourself before we present you to the Queen," Gustav instructs, and a full-length mirror is wheeled in front of me.

You know when you see makeover scenes in movies and the people regard their new selves in disbelief after their transformation? Well, I hate to be a copycat but that is exactly what happens to me.

I gawk at my reflection, half wondering who this totally put together woman is gazing back at me. I know it sounds insane, but for a moment, I think it's actually Kate Middleton. As in the real Kate Middleton, only she has a look of shock and wonderment on her face. It takes a full five seconds for my brain to catch up to the fact that the woman looking back at me is... me. Only the very best version of me I could ever imagine.

My once mousy brown hair is now highlighted to perfection, my once frizzy ends now fall in soft waves. My makeup is subtle and natural but makes me look ten times better than I've looked before in my life, my figure complemented by the cut of the blue dress, cinched at the waist with a silver belt that matches the pumps on my feet.

I look like a well-heeled East Coast WASP, on my way to a charity luncheon—and one hundred percent not like the girl from Texas who visits Taco Bell way too often for her health.

"You love it," Gustav instructs, and I can't help but agree.

"You've made me look—" I'm not quite sure what the word is to describe this complete and utter transformation.

"Like a princess," he finishes for me, his chin lifted in triumph.

I let out a giddy laugh, still gazing at my reflection. "Yeah. I guess you did." I turn to him. "Thank you. I thought you were going to make me look like a drag queen."

He pulls his brows together in confusion. "But you are a woman."

"You've got a good point there."

"Now, we shall present you to the Queen."

"Right." I run my hands over the silk fabric of the dress. "She sure is going to love this."

Gustav's lips lift. "Of course she will. You are my masterpiece."

"I'm not sure I'd go quite that far."

"But of course. You must. You are a masterpiece. You are a princess," he states with an assuredness I can only dream to possess. "A beautiful princess who will be presented to the world at the ball in the most exquisite dress and tiara!"

I swallow.

Geez. Talk about pressure.

Gustav had me try on at least a dozen ball gowns until

we landed on one that I didn't feel completely ridiculous in. Seriously, the guy had me looking like 80s Princess Di, with sequins and bows and big puffy sleeves. Which was all very well for 80s Princess Di, but not so great for 21st century Princess Maddie.

The dress we agreed on is perfect. It's a Kate Middleton-inspired satin floor-length gown in Malveauxian blue, paired with sparkly heeled sandals and a silver clutch, the overall effect of which makes me look...well, it makes me look like a princess.

Kind of appropriate, don't you think?

The queen is sent for, and I find myself turning back to my reflection. The girl gazing back at me has got this. She's a bonafide princess, from the top of her head to the tips of her (newly painted) toes.

Now, all I've got to do is start feeling like one.

Chapter 8

Alexander

> Good people of Malveaux, I cannot tell you how lucky you are. The Prince of Passion himself is gracing you with his presence for the ball to formally welcome your new princess. All this reporter can say is watch out, Princess Madeline, your heart could be snapped right up if our Prince McHottie has anything to do with it. It would take a strong woman to be able to rebuff his scrumptiousness. Good luck!

#HeartThrobHavoc
#HeartGuardOnDuty

Yours always,

Fabiana Fontaine xx

I grab a couple of drinks from the passing waiter, who bows his head in greeting, and hand one to Amelia. Of course, being a royal event in Malveaux, the only drink on offer is locally made champagne which, along with their allegedly delicious tea—if you think tea that tastes like it was made by someone with a vendetta against its drinkers is delicious—is about the only thing I'm ever offered to drink here.

But, as the Americans say, this isn't my first rodeo, and I have come prepared to this ball. I pull a hipflask out of my top pocket and unscrew the lid.

"Alex! You can't do that!" Amelia hisses, glancing around in the crowded palace ballroom.

"You sound like Sofia."

"How deeply insulting of you," she quips before she thrusts her glass at me. "Is it whisky? Bourbon? Vodka? Oh, say it's vodka."

"Sorry to disappoint. It's orange cordial." I pour some of the liquid into my own glass.

She gives me a puzzled expression. "Why would you smuggle cordial into a ball?"

"You have tasted the champagne here, haven't you?"

"Good point."

I pour a splash into her glass before I slip the hip flask back into my pocket. "Tell me, do you make it a habit to spike your own drinks with hard liquor?"

"Of course not. I'm so much more sensible than you. You're the Party Prince with a different woman on your arm every night of the week, remember? Whereas all they say about me is that I'm blossoming into a lovely young lady."

I frown. The Party Prince moniker has proven to be one that's been hard to shake, even though I've hardly been the life and soul of the party for some time. I suppose being *The Sensible Prince Who Gets Home by 11* doesn't have quite the same alliterative appeal.

"I've given all that up," I tell her.

"What? Womanizing?"

"You make it sound so sordid."

"Serial dating. Is that better?"

I chortle. "Not really."

"What do you mean you've given it up?" She takes a sip of her drink. "Much better with the cordial."

"I haven't been involved with anyone for at least a year."

"Heavens! Why ever not?"

"Don't tell our parents."

She crosses her heart. "Promise."

"I'm…ready."

"Ready?"

"To you know, find The One."

She reels back from me. "As in fall in love and get married?"

"Amelia," I warn.

"Sorry, Alex, it's just so very *not* you."

I shrug. "It's the new me."

She lets out a low whistle. "Any luck finding this elusive woman?"

"Sadly, no." I think of Freya and many others like her. "The women of the world seem only interested in the fact that I'm a prince."

Amelia pushes her lower lip out. "Poor Alex. Adored by many, loved by few."

"Not helping."

She rubs my arm. "I'm only messing around. I think it's fabulous that you want to fall in love. I've got the most splendid idea! I could be your wingman."

I shake my head. "No. Absolutely not."

"Please? It could be so fun looking for your queen. Oh, I know! The new princess. She's gorgeous. She would be perfect for you."

"The American?" I scoff, barely believing my sister could think such a thing. "That would be a hard no."

"Don't dismiss her outright, brother. You haven't even met her. When do you think they're going to present her?"

"I'm sure she'll have chosen a very dramatic moment so we all sit up and pay attention."

She pokes me in the ribs. "What happened to make you so cynical?"

"Why, I was born into the royal family of Ledonia."

She lets out a laugh. "By that assessment I should be cynical too, and I'm not in the least."

"You're also only just out of nappies. There's plenty of time for you to become cynical, believe me."

"Just out of nappies? Alex, I'm 22," she protests, even though we both know I'm only winding her up. It's a lot more fun with Sofia. She takes the bait every time, whereas Amelia and I seem to share the same sense of humor and know innately when one is teasing the other. Which we do constantly.

If it wasn't for my darling younger sister, life would be a whole lot more boring .

"Your sash is skew-whiff. Hold this and I'll fix it." She passes me her glass and sets to work on straightening the blue satin sash that runs diagonally across my Ledonian red jacket from my shoulder to my waist.

"What on earth are you drinking?" Mummy asks as she and Sofia appear at our side. "And you have two of them? Alex."

"Crazy party animal that he is, Alex spiked our drinks with orange cordial," Amelia explains tongue-in-cheek as she takes her glass back. "It's so much better. Want some?"

"It's also a potential headline," Mummy grumbles.

"She's right. The optics aren't ideal," Sofia agrees.

"Optics?" Amelia asks. "Who's watching us? Everyone's here to meet the new American princess. We're a sideshow."

"Alex is never a sideshow, Ami. He's the darling of the press," Sofia says with a familiar note to her voice.

It's true that I get a lot more media attention than her. She's always been so much more sensible than me. Typical first born. She'd never be caught dead playing poker in Las Vegas, surrounded by what Amelia referred to as my "bevy of beauties". She couldn't even point to where Las Vegas is on a map. Or even Monte Carlo, for that matter, which is a mere hop, skip, and a jump away.

Although those partying days are behind me now, my reputation still lingers, and there are a few devoted journalists out there who love nothing better than to create a story about me and some new woman completely out of thin air.

Last week, I had torrid affairs with at least two American heiresses, seduced a senator's daughter, and partied all night with a rap star. Allegedly.

Sofia, on the other hand, has dated a total of two men in her life, one of whom was way back in high school and lasted for about six weeks. And the other? He's the one who broke her heart. Not much of a fun story for the media to get their grubby mitts on. It was a headline for about a week, after which she's been regarded as the Pitiful Princess ever since.

Party Princes get a lot more coverage than Pitiful Princesses, I'm afraid, even when they've hung up their dance shoes.

"Quick, you two. Get rid of your peculiar-colored drinks before anyone notices," Mother demands.

"If I must." I drain my glass.

All three members of my family regard me with wide eyes.

"What? I did what you said."

Mummy pulls her lips into a line. "Hmm."

"You're so literal, Alex," Sofia complains, but really, I did what I was asked so there should be no problem.

Amelia is still clutching onto her glass.

"Go on then. Down in one," I instruct her with a grin.

Amelia lifts the glass to her lips but Mummy puts her hand over the top of it before she has the chance, and whisks the glass away, depositing it on a passing waiter's tray.

"Mummy! I was going to drink that," she complains.

"We don't need a drunk princess," Sofia replies.

"As if one glass will do that," Amelia mumbles under her breath.

"What did you say?" Sofia asks.

"I said you are very wise, dear sister," she replies and I huff a laugh.

A man in Malveauxian royal uniform arrives at our group and bows his head. "Your Majesty, Your Royal highnesses. The Princess Madeline will be arriving shortly and we require your Majesty for the formal presentation, if you please."

"What about us?" Sofia asks. "Are we required, too?"

"Not at this present moment, ma'am," he replies.

Sofia bristles. She lives for this kind of pomp and ceremony.

"The three of you behave while I'm away," Mummy instructs.

"Of course we will," Sofia replies.

"It's not you I'm concerned about, my dear." Mummy throws a meaningful look at both Amelia and me.

"We'll behave," I promise her.

Even my own mother thinks I'm a wild party animal, set to make an embarrassing scene.

She arches a sardonic eyebrow at me. "No fountains."

"One time, Mummy. One time," I protest, knowing exactly what she's referring to. We were here for another royal event when I was back from university for the summer holidays. I had rather too much to drink, thanks to the fact I was new at it and had no clue what my threshold was, and nor did I care a whole lot, either. My friend, Renee, and I found a rather pretty group of women, all of whom seemed to want to flirt outrageously with us, and we got up to no good together. Cutting a long story short, I ended up in the fountain with three of the ladies, fully clothed in my regal attire, and drenched from head to foot.

As adept as they are at photographing you at your worst, a paparazzo appeared from behind a bush some-where to record it all, and me, the fountain, and the three lovely ladies were immediately splashed over all the media the next day, from which the moniker Party Prince was born.

As our mother disappears into the crowd, my attention is claimed by Jacob Lowland, a business leader who has fingers in pies both here and in Ledonia, and a couple of other men.

"We'll have to keep our new princess away from the likes of you, eh, Prince Alexander," he says, his eyes bright.

"The Party Prince," one of the other men adds. "Breaking hearts wherever he goes."

"Oh, I'm sure—" I begin, but am cut off.

"You chew them up and spit them out faster than I can eat a hot meal," Jacob says, and all three of them laugh.

"What's your body count these days, eh?" one of the other men asks.

"Body count?" I question, barely believing how crass they're being.

"What I wouldn't give to be born a prince and have that amount of female attention," Jacob continues.

"Bloody fantastic," one of the other men adds, and they all nod their agreement.

I, on the other hand, do not.

I've had enough.

"If you'll excuse me, gentlemen," I say.

Jacob nudges one of his friends. "He's spotted his latest target, I bet. We won't stand in the way of the Party Prince."

"Something like that," I mumble as I make my exit.

With reluctance, I greet people as I make my way through the crowd, pausing to shake hands with a duke and exchange a few short sentences with Prince William of Britain, before I push through to the exit and find myself alone but for wait staff scurrying past with trays full of drinks.

I take a deep breath and lean up against the wall.

Will I ever shake off this image? I get it. I was a total bad boy. But those days are in the rearview mirror.

Does anyone actually care enough to get to know the real me?

A waitress in a black, form-fitting skirt and white shirt

throws me a smile as she breezes past me. "Your Royal Highness," she coos.

I give her a brief smile before I push myself off the wall and walk away from her down the hall.

"Do you need anything?" she asks as she trails behind me.

"No, I'm perfectly fine, thank you," I tell her, pausing and turning back so as not to offend.

She bites down on her bottom lip. "I get off at midnight if you want to…you know."

I regard the pretty waitress with a look of hope in her eyes and I know I need to find a way to let her down gently so that a) I don't hurt her feelings, and b) she doesn't run to the press, telling them some inflated story about me.

"You're so very kind, but sadly my duties won't allow it," I tell her and her face drops. "Enjoy your evening."

I turn and walk down the hall until I find myself outside a closed door. A furtive glance inside the darkened room suggests it's an empty cupboard, so I slip inside and close the door over behind me, stealing a few moments of isolation before I head back to the throngs—and their opinions of me.

Of course, now that I've closed the door over it's completely dark, and I fumble around, trying to find a light switch.

No luck.

I suppose I'll just stand here like a loser in the dark. Alone.

Perhaps I should meditate? Women I meet are always going on about things like yoga and meditation. I've always assumed it's because they want me to know how bendy they are, but maybe they're onto something?

I pull out my phone and search for a meditation app. They've got apps for everything, I'm sure there will be a bunch for meditating. I land on one and as it begins to download I use the light to look around me.

It's a sizable closet, filled with things like mops and brooms and linens. There's a distinct smell of silver polish and ammonia, both of which have begun to fill my nostrils, much to my irritation.

Why isn't this app downloading faster?

"What are you doing in here?" a high-pitched voice demands, and I almost jump out of my skin.

Someone is in here?

"Hello?" I fumble with my phone to locate the torch app, which suddenly seems to have disappeared. "Who's in here?" I demand, half expecting to find a murderer or some kind of psychopath, wielding a knife, ready to attack.

"Who are *you*?" an indignant voice responds.

Finally, I locate the torch app and flick it on, scanning the closet.

I suck in a breath as it illuminates a woman, her features lined with fear as she squints at me, her hands held in tight fists in front of her chest.

I relax. She doesn't look like a murderer or a psychopath, or even a ghost. Well, a little like a ghost. The woman is rather pale.

But there's something recognizable about her. The look in her eyes is like a deer in headlights. A beautiful deer. A *familiar* deer.

I take a step closer to her.

"Get back!" she screeches. "I'm warning you; I know tai chi."

I press my lips together to stop a smile. "You know how to do slow, controlled movements at sunrise?" If I tried to keep the amusement from my voice it wasn't much of an effort.

"I meant... karate. I know karate and I'm not afraid to

use it!" She unfurls her fists and brandishes her flat hands at me.

A laugh bubbles up, and I do my best to style it out as a cough. "I come in peace, I assure you."

"How do I know that?" She does a chopping motion with one of her hands, presumably to demonstrate her karate prowess.

"Why don't you put those weapons of yours down?" I reach for her hands to hold them in mine reassuringly. This woman is freaked out and I need to do *something*.

As my hands fold over hers she snaps them away, raises one in a fist, and before I have the chance to ask what she intends to do with that fist, she jabs it straight at my face.

"Argh!" I call out, my eyes watering as my nose throbs in pain that pulses painfully across my cheekbones. I stagger back, clasping my nose "What did you do that for?"

But no sooner have the words left my mouth when she yanks the cupboard door open and bursts from the room, her skirt billowing behind her as she rushes away from me down the hall.

"What the—?!" I trail after her, muttering in disbelief. Who punches someone in the face in a hallway cupboard when all they were trying to do was show they weren't a threat?

Through watering eyes, I blink at her as she tears away from me down the hallway—only to fall flat on her face, her skirt billowing up behind her to expose her plain white cotton underpants, and her tiara pinging off her head and bouncing across the carpet.

Who is this woman and what the heck is she playing at?

My instinct kicks in, and before I have the chance to second guess myself, I hurry down the hallway to her aid.

"Are you all right?" I ask.

Her eyes are wild as she yells, "Stay away!" She clamors back to her feet, clutching her head.

"Are you hurt?" I ask, and she shakes her head, her eyes searching the floor.

She must be looking for her tiara.

"It's over there." I point at the tiara on the ground, still in one piece.

She grabs it and turns back to me. "I—please don't tell anyone."

"Okay."

She doesn't say another word, instead she turns on her heel and dashes away, rounding a corner and disappearing from sight.

I stand, rooted to the spot, my brain scrambling to make sense of what just happened. I sought a brief moment of refuge in a cupboard only to be attacked by a beautiful woman in a tiara with an American accent.

My nose throbs painfully as realization dawns on me.

She's Madeline, the American here to claim the throne. The woman a nation has pinned their hopes on.

The woman who wields a strong right hook.

Chapter 9

Maddie

Barely believing what just happened, I round a corner. My heartbeat is racing, my hand throbbing as I hold onto my skirts, the tiara I feared broken or lost digging painfully into my palm.

My dignity? Well, I'm not sure what my dignity is doing right now, but it sure as heck left me a while back.

All I know is that man could have been anyone and he could have done anything. I *had* to hit him. I had to show him that I wasn't some pushover he could take advantage of. Or murder. Or worse! Who knows what his intentions were?

I mean now that I think about it, I did hear him muttering about a meditation app.

Do murderers use meditation apps?

And do murderers check if you're okay when you run away from them and accidentally land flat on your face, and then show you where your tiara landed?

And, if I was being entirely honest with myself, I'd admit that dressed in his red jacket and sash he looked a lot like Prince Alexander. The Party Prince himself.

But it couldn't have been him. What would a man like him be doing in a hallway closet, searching for a meditation app? Isn't he the prince of all things fun and sexy? He should be flirting with women and telling jokes, the life and soul of the party.

Oh, I don't know.

I did what I did and all I can hope is that the man—Prince Alexander or not—is true to his word and doesn't mention what happened to anyone. Then we can all get on with our lives.

Now, I'm horribly late for this whole princess presentation that, personally, I'd like to skip altogether. And not only because I'm dressed up like a doll, from the tiara that's supposed to be on my head to my blue gown and high heeled shoes covered in diamantes. But I'd barely managed to get past feeling overwhelmed by the whole thing—the very reason I was taking time out in the closet in the first place—when my intruder turned up and it all took a turn for the crazy.

Talk about *not* the way I wanted things to go tonight.

"Princess Madeline!" a familiar voice calls and I slow my pace.

Turning, I plaster on as brave a smile as I can manage as Vladimir strides toward me.

"Vlad, there you are," I say as though I haven't been hiding from him and everyone else for the last 10 minutes.

We both know I'm bluffing, but he has the good grace not to mention it.

"I've been looking for you for some time, ma'am. I was concerned about you," he says in a surprisingly fatherly and tender way, and I feel bad for giving him the run around.

"Well, I'm right here. All in one piece." My hand throbs. I shove it behind my back.

Vladimir gives me a questioning look. Who knew punching someone could hurt so much? Clearly people who get into fights would, but I'm not one of those people. In fact, I've never hit anyone before in my life, and I can safely say I have no intention of ever having to wield my fists again.

"Shall we join your father and the King and Queen? They're waiting for you for the presentation, ma'am."

The mention of my dad makes my chest tighten.

"I guess."

"May I make a suggestion before we do?" he asks and I nod. "You might like to reattach your tiara and perhaps straighten your hair."

I unfurl my hand, in which I've tightly clasped the tiara. Dang it! I must look like a hot mess.

A short walk later and Vladimir delivers me to Alice, whose eyes flare at the sight of me. I'm thankful when she doesn't ask any questions. She simply fixes my hair and makeup and places the tiara carefully back on my head. As she's putting on the finishing touches, trumpets sound and Vladimir rushes me down the hall to where my family are waiting patiently for me.

"Where have you been?" Dad asks.

"Alice was just making sure I looked perfect," I tell him, which is the truth. I just left out why.

He takes my hands and gives them a squeeze. I try not to wince.

"You look more than perfect. You look beautiful."

"Thanks, Dad."

"They're ready and waiting, Madeline," Grandpapa says and instantly my pulse quickens.

Dad places a kiss on my forehead. "You've got this, princess. You're brave and strong and I love you."

A guy in a fancy blue suit with gold trim makes an announcement in Malveauxian, and a heavy velvet curtain is pulled open. I step out onto a balcony, flanked by my grandparents, to the sound of polite applause from the crowd of people below.

I blink at my surroundings. I'm high above the sea of people, the place more like the size of a stadium than a hall. There are huge chandeliers hanging from the ceiling, the walls covered in gold patterned wallpaper and long gilded mirrors. The guests are all wearing super fancy evening clothes.

It's like a scene from a movie, only it's all real—and I'm right at its center.

I stand and wave and smile, just as I was taught to do during the rehearsal.

Just keep smiling, I tell myself as I'm chaperoned down the stairs by the dependable Vladimir, who holds on tight to me, probably because he's seen me get out of a car before. The last thing anyone wants is for me to trip and land on my face during my official presentation.

We reach the bottom of the stairs where there's a line of dignitaries for me to greet.

And so it begins. So much smiling. So much nodding.

So much hand clasping. So much pretending I can understand whatever language it is that they're using. Lucky for me, a bunch of them speak English, telling me how wonderful I am and how wonderful it is for me to be here, and how all their hopes lie with me, wonderful me.

Zero pressure.

"Remember, Princess, when you meet royalty, you only curtsy to the senior members of the family, the King and Queen," Vlad explains under his breath as we reach a group of people in red with crowns on their heads. "You are meeting the prince and princesses as equals."

"Shame. I was getting used to all the curtsies and bows," I murmur back.

"Princess Madeline, may I introduce you to the members of the Ledonian royal family," Vlad announces.

Oh, no. Prince Alexander is a member of this family.

I slide my eyes down the line, but I don't see him.

My shoulders drop as I release a relieved breath.

A man about my dad's age gives me a stiff, humorless smile, after which a kind looking woman who must be his wife, the Queen, says hello. She's accompanied by two gorgeous women about my age. They're all dressed in red, and all have crowns of varying sizes atop their heads, and together they look like a charming royal fairy tale family.

Vladimir announces, "King Frederic of Ledonia, Queen Astrid of Ledonia, Princess Sofia of Ledonia, and Princess Amelia of Ledonia, may I introduce Princess Madeline of Malveaux."

Well, that's a mouthful.

Does he have to mention the place we're all from each time? That's like me meeting a new staff member back at the glazing company and introducing myself as Madeline Turner of the wrong part of Houston. It would be just plain weird. But I guess they have different rules here in

Europe, particularly when everyone's sporting priceless crowns and tiaras.

"I'm very pleased to meet you, your Royal Highnesses," I say with my best winning smile as I curtsy to the King and Queen. I stretch my hand out to shake the King's hand.

But instead of a handshake, King Frederic clasps my shoulders with firm hands and plants a purposeful and very dry kiss on each of my cheeks, the bristles of his moustache sharp and uncomfortable against my skin. Not that I'm complaining about the dryness of the cheek kisses, because sloppy, wet cheek kisses from a middle-aged man I've just met? *Ew.*

"Woah!" I say in the surprise, staggering back as he unclasps me.

It was made clear by Vladimir that when I meet a King or Queen, I'm supposed to shake their hands as though they are my equals—not get manhandled and poked in the face by surprisingly wire-like moustache hairs.

King Frederic pulls his brows together, looking thoroughly unamused.

Can this kind of thing cause an international incident?

I decide to style it out as best I can. "Well!" I exclaim exuberantly. "Well well well. You do look so well."

"So well?" he questions, looking at me like I'm some kind of simpleton.

I really can't blame the guy.

I need to do some quick thinking.

"You are looking so well, King Frederic of Ledentia."

"Ledonia," Vladimir corrects.

"Ledonia," I repeat.

How could I have gotten that wrong when it's been repeated so many times?

"Which is awesome to see and makes me super happy

because I am so very concerned that you are well and healthy and all those things."

He looks at me blankly.

"So." What do I say now? I've already messed this one up royally—no pun intended—but I guess at least I haven't punched the guy. That, it would seem, I reserve for strange men who may be related to these people, appearing out of thin air in hallway closets.

My hand throbs.

At my side, Vladimir clears his throat "I believe it's customary for Americans to comment on the health of the people they meet, Your Majesty. It's a very endearing quality, don't you think?"

I flick a thankful smile to him. Vlad to the rescue.

I jump on it. "We Americans are super concerned that everybody is well and healthy. You know, after the pandemic and all." I tilt my head to the side and pull my features into a look of concern. "Wellness has to be a top priority. For all of us."

Have I taken it too far?

Who am I kidding? *Of course* I have. He's looking at me like I'm some kind of a babbling idiot.

If only there was a way I could stop myself from talking.

"Princess Madeline. We are also very pleased to meet you," Queen Astrid says with a smile that is so generous and warm, and in such strong juxtaposition to her husband's icy glare, that I instantly like her. "I'm sorry our sons are not here to meet you. Our younger son, Maximilien, is currently at university at Cambridge in England, and our other son, Alexander, appears to have been detained."

She, too, places a kiss on each of my cheeks, but this time I'm ready for them. And anyway, she doesn't have a moustache to stab me with, and she smells like a spring meadow filled with pretty flowers. It's altogether a much more pleasant experience.

"It's great to meet y'all," I reply as I smile at the Queen and the two princesses. "I love your red dresses. You stand out so well against all the blue we've got going on here."

"Blue has been the color of Malveauxian royalty for a millennium," King Frederic explains in that super friendly tone of his that somehow manages to fit judgment, irritation, and condescension into a few short words all at once.

It's a skill.

"You're right. In fact, I believe it was King Ivan III back in 1473 who first wore this particular shade of blue and made a royal decree that all subsequent monarchs must prefer it over all other colors," I say.

I'm quoting Wikipedia's Malveauxian Royalty page almost word for word.

The King's eyes skim over me briefly before he pulls his lips into the least genuine smile I've seen all day. "Quite."

I chat for a short time with the Queen and the two princesses, all of whom seem super nice, before Vladimir moves me along to greet the rest of the dignitaries. Once we've finally reached the end of the long line and my face feels like it's frozen into a smile, I see Princess Amelia making a beeline for me.

"I want to talk to you on your own with no bodyguards or pesky parents listening," she tells me as she hooks her arm through mine.

"Sure thing." I shoot Vladmir a look and he nods his assent.

She leads me to a quieter end of the hall. "How have you found it all, Princess Madeline? I bet it's so very different from your life back in America. Do you miss it? Do you miss your friends? Do you wish you were back there? Or do you prefer it here now?" Princess Amelia's pretty face is bright, her big brown eyes shining.

"That's a lot of questions."

"Answer as many as you see fit. I don't mind. I just want to get to know you."

"Sure." I count them off on my fingers. "I'm getting used to being here and everyone is super friendly and nice; it's so very different from my life back home, but that's not to say it's not awesome; and I do miss my friends, my best friend in particular, but we chat a lot and I'm sure I'll make new friends here."

Princess Amelia beams at me. "Well, we find you very, very fascinating, and I for one am more than eager to be one of your new friends, if you'll let me."

I grin at her. "Of course I'll let you. But we probably won't see all that much of each other. Don't you live in another country?"

"Oh, but we do so many things together. Our countries have a long history of rivalry, and then once the rest of Europe started rising up against their royal families a few hundred years ago, that rivalry morphed into a history of sticking together and looking after each other. But I imagine you know quite a lot of that from Wikipedia."

I widen my eyes at her in embarrassment. "How did you—?"

She waves my concern away. "I've contributed person-ally to those pages a number of times, although my points often get taken down."

"What kind of points do you make?"

"Insider tips. You know, things like how Father can be so beastly about allowing me basic freedoms like popping to the shops to buy some new water color paints, or how sometimes it might be nice to wear something other than a red dress to these sorts of occasions."

I huff a laugh. "You did not write those."

"I did," she replies proudly. "Although Father had me blocked from Wikipedia, so now I can't make any changes at all. He said he didn't, but I know he did."

We share a smile and I feel like she's already my friend, even though I've only just met her.

A waiter offers us glasses of champagne, and I take one from the tray.

"I could really use a drink about now. This evening has been a lot," I tell her before I raise the glass to my lips to take a sip.

She places her hand lightly on my forearm as she makes a face. "Oh, you shouldn't drink that. It's utterly ghastly, if you don't mind me saying because I know it's Malveauxian champagne, but really it's just as bad as the tea. That's what my older brother always says. He carries a flask of cordial in his top pocket to put a splash in the champagne, although I had hoped it would be whisky. Much more fun."

"Wait. Your brother is Prince Alexander, right?"

Amelia rolls her eyes in good humor. "Of course you know who he is. Everyone does. He's famous. Father's not wild about it, but Mummy thinks Alex's profile does wonders for the country, and I agree."

I arch an eyebrow. "You mean his profile as the Party Prince?" I ask and instantly realize that sounds a touch judgmental. Okay, a *lot* judgmental. "He's got that reputation, but I'm sure he's an awesome brother."

She beams at me. "He's the best. I adore him. But then of course I do. He's my older brother. I've also got another brother, Max, but he's at university and can't be here. He's the clever one. He's almost as wonderful, but not quite, mainly because he's not as much fun as Alex. You met my sister, Sofia, too. She's great but a touch bossy. You know how older siblings can be."

"Actually, I wouldn't know how it feels to have an older sibling, or any sibling. I'm an only child," I admit. "I always wanted a brother. I'm jealous you've got not one, but two, and a sister."

"You'll have to meet both my brothers. I don't know why Alex wasn't in the official lineup before. Probably off being naughty somewhere, knowing him, although he did insist he's changed." She shrugs.

From what I know about the guy dubbed Prince McHottie, I imagine he was.

"Oh, look. There he is," Amelia says as she waves and smiles at someone behind me before her features drop. "Goodness. What happened to his face?"

I turn to see a man in a red buttoned-up jacket, a blue sash crossing his body from shoulder to hip, his stride strong and confident. His face looks like the image in Chloe's magazine, extremely handsome with a head of dark hair, a strong jaw covered in a cropped beard, and the kind of olive skin I always wished I had instead of my pale skin prone to freckles. Although now that I look at him, his nose is red and swollen and looks like he might have been—

Wait.

His nose looks like it's been…punched?

Ice cold seeps across my chest.

It *was* him. It was Prince Alexander in the closet!

I freeze, every nerve in my body on high alert.

He stops to speak with someone and although I wouldn't have thought it possible, he looks so much more handsome in person. Dangerously handsome.

And angry. Definitely angry.

I swallow, my mouth suddenly dry. The guy in the

closet was Prince Alexander. The guy I went NHL in a bad mood on, who I thought was a murderer or worse, is in fact the Crown Prince of Ledonia, heir to the throne, brother to my new friend.

And the worst thing of all? He's heading our way.

Chapter 10

Alexander

As I make my way through the crowd to Amelia, I spot the woman standing with her. She's about Amelia's height, her hair piled up on top of her head in an elaborate updo that probably took hours. I know. My sisters have complained to me about the process many times.

She's in a blue satin dress, which clearly marks her out as Malveauxian royalty. If there's any doubt, she's also wearing a tiara on top of her head.

She must be the new American Princess.

As I get closer, I size her up. I admit she's a beautiful woman, with classically high cheekbones, wide eyes, full lips, her brown hair an attractive shade of chestnut.

As I get closer, it hits me.

It's her. *She's* my cupboard attacker.

She's the woman with the shockingly firm right hook who not only damaged my face, but then treated me like the enemy even after I tried to help her back to her feet when she fell.

I narrow my eyes at her as hers do the opposite, widening in recognition.

She's about to stutter a heartfelt apology, and I'll do my best to forgive her. Eventually. But not until I've made her squirm. What she did was entirely unnecessary and needlessly violent. Not the behavior of a princess.

"Alex! Where have you been? And what on earth happened to your face?" Amelia exclaims.

I wave her concern away. "It's nothing."

"It doesn't look like nothing. It looks like you've been smashed in the face by an anvil."

I glance down at the American princess's hands. She's clasping her right hand in her left, and I'm quite certain the hidden hand would show a battle scar almost as bad as my own.

"Not an anvil, because I'm not a cartoon character," I reply, my eyes trained on the woman with the strong right hook. "Something else."

Princess Madeline appears to have some control over her features now, and has the good grace to avert her gaze, her face turning as pale as a sheet. She must have concluded that the man in front of her, sporting a damaged face, is in fact her would be assailant—or rather her innocent victim who accidentally stumbled on the scrappy fighter. And paid the price.

"I don't believe we've been introduced. I'm Alexander." I offer her my hand.

She opens her mouth to speak but then seems to think better of it and closes it again.

I suppress a scoff. Of course she doesn't know what to say to me. She could lead with "sorry". That would at least be a start. In fact, that would be the bare minimum I would expect of her, given the circumstances.

When she doesn't respond, Amelia jumps in for her. "This is Princess Madeline of Malveaux. Madeline, this is my brother, Alex, the one I was telling you about."

I arch an eyebrow and it pulls on my swollen nose. "Princess Madeline of Malveaux," I repeat as I bow my head with my hand held over my heart. I'm hamming it up, just to irk her. "I'm thoroughly enchanted to make your acquaintance." I pause before I add, "For the very first time."

I lift my head and look at her wide-eyed expression. She doesn't know what to say or how to behave. I've totally thrown her—and I've begun to enjoy this. After all, this woman attacked me for no good reason, leaving me with a painful and swollen nose that may or may not be broken. Although the kind member of staff who provided me with an ice pack assured me it wasn't in fact broken, it certainly feels bruised and battered.

She still hasn't taken my hand, so I purposefully move it closer to her. After a beat she takes it in her left hand and gives it one singular shake.

She's acting like a petulant child, which is totally ridiculous considering I'm the injured party in this instance.

"I'm *thoroughly enchanted* to meet you, too," she says with a smile that gets nowhere near her eyes.

"I'm sure not quite as enchanted as I am to meet *you*," I reply, layering it on thick.

"Perhaps we're equally enchanted," she offers.

"Oh, I very much doubt that. I'm the enchanted one."

We stare at one another like we're in a face off.

Amelia is watching us. "You're acting weird."

"Who? Me?" I ask.

"What did happen to your face, because from where I'm standing, it seems to have affected your brain."

I glance at the American Princess. She's studying the floor as though it's become rather fascinating.

As well she might.

She's hardly going to volunteer the information that my face met the wrong end of her fist in an entirely unjustified attack.

I clear my throat and wait, giving her the chance to confess.

But it would seem the floor remains so much more fascinating.

"My brain is absolutely fine, but thank you for your concern, Ami. It was a case of waiter's tray meets face," I lie, wondering how this new princess will react.

That makes her snap her attention to me.

She must know I'm protecting her. Of course I am. I gave her my word. I'm not planning on telling my sister about what actually happened. Or anyone else for that matter.

What do you think of me now?

"Ouch!" Amelia declares. "But good news on the brain sitch."

"It's fine." I offer my sister a benevolent smile before I return my attention to Madeline. "You should see the tray."

Amelia giggles. "As long as you're okay."

"Nothing damaged but my ego. And my nose. Clearly," I reply. "Ami, would you mind hunting down a real drink for me, not this horrible cough medicine masquerading as champagne?"

"I'm sure a member of the wait staff will be here soon," she protests. "I'll protect you from their trays. Don't you worry."

"I'd prefer a glass of brandy, if I'm honest. Why don't you get one for each of us? I'm assuming you could do with a brandy, too, Princess Madeline? You look a little...shaken."

"Shaken? No, I'm good," she replies with a scrunch of her nose—something I can't do without wincing.

Show off.

Amelia's eyes brighten. "That's the best idea you've had all day, Alex. I'll be right back with three glasses. We can have a toast to you, Madeline. Welcome you to the fray."

"Oh, I'm not much of a brandy drinker," she replies. "I'll stick with this." She raises her champagne glass, which I notice is full.

"I wouldn't do that," Amelia warns, and Madeline lowers the glass.

Pity. I was rather looking forward to the look on her face as she attempts to swallow her first sip.

"Because it's utterly dreadful, remember? Wait until I've got the brandy, promise?" Amelia says.

"Sure," she replies uncertainly.

Amelia leaves me with the newest princess in the room, aka Right Hook Madeline.

I lean toward her so only she can hear—did I catch a hint of her scent? Something feminine and evocative.

Not that I plan on being evoked.

"Tell me, Princess Madeline, do you make it a habit to attack first and ask questions later? Or is that a new dimension to your charming personality, now that you're suddenly a princess?"

She twists her mouth. "I thought you'd followed me in there and that you wanted to do something not very nice to me."

"Not very nice? Like what?" I ask with my eyebrows raised suggestively, a smile on my lips.

Yes, I know, I'm teasing her. But this is the woman who attacked me and failed to even apologize. I can't just let her get away with it, now, can I?

"What?" she snaps.

This woman is a real charmer.

I double down.

"Two unattached people of the opposite sex, alone in a darkened room while everyone else is occupied. Hmm. Tell me, princess, what are the possibilities?"

She looks at me, incredulous, her eyes wide as her jaw slackens.

Target struck.

"You're *hitting* on me?" she asks in obvious disbelief.

"I'm merely asking a question."

"Oh, you're definitely hitting on me."

I scoff. Who does she think she is? So irresistible to men that even after she's punched me, I want to seduce her? The cheek of this impostor!

Not that she's an actual imposter per se. I'm sure she really is Princess Josephine's daughter. They would have DNA checked her before they did anything else. The Malveauxian royal family are no fools. But I'm not feeling in the least charitable toward her.

"Princess—" I begin only for her to lift a finger to scold me like I'm a naughty schoolboy.

"I know your reputation, Prince Alexander. Not going to happen. Not now. Not *ever*. Got it?"

Now she's insulting me on top of the punch?

This woman!

"I assure you, princess. I'm not 'hitting on you', as you so delightfully put it," I tell her, despite the fact I quite possibly crossed the line from teasing into flirtation just now. What can I say? Notwithstanding the fact she's clearly not remorseful for what she did back in the hallway cupboard, she's breathtakingly beautiful, and feisty, to boot.

A lethal combination.

"It's not like I asked if you wanted to get out of here, or anything corny like that."

She balls her hands into fists and thrusts them to her hips, and I note with satisfaction that she winces. Good. Her hand clearly hurts.

"I wasn't born yesterday you know, dude."

I suppress a smile. "Dude?"

"You heard me, *dude*."

"Is that because to show interest in somebody you punch them? Seems rather violent to me, but then you are from Texas and things are different there, I'm told."

She glares at me. Is it terrible that I think she looks hot angry?

Yes, yes it is.

"You're insulting me *and* where I'm from? Wow. Just wow."

"Take it as a two for one."

She raises her brows. "Whatever. You were definitely hitting on me just now, which is so outrageous I can't even."

I lean a little closer and murmur, "Believe me, Texas, if I were hitting on you, you would know."

She pulls back. "Texas?" she scoff-laughs.

"Texas," I confirm.

I don't think she knows quite what to do with the nickname I've bestowed on her.

"Is that because you're Prince Charming and women simply fall at your feet with a mere glance in their direction?"

I do my best to ignore the way her instant judgment makes my heart sink.

I'm never going to shake my image, not even with someone I've just met.

"Something like that."

"You're just as I imagined." She gestures at my face. "Only with a slightly enhanced nose."

"Thanks to you."

She shrugs. "All part of the service."

"Remind me never to stumble across 'the service' from you again."

"Oh, I can guarantee you will never stumble across *my* 'service' again in your life."

We stand in irritated silence, both of us glaring at the other. How did this turn from being vaguely fun to outright hostile? Oh, that's right, my damaged face and this obstinate American.

"What were you doing in the hallway cupboard, anyway?" I ask.

She lifts her chin. "That is none of your business."

I gesture at my face, my nose giving a little throb, right on cue. "I would say you made it my business, princess."

Her eyes drop from mine to my nose before she lifts them back up again. "I was taking a break, that's all."

"Aka calling your publicist."

"What?!"

"Tell me, which magazine are you going exclusive with? *The Malveaux Telegraph* would be a good choice because it's got a wide national circulation, but you probably want to go global for maximum financial reward. Probably an American publication, I would say."

"I'm not going exclusive with any magazine, Malveauxian *or* American!"

"So you're spreading yourself around. Good thinking, although you'll probably make less money that way, and knowing what I do about you, I imagine that is your main goal."

She rounds on me. "Who do you think you are suggesting that I'm using this massive, unexpected life change to make money? It's…it's not fair."

She almost stomps her foot like a toddler having a tantrum.

I bite back a smile. "Not fair?"

She scowls. "You heard me."

"Look, you and I both know that this"—I gesture around us—"could all be gone tomorrow if Prince Nicolas decides against abdication. Which he may very well do once he comes to his senses and realizes what the country's alternative is. You're here as a backup option for the Crown. You may as well cash in while you have the chance."

Her eyes widen in disbelief. I know I've crossed the line from teasing to insults. What can I say? This new American Princess brings out the worst in me.

I'm not proud.

"You're calling me a what-now?"

I know I've been harsh, but I'm merely parroting what they're saying in the media. One journalist called her Malveaux's Backup Princess on national TV yesterday. But despite the fact that's clearly what she is, I don't need to be the one rubbing her face in it. Which, I've noticed, is rather beautiful.

I temper my approach, despite the throbbing pain in my nose, reminding me what this woman is capable of. "You must know you're here in case Nicolas follows through with his threat to abdicate, and there's nothing wrong with being a backup. Heck, we've got three of them in Ledonia, aka my brother and sisters."

She's not having a bar of it.

"You're a real piece of work, you know that?" she growls, and I notice tears welling in her eyes. She sniffs them back as she raises her chin once more in defiance.

I feel sorry for her. I know I've taken it too far. She might have punched me and run off, but looking at her now in her tiara, she looks like a lost little lamb, almost entirely overwhelmed by this new life she finds herself in.

And here I am being horrible to her.

I soften.

"Look, let's call it a truce, shall we? My nose for your presence?" I suggest.

Her jaw tightens, her features set, and I know there's no getting through to her now.

"It was a pleasure meeting you, Prince Alexander. I hope never to repeat it," she spits, before she turns on her heel, her skirts rustling around her as they did when she bolted from the hallway cupboard.

I watch her leave, feeling a surprising mixture of emotions. Annoyance, attraction—don't judge me—and worst of all, guilt.

Perhaps I got this new princess horribly wrong?

Chapter 11

Maddie

66 We are distraught! Our poor darling Prince of Gorgeousness was spotted leaving last night's ball for the new Malveauxian princess with a swollen nose that frankly makes this reporter weep! Who in their good mind would want to damage such a perfect, perfect face? As I write these words, I know it must be a jealous man, intent on damaging the dashingly good looks of our Prince of Perfection after he no doubt attracted the attention of his wife. Doesn't he

know his attempts are futile? Not even a swollen nose could impair his looks, and those who have taken to calling him Rudolph the Red Nosed Prince should be ashamed of themselves. He is and will always be forever in our hearts, our most treasured Prince Alexander.

Princess Madeline looked nice in her blue dress.

#StopTheRudolphReferences
#StillCrazyHot

Yours in the very deepest of concerns,

Fabiana Fontaine xx

"Ugh!" I slap the paper down on the table in disgust.

You heard me right. A paper. As in a newspaper, something I think Dad got once in my adult life when Houston won the World Series, insisting it was for posterity.

How can anybody write such sycophantically ridiculous drivel about that horrible man? It's clear they can't see past the fact that he's a handsome prince—in itself such a cliché. Like either of those things means anything at all.

They don't.

He's rude, he's mean, he's full of himself, and he's flirtatious in an absolutely inappropriate and revolting way. I'm glad it was me who punched him, not some jealous man. Although the idea of Alexander flirting with someone's wife rings a hundred and fifty percent true. I know. I'm the one who punched him and still he found it within himself to flirt with me. Even though he denied he did because he *so* did.

Un-*freaking*-believable.

What annoys me the most, however, is the fact that I let his words get to me. Suggesting that I'm jumping at this opportunity to become a princess so that I can cash in is deeply insulting and so unbelievably inaccurate. Doesn't he know that I'm wrestling with this whole thing? That I've got one foot in and one foot out, hoping that at any moment I'll get a clear sign to help me decide which life I should choose?

Of course he doesn't because he's an arrogant, self-satisfied man who thinks so much of himself he doesn't even bother to ask me how I'm feeling about becoming a princess. He just jumped to a deeply insulting conclusion.

I huff out a breath.

And what's more—if there even needs to be any more —he called me a backup princess, heir to the throne only if my Uncle Nicolas, who is apparently sailing around the Mediterranean, decides to follow through with his threat of abdication. The cheek of the man! I'm no one's backup, thank you very much, and everyone says Nicolas will officially abdicate anyway, so…so…*argh*!

I hate him. Hate him!

I hope I never have to lay eyes on him ever again, as long as I live. And if I do have to see him, I refuse to speak with him or have anything to do with him at all.

There. Decided.

I feel better already.

My phone vibrates with a message and I pick it up to see it's from Chloe.

> Hey, Princess! I cannot get used to saying that. What's the haps? I bet you're doing amazing princess things while I'm stuck here in the office with Denise breathing down my neck and Eric looking like his favorite toy's been taken away.

My breath catches in my throat. Eric is missing me? I type a message.

> Say more things about Eric.

That's what you got from that? What about the fact I'm your bestie and I have to read about your life online now that you're on the other side of the Atlantic leading a crazy new life while I'm stuck here at Fontana?

> Sorry 😦 But to be fair to me, the fact that Eric misses me makes my LIFE.

Why are you even bothering to think about Eric when you have McHottie himself? 😍

> I don't have Prince McHottie, as you put it, and I wouldn't want him either. He's a completely horrible human being who thinks so much of himself he could strut sitting down.

My phone rings in my hand and I barely have the chance to say hello when Chloe launches into a tirade.

"Are you drunk? Who wouldn't want Prince Alexander? He's gorgeous. He looks great in a tux. He's a *prince*. If you can't see what the entire world sees, I can't help you."

"Those are all super excellent reasons to want to be with someone, Chlo." My voice may be dripping in gooey sarcasm.

"They're enough for most of the women in the world," she retorts. "Did you not hear me? He's a prince. He's hot. He's a hot prince. He's Prince McHottie."

"The fact he's a hot prince is not enough reason for me to want to spend any time with the man. That I can tell you for sure."

"Why? Has something happened? I mean, I know you

met him at your big princess thing last night because there are super cute photos of you two together. And can I add that it is beyond amazing to get to see you on TMZ being talked about as this new exciting thing?"

"I'm on TMZ?"

"Are you kidding? You are all over it, girl. All. Over. It."

I turn the paper over again and my eyes land on one of several photos of me with various people last night. I'm standing with Amelia and Voldemort—sorry, *Prince Alexander*—looking down at my feet as Alexander smiles his dashing smile. I begrudgingly admit his swollen nose doesn't diminish his good looks, which makes him doubly horrible. If you're sporting a damaged face, you should at least have the good grace to look bad. It's not fair for us mere mortals otherwise.

"I look all awkward and shy."

"Sure, you're looking down, but your dress is so pretty, and you're standing next to Prince Alexander. No one is going to look as good as him."

I roll my eyes. "I get it. You want to marry him and have his babies."

"Oh, I would so marry that man and have his babies. Just give me the chance."

"You're welcome to him."

"Okay, spill the tea, girl. What happened with you guys? You have to tell me."

I let out a sigh. "You've gotta keep it to yourself."

"When have I ever betrayed your confidence? I want to see that tea spilled all over your fancy palace room."

"Okay," I begin reluctantly. "I was hiding out in a closet last night before the big event and—"

She interrupts. "Why?"

"Because… you know. It was super scary. Everyone was

waiting to meet me and I was all dressed up with a freaking tiara on my head. It was… a lot."

"Girl, you looked gorgeous."

"I didn't feel gorgeous. I felt totally out of place and totally freaked out about it all."

"That's not how to respond to a compliment. Say, 'thank you, Chloe'," she instructs.

"Thank you, Chloe," I parrot.

"Of course you're going to feel weird, Mads. This is all totally new for you."

"I was on my way to meet my dad and my grandparents when it all felt like too much for me. That's when I decided a few minutes in a hallway closet, taking some deep breaths, would be a good idea."

"Were you having a panic attack or something? My cousin used to get those when we were teenagers. They sound horrible."

"Oh, no. Nothing serious like that. It was just all too much, you know?"

"It's a lot, girl. I can't believe you hid in a closet in your tiara and gown."

"It was all good until someone rudely burst inside and I had to press myself up against the back of the closet so he wouldn't see me hiding in there."

"Wait." I can almost hear the cogs in her brain clicking. "Don't tell me it was Prince Alexander."

The memory has my insides tying in knots. "I could tell you it wasn't, but it'd be a shamefaced lie."

"You were in a closet with the world's most eligible royal bachelor?"

"Mm-hm."

"Did your gazes meet before he pulled you into a passionate embrace, giving you the kiss of your life?" she asks breathlessly.

"Chloe, this is not your fantasy. This is what actually happened."

"Can't a girl dream? Tell me he's an amazing kisser."

"There was no kissing."

She sounds deflated when she says, "No kissing."

"No, and I can assure you there will never be any kissing with Prince McHorrible."

"Prince McHorrible? How old are you?"

"It was the first name that came to mind, and besides, you call him Prince McHottie."

"The *world* calls him Prince McHottie because he's super hot and he's a prince."

"The hot part is debatable," I grumble.

"So, if you didn't kiss him, what did you do with the delectable Alexander in the closet?"

"I punched him. In the face." I feel weirdly proud of this fact, as well as deeply mortified. It's an unusual combination.

"You did *what*?!" She squeals so loudly, I'm forced to pull the phone from my ear for fear she may burst an ear drum. "Why did you go and do something like that?"

"It was in self-defense."

"Because he was trying to kiss you?"

"Can you drop that, please?"

"The photos of him show a red, swollen nose. Are you telling me that's *your* handiwork?"

"I'm not proud of it," I tell her, even if I am a little proud. Have I mentioned the guy's a jerk?

"Madeline Josephine Turner, I cannot believe you punched Prince McHottie in the nose."

"Can you keep your voice down? No one knows about this."

"Prince McHottie does," she singsongs.

"To be fair to me, I didn't know it was him. It was dark

and I freaked out and hit him before he had the chance to do anything to me, and then I took off, only I was wearing these stupid high heels with a floor-length dress and I tripped and landed on the carpet."

I conveniently leave out the part about Alexander trying to come to my aid as I landed flat on my face. It doesn't fit my rhetoric about him, and anyway, who knows whether he was actually going to help me? I was so freaked out, I had no idea what he was going to do.

"He is such a great guy," she says dreamily.

There's no getting through to her. "How the heck do you get that from what I just told you?"

"He came to talk with you after you attacked him. That makes him super nice."

"He had to. It was my presentation ball."

"Did he flirt with you?"

"A little," I reply. "But I think it was more of a reflex because I'm female." I roll my eyes.

"Prince Alexander flirted with you." She lets out a sigh. "Girl, you are so lucky."

"Lucky?" I huff out a bitter laugh. "He accused me of milking my new status for money."

"Shut the front door."

"And he called me a backup princess."

"No way."

"I know you think he's the perfect man who can do no wrong, but believe me, Prince Alexander is a horrible human being and I have no idea why women the world over think he's so great. He's not. So not."

"Interesting."

"He's not interesting. Trust me."

"No, I mean it's interesting how impassioned you are about him."

"I'm not impassioned." I keep my tone light and

less…impassioned.

"You know what they say: there's a fine line between love and hate."

I chortle. "You cannot be serious, Chlo."

"Maybe I am, maybe I'm not," she teases. "When are you seeing him again?"

"I hope never. I don't want to talk about him anymore. Tell me all about Eric pining for me."

She chortles. "He's been telling everyone who'll listen how much of a crush you have on him, and how he could have dated you just like that."

It's as if the room's oxygen was sucked out in one swift breath.

"He said that?" I ask, my voice small.

"I've been telling you for ages. He's a jerk. Forget about him. Besides, you've got way hotter fish to fry."

An image of Alexander's head imposed on a fried fish pops into my head.

There's a knock on the door and it drags me from my sweet, sweet dream. Vladimir enters, and I know he's here to begin today's instruction, aka my princess lessons. He's accompanied by Dad, who's been packing his bags, ready to leave for the airport.

"Chlo, I've really got to go. Big kisses. I miss you."

"I miss you so hard, girl. It's not the same here without you. Call me later?"

"I've got more princess training and then I'm meeting the royal peacocks with this super nice princess called Amelia, so I'm not sure when I'll get the chance."

"You're meeting royal peacocks?"

"It's a whole thing, apparently. The peacock is the symbol of Malveaux and I need to be formally introduced."

"Sure. That's a normal, everyday kind of thing to do,"

she says on a laugh.

"I'm going to the Tleurbonne Children's Hospital here in the capital soon to chat to some of the kids. It's part of one of the charities that I have as princess. Apparently, my mom was the patroness."

I smile to myself. Not only do I get to be the patron of a bunch of charities, such as the Children's Hospital, but I get to do what my mom used to do when she was Princess Josephine, and not just Jo Turner, my mom and co-owner of Doug's Hardware.

"Girl, your new life is amazing."

I'm not as convinced. "We'll see. Love you." I hang up.

"I've come to say goodbye, honey," Dad says with a hesitant smile.

I bounce up from the sofa and he wraps me up in a hug. "Do you have to? Can't you stay a little longer?"

"I've got to get back to the store. But honey? You know I'll support you in whatever decision you make about this whole thing,."

A lump forms in my throat. "I know."

"You looked so beautiful last night. Like a real princess. Didn't she, Vladimir?"

"You were absolutely enchanting, ma'am," Vlad says, and instantly I'm reminded of Alexander using that exact same word.

I harrumph. I don't want to think about that passive aggressive man.

"I think it's one thing to look like a princess, but I think it's going to take some time for me to actually *feel* like one," I admit.

Dad squeezes me in another hug, and I hold on, knowing I won't see him for a while. He's got a business to run and a life back in Houston. I can't have him staying here babysitting me like I'm a kid forever. And he's right. I need to make up my mind, but it feels amazing to know I have his support either way.

Dad places a soft kiss on my forehead. "I love you, my girl."

That lump in my throat grows to the size of Texas, my eyes pooling with tears. "I love you too, Daddy."

"It's time to go. No fancy private royal jet for your old man this time around."

"Back to regular old commercial? How will you cope?"

"Your grandparents sprung for first class, so at least I can miss you lying down as I catch up on baseball."

A laugh bubbles up and the tears I've been holding back spill down my cheeks. "I'm going to miss you so much."

"I'm only a flight away, and you can come home anytime you like."

Vlad clears his throat in what I'm learning is his subtle way of interrupting.

I wipe my tears away and plaster on a brave smile.

"Love you," Dad says at the door before he shoots me a smile, and then he's gone.

Vlad hands me some Kleenex, which I promptly sob into like a little girl. I haven't lived at home since I went to college, but somehow seeing Dad leave is much harder than I expected. I'm left here alone with a huge decision resting on my shoulders.

I know he could never make that decision for me. I know I've got to do it myself. But having him here made it all feel somehow less overwhelming.

"Are you ready to start your lesson?" Vladimir asks in a kind voice.

I suck in a deep breath, balling the used Kleenex in my hand. "You know what? I'm as ready as I will ever be, Vlad. Let's do this."

Chapter 12

Alexander

"But Father, be reasonable. Why can't Sofia stay instead? She loves this sort of thing," I protest. "It's right up her alley."

My father leans back in his chair, his fingers interlaced as he studies me. "You know exactly why, Alexander. I'm surprised you're arguing with me about this."

"Of course I understand why you want me to stay—" I begin but I'm immediately cut off.

"You are my son and heir. As such, you are an extension of me. With business back in Ledonia, I must return and can only come back for The Games at the end of the month. You must stay in my stead. You're the next best thing after me."

Ah, what every child wants to hear from their dad.

It's a line of rhetoric I am all too familiar with, and one I've never successfully argued with.

I know one day in the not-too-distant future I'll be making decisions in the best interests of Ledonia, a heavy metaphorical—and literal at times—crown on top of my head. In seven years in fact, when Father stands down, as is Ledonian tradition.

The thought has my insides shriveling up into something the size of a raisin.

That's the problem when you're born into a job. You get no say. No choice. Well, not unless you're Prince Nicolas and decide to do a runner.

But that's not my style.

"I want you to stay here in Malveaux to spend as much time as possible with the new princess. Get to know her. Find out how she ticks, what she likes."

"She's American, so she probably likes burgers and Coke," I jest.

Father is not amused. "Let's try to get a little deeper than that, shall we, Alexander?"

"Of course, Father. That was a flippant comment."

"Hmm," he grunts.

My father is a tough crowd of one. I continue to try to charm him, but so far, any success on that front has eluded me. Idiot that I am, I can't help but try.

"I can't say I've exactly warmed to her."

"You need to. And besides, you're good with women,

from what I've seen, when you can fit it in with your endless parties."

Can't I shake my reputation, even with my family?

"That's the old me, Father. I'm not into all that anymore. I've left it behind."

He cocks an eyebrow. "Why ever would you do that?"

"It got old," I reply simply.

He narrows his gaze, as though assessing me in light of this new information. "What's the 'new' you?"

I pause, not sure how much to share with him. We've never been what you'd call close. Keeping me at arm's length my whole life saw to that. Of course I love him and would do anything for him. That's the way it is with children and their parents. No matter what they're like as human beings, you desperately want their approval. Their love.

My father? He sees me more as an employee, someone to train and prepare to eventually take over the family business once he retires. I don't doubt his love, but it's barbed like a wrought iron fence—as beautiful as it is dangerous.

"I suppose I'm less interested in partying and all that goes with it," I reply simply.

"And the women?"

"I haven't been romantically involved with anyone in over a year, Father."

"A year?" He looks positively stunned. "That's not what I see in the papers."

"Because you and I both know how accurate they are."

"Hmm. Yes. Well, now's not the time to bring out this new you, Alexander. Stick with the old where the American is concerned. Charm her. Show her how important we are to Malveaux. You'll be King when I retire. It's about time you stepped up. Proved yourself useful."

His words burn like the flick of a stingray's tail.

I let out a resigned sigh. I'm not going to win this one. "What do you want me to do?"

"Where she goes, you go. I'll see to it. I'm sure she'll be introduced to her charities and have to attend various functions, among other activities."

"Father, I hardly think—"

He cuts me off. "Yes, I do, and you should too. She's being introduced to Parliament next week. Go with her. Be seen together."

"I can't imagine the Malveauxian Parliament is going to welcome a Ledonian royal with open arms. They were rather negative about your decision not to change the royal succession to include women when you ascended the throne."

In fact, the government of Malveaux didn't hold back from commenting about how archaic our law had remained. Of course the royal family didn't comment, because that would have been unseemly and rather unroyal, but it was implied by their silence on the matter that they agreed with their government.

"They will be honored to have you present," Father replies, either missing my point or ignoring it. It's not clear which.

I decide to level with him. If he's not going to listen to reason, perhaps he'll listen to the fact that the woman hates me, and I strongly suspect she would prefer to spend a night in the old palace dungeon then spend an afternoon with me.

"The thing is, Father, I hardly got off to a flying start with the new princess last night. She's not what one would term my number one fan."

"Make her your number one fan."

So much easier said than done.

The last thing I'm going to tell him is that she was the one who punched me in the face last night. I'm keeping that little gem to myself. As far as he's concerned, my nose met a waiter's tray, just as I told Amelia and anyone who's asked me since. I might not like her, but she doesn't need that kind of story getting out.

He flips the leather cover closed on his phone and rises to his feet, symbolic that this conversation is well and truly over—and I've lost.

"I'll have more clothes sent to you. You'll be very comfortable here in the rooms on your own for the next few weeks."

There's a knock on the door, and before I've even got to it, in bursts Amelia, all enthusiasm and excitement, followed by the entirely more mature and sedate Sofia.

"Alex!" She gives me a squeeze. "I can't believe you get to stay. You're so lucky."

That depends entirely on your definition of the word "lucky."

"It's only because he's the heir." Sofia greets our father with a kiss to his cheek. "Hello, Father. Going somewhere?"

"I have a call to make," Father replies as he leaves the room.

"How's your nose?" Sofia inspects my face. "It seems improved today. You looked quite shocking last night."

Gingerly, I lift some fingers to my face. My nose is still a little swollen, and I woke more than once in the night as I rolled over and knocked it painfully against my pillow. But I've been assured by the palace doctor that it's not broken.

Amelia leaps to my defense. "No, he didn't, Sofe. He looked as handsome as ever."

"You always say nice things about him because he's your favorite," Sofia accuses.

All Amelia does is shrug because I *am* her favorite, and we all know it.

Although I'm actually closer to Sofia's age than Amelia's, I've always been closer to my little sister. She's so easy to love. She's full of life and happiness and wonder, and now that I'm hurtling headlong into middle age—all right, I'm 26, but still, it's not very young anymore—I can do with as much positive, life affirming stuff as I can get. Of course I love Sofia as well. Although she's more serious than both Amelia and me, she has a good heart and I know she would do anything for us.

Then there's my younger brother, Max. He's almost as much fun as Amelia, but being five years younger than me, we didn't spend as much time together when we were growing up as Amelia, Sofia, and I did.

"Did you see that the papers are calling me Rudolph the Red Nosed Prince," I say and both my sisters laugh.

"That's just too funny," Amelia says as she sits down onto the sofa next to me.

"Funny but also quite appropriate, don't you think?" Sofia adds with a sly grin. "We're so used to you looking like the dashing Prince Perfect. It's good to see that you're human after all."

"Prince Perfect?" I guffaw. "I get enough name calling in the press without having to endure it at home."

"Yes, poor you being adored by not just the nation's press, but the whole world's," Sofia says. "They think you're perfect and I'm boring."

"It's only because you don't have wild affairs with gorgeous people," Amelia explains. "Maybe you should try it? You might change everyone's opinion of you as well as have a little bit of fun."

"That's about as likely as—" Sofia begins.

"Me winning the American princess over," I finish for her.

Sofia places her hand over her heart in mock surprise. "Are you telling us there's a woman outside of our family who isn't swooning at your feet, Alex? Never!"

I chortle. "Trust me, Madeline Turner isn't swooning."

"She can't resist you for long. None of them do," Amelia says with confidence.

I think of Madeline's and my conversation last night, how I hit a nerve and made her cry. Guilt worms its way across my chest. I've never purposely made a woman cry before. It doesn't feel good.

I pour myself a cup of tea at the sideboard and add a dash of milk. "Something tells me our American princess will be more than capable of resisting me."

"Rubbish. She's a woman. She's got eyes, hasn't she? You'll have her eating out of the palm of your hand before you know it," Amelia says.

I take a sip of my tea, somehow forgetting how horrendous Malveauxian tea actually is. "Oh, this stuff is truly awful. Can't we get some coffee?"

"Why don't you add some of your magic cordial to it?" Amelia suggests.

I chortle. "To tea?"

"I think you're going to adore her once you get to know her, Alex," Amelia says assuredly.

"Perhaps."

Madeline and I may have had a poor start, but she's certainly feisty, and I can't say that's something I dislike in a woman. Last night she oscillated from looking as comfortable as a mouse in a roomful of hungry kittens, to haughty defiance.

It's an intriguing mix.

Part of me would rather clean up after the famous Malveauxian peacocks than stay here and "woo" her. The other part? I can't deny it, even to myself. The other part of me wants to know this feisty, vulnerable, beautiful American more. Even at the risk of once more suffering her impressive right hook.

Chapter 13

Madeline

I lower myself gingerly down onto the chair, concentrating super hard on, a) not wobbling or jerking, b) not looking like I'm about to be executed—Vlad's exact words from a few moments ago—and, c) not hurtling myself into the chair like a cricket ball into a wicketkeeper's mitts. Again, Vlad's exact words from a few moments ago. Because cricket? No clue.

"Well done," Alice exclaims as I let out the breath I've been holding during the maneuver—a maneuver that up until a few days ago I'd never given a second thought to in my life. It's this exciting new thing called "sitting". Apparently, there are lots of rules on sitting here in Malveaux, for a princess, anyway. Where I'm from, you sit down. Period. Now, sitting has to be done elegantly and carefully so as not to look like a common peasant—Vlad's exact words yet again—and definitely not flash anyone anything they shouldn't be seeing.

"May I make a suggestion?" Alice asks.

"Shoot," I instruct.

"Perhaps you could cross your ankles in the other direction. It may feel more natural," she suggests tactfully.

One glance in the mirror positioned in front of me and I see that, although I look the part in my pale green shift dress and matching pumps, I'm sitting like a contorted piece of string. Quickly, I switch ankles.

Alice smiles. "Much better."

"Awesome. I'm a 24-year-old who's successfully mastered sitting."

"Now, perhaps you could stand?" Vlad suggests.

"Easy as pie, Vlad." I hop to my feet.

"In the way we taught you might be preferable."

Oops.

"All righty." I repeat the sitting maneuver, this time crossing my legs in the correct direction, and then concentrate on uncrossing them and rising to a stand as I hold my hands delicately in front of my belly button. "Good, right? I have so got this."

"Wonderful," Alice exclaims.

I liked her from the moment I met her and since then, we've become friends. I know she's my servant and not appropriate for me to be besties with *yadda yadda yadda*—thank you, Grandmama—but she's also only a year younger than me and she likes a lot of the same music and movies and books as me. We've bonded, and I've needed it. With Dad now back home in Houston, I need all the friends I can get here in Malveaux.

"Sitting and standing now checked off the list. What's next, peeps?"

"Next is your appointment with Princess Amelia of Ledonia to meet the royal peacocks, ma'am," Vlad informs me.

I grin at the thought of seeing Amelia again. I so liked her when we met at the ball, despite her despicable brother.

Not that I'm going to think about Prince McArrogant Alexander. That guy is dead to me and I for one am ecstatic that he's now left the country for Ledonia, where I hope he stays for the next 70 or so years.

"Maddie, remember?" I say to Vlad. "Alice uses it. You can, too."

"Maddie," he repeats.

"Now, when I meet these peacocks, do I shake their wings or is it more appropriate for me to smooch them on their beaks?" I ask solemnly.

Alice suppresses a giggle. Vlad presses his lips together.

"I'm only kidding, you guys," I reassure.

"You will observe them. Simple as that," Vlad replies.

I nod. "Observe. Got it."

"Might I suggest you comment on their beauty as well? After all, they are the symbol of our country, after which the Malveauxian blue was developed," he adds.

"Comment on their beauty. Got it," I say. "Let's go meet me some peacocks."

I charge from the room, knowing Vladimir will be frowning at me. We've got a kind of father-daughter thing going on. He tells me what to do, I tease him about it, and, eventually, I do it.

Between him and Alice, and the way in which my grand-parents are so eager to relate to me and make me feel at home, my time in Malveaux has been much less daunting than I'd anticipated. It might be too soon to tell, but coming here to meet everyone and see how it feels to be a princess has been the right call. I'd even go so far as to say that I'm glad I'm here.

Later, on a walk through the palace grounds, we meet a group of people wearing rubber boots, who greet me with curtsies and bows.

I may have been a princess for a few days now, but I still cannot get used to that part. I feel like one of my grandparents must be lurking behind me and they're all greeting them, not this brand-new princess who has next to no clue about anything—other than sitting. I've got that nailed.

"It's great to meet y'all," I say with a smile. "Should I be in rubber boots, too?"

"By rubber boots do you mean wellingtons?" the game-keeper, who introduced himself as Ralph, asks.

I point at his feet. "Those."

"Naturally," he replies as he gestures for a woman to step forward and present me with a pair of blue royal monogrammed—what else?—rubber boots, which I sink my feet into, grateful to be rid of the pumps Grandmama insists I wear for my princess lessons.

"Okay, I'm ready to meet the birds," I announce.

"We're waiting on the representative of the Ledonian royal family," Ralph instructs.

"Princess Amelia. Right. It'll be so nice to see her again."

"Princess Amelia? No, miss." He looks over my shoulder. "Ah, here he is."

Wait. *He?*

It can't be. The universe isn't that mean.

I turn to see the smug prince of all things flirty and rude himself, sauntering toward me with the same confidence and swagger he had at the ball last night.

Thanks a lot, Universe.

Everyone around me curtsies and bows. Me? I just glare at him. Grandmama might want me to be friends with him, but she didn't say anything about glaring.

Alexander's nose still sports redness and some swelling, but it's not nearly as painful looking as it appeared last night. Pity, really. His good looks could do with a dent or two to make him look less like a Ken doll.

I bet he'd be proud of his "beach" skills.

I stifle a snicker.

"I apologize for being a touch late," he says in that smarmy way of his that makes my skin prickle. "I do hope I haven't held you up."

"You're right on time, Your Royal Highness," Ralph replies.

"I'm pleased to hear it." His eyes land on mine and a cold shiver crawls down my spine. "Princess Madeline. How nice it is to see you again." He offers me his hand and I take it reluctantly in mine, only because it would appear rude if I didn't. But seriously, that's the last time I ever want to touch this man.

Are you listening, Universe? You let me down before so you owe me this.

"Good to see you, too," I reply stiffly as I snatch my hand back.

Of course he looks shockingly handsome in his buttoned-up shirt, open at the neck, tucked into a pair of pants that show just how V-shaped his torso is, the crisp whiteness of his shirt contrasting with his olive skin. I glance down at his feet. He's come prepared in his rubber boots.

And then the worst thing imaginable happens, worse than Eric not asking me out when I lived in Houston. Way worse.

As I look into his eyes, I feel a faint but distinct electric spark firing up inside of me.

Nope. Not happening.

There is no way on this sweet earth I'm going to be attracted to this…this…*man*. He's horrible and arrogant and rude and I do not like him one little bit.

I unplug the spark from its electric socket and promptly turn my back to him.

I know it's just some simple physiological reaction to seeing a potential mate. He's a man, I'm a woman. It's basic reproductive science. If I ignore it, I know it will go away because Prince Alexander is absolutely the last man I ever want to feel anything for, especially anything even vaguely related to reproduction.

Ugh.

"Shall we walk this way?" Ralph asks.

"I'd love to," I reply and begin to follow him, only for Alexander to fall into step beside me.

"I like the wellies," he says, his eyes on my feet.

"Thank you," I sniff. I don't risk looking back at him. "I would have thought your boots would be Ledonian red."

"I thought I'd leave the red boots to Father Christmas."

"You mean Santa? His boots are black, actually."

"Good to know. I'll be sure to wear black boots when I dress up this Christmas as Santa, as you call him."

I throw him a look. He has to be the least Santa-like guy I've met in my life, unless of course Santa has deliciously broad and muscular shoulders that taper into a slim waist, where he sports an impressive, tan six-pack that would make many a woman weep.

I may or may not have Googled Alexander last night. And I may or may not have seen shots of him on a beach vacation in nothing but his swim trunks.

Not that I wept. For all his good looks and masculinity, Alexander's arrogance, superiority, and sheer rudeness are the only things I see.

Take that, spark.

"You do that," I say.

"I will."

"Who do you dress up as Santa for?"

As the words leave my mouth, I have a terrible image of it being some weird sexy thing he does with some girl, and I immediately backtrack.

"Actually, don't tell me. I don't want to know."

"I would be happy to tell you." His smile does weird things to me.

Things I ignore.

"For the last few years, I've been Father Christmas for the children's charity I support."

I snort laugh. "Sure, you have." Prince McHottie wearing a Santa costume for a bunch of kids? *So* likely.

"Is it so hard to believe?" he asks, his dark eyes trained on me.

I slide my gaze from his. "I was told Princess Amelia was attending," I reply, changing the subject away from thinking of Alexander being nice to kids. Which I'm certain is an outright lie, anyway.

"My dear sister has returned to Ledonia along with the other members of my family," he replies. "I'm afraid we'll need to put up with one another for a week or two."

My jaw drops open. A week or two of Prince Alexander, the man I would vote most likely to make me run for the hills?

The Universe and I are definitely in a fight.

"Awesome," I reply brightly. "I hope you enjoy your stay here in Malveaux. I'm super busy, though, so this might be the only chance we get to hang out."

"I assure you it won't be," he replies, his lips curving into that knee-weakening smile of his.

Not that it weakens my knees whatsoever. Nope. My knees are firm. Firm and solid. There will be no weakening where I'm concerned. Rock hard knees.

"We will be 'hanging out' every day." He uses air quotes to mock me, because he's that much of a nice guy.

"No, we won't."

"Yes, we will."

I shake my head. "I've got a lot going on."

"I know. Your press secretary has already been in touch with your schedule."

I have a press secretary?

I eye him cautiously and see he's still smiling at me as though this is a great idea. But surely he's not *happy* about this? I bet I'm the last person he would want to spend any time with after our whole meet un-cute last night.

"Have you become my new stalker?" I question.

"Do you make it a habit to always have a stalker, princess?"

What kind of question is that?

"I'm just making light of the situation." I lean closer to him so only he can hear, and I catch a hint of his scent. It reignites that dang electricity and I'm forced to perform another swift unplug. "I'm sure you're about as happy about this as am I."

"Follow me, your Royal Highnesses," Ralph says, and I take the opportunity to walk away from Alexander.

But he's a slippery eel, and before long, he's back beside me.

"How have you been since the ball?" he asks.

"Fine."

"I hope your hand has recovered."

I snap my attention to him. "It's fine, thanks. How's your...you know?" I inspect Alexander's face. The swelling and redness in his nose from last night has lessened.

Is it terrible that I think it's a shame?

Probably, but I'm not going to dwell on it.

"You can say it, you know, and it's perfectly fine, no thanks to that waiter's tray."

So, he's sticking with the story. I squirm, uncomfortable. "I'm sure the tray didn't mean it."

"Is that so?"

"I imagine it did it in self-defense, as misguided as it turned out to be."

"That sounds like an apology, Texas," he replies.

He's calling me *Texas* again?

I open my mouth to reply, but no words come out.

What *is* this guy playing at?

"If you're ready, your Royal Highnesses, we'll enter the wooded area for the Princess's formal introduction to our most treasured national bird," Ralph announces, and I'm relieved for the change of topic. "We often see them on the lawns, but they appear to be a little elusive today."

"I'm ready," I tell him eagerly, stepping away from the increasingly confusing Alexander.

I don't like thinking that he might actually have some nice traits, like not sharing what really happened in that closet, and dressing up as Santa for the kids. Although I'm still deeply suspicious he actually did that.

I sidle up to Ralph and together we make our way into the woods. We're trailed by Alexander and Vlad and another guy in a black suit named Paulo, who's probably Alexander's long-suffering bodyguard.

The stories he could tell.

Not that I'd be interested in knowing.

I look around the lush lowland forest. Sunlight filters through the canopy, casting a dappled glow across the floor.

"I wonder where the peacocks are?" I say, more to myself than anyone else.

"At this time of year, I imagine the females will be nesting," Alexander replies, and incredulous, I turn to see him beside me once more.

What is this guy, *superglue*?

I give him the side eye. "You know a lot about peacocks?"

"I know enough."

I bet he does, thanks to being a poor imitation of one himself.

I bite back a smile at the image of Alexander wearing a peacock plume, strutting around the forest floor.

"And it's pea*fowl*, Texas. Peacocks are male," he adds and I shoot him a withering look.

"We have a long tradition of the monarchy caring for peafowl, much as the British royal family is responsible for the country's swan population. The royal family, yourself included, ma'am, is responsible for their habitat, to check them periodically for injuries, and to conserve them," Ralph explains.

"Who exactly in the royal family?" I ask.

"Are you worried it's you?" Alexander's eyes are dancing.

"Not at all," I reply curtly. "Is it the King? The Queen?"

"It's the monarch, ma'am. The King, in this case,"

Ralph replies. "Now, please do remember to tread carefully."

"Do they spook easy?" I ask.

"They are known to, yes," Ralph replies. "We need to refrain from speaking, if that is acceptable to you, Your Royal Highnesses."

"Totally acceptable," I reply and turn to Alexander, who gives Ralph a simple nod.

We walk in silence until we come across the most incredible site I've seen. It's a whole congregation of peacocks—sorry, pea*fowl*—in a clearing. It's like being at the most extravagant fashion show, with the males as the divas, strutting around with their tail feathers fanned out like oversized, psychedelic fans. They're the peacock equivalent of runway models, showing off with a *just look at how fabulous I am* attitude.

Shame Ledonia's national symbol isn't the peacock. It would suit Alexander to a T.

Then there are the females, who seem more like the sensible audience, totally unimpressed by the males. Every now and then, a male makes a dramatic display, and the females just glance over with a look that tells them they've seen it all before.

Good work, ladies. I should take a page from their book where Alexander is concerned.

Ralph whispers, "It's wonderful to find an entire ostentation of peafowl, ma'am."

"An ostentation?" I whisper back.

"That's the term used to describe a group of peafowl."

"Got it. Are they native to Malveaux?"

"Oh, no, ma'am. Much like the lion is the symbol of England, the peafowl is not native to Malveaux. In fact, the first peafowl to live in our country were a gift to King Leopold by an Indian Maharaja some 800 years ago."

"Seriously? That's so cool," I reply. "Okay if I get a closer look?"

"As long as you tread carefully and not try to touch any of them."

"No touching. Got it."

I creep closer, watching my step. Closer, closer. Then, I step on what can only be described as the loudest twig snap on record, like a firecracker on the 4th of July.

Uh-oh.

The peafowl erupt into a frenzy, flapping and squawking like I've just announced a pop quiz in calculus class. It's a flurry of wings and indignant bird noises. One particularly flustered peacock flies straight up like a rocket, while others run around like they've lost their GPS signal.

It's unsettling and loud, and I steel myself before I turn back to face the others. What does it mean that on my formal introduction to Malveaux's national bird, I give them the fright of their lives?

"Oops," I say, hoping I can somehow style this out.

Not happening.

Ralph presses his lips together, probably to stop himself from telling me I'm a total idiot; Alexander shakes his head at me with a smirk teasing his lips, and I wish I could spook him so he'd fly away, too; and Vlad and Alexander's bodyguard suddenly pretend to be searching for snipers, hidden in trees.

"Thank you so much for all of this," I say to Ralph with a strained voice.

I don't look at Alexander. I know he must be loving this, seeing me make a fool of myself with a bunch of birds.

Ralph's jaw is slack as he watches the last of the birds scamper away. "You are very welcome, ma'am," he says with uncertainty.

"I'm going to head back now." I gesture in the direction of the palace with my thumb. "People to see and things to do. Princess things. So…yeah."

Smooth.

Without waiting for a reply, I turn on my heel and stomp away, humiliation flooding my bloodstream with each and every step.

Chapter 14

Alexander

"She's not going to last a full month," I say into my phone as I wander past a fountain in the grounds immediately outside the palace.

"Why not?" Sofia replies.

"Because she makes a mess of things. Only yesterday she spooked the royal peafowl on her formal introduction, causing them to flap and carry on like she was about to pull off a full-scale military attack on the poor creatures."

I think of the way she terrified her country's most treasured birds into flying away, then raised her chin and stormed off as though she'd done nothing wrong.

"No!"

"I actually felt quite sorry for her. It must have been so embarrassing."

"You're right. All of this must be so hard, coming here from living a normal life in America. Embarrassing herself like that would be utterly mortifying for the poor girl."

"True, but also not my problem," I reply.

"Alex, you're so uncharitable. I get that you don't particularly like her, but you could at least try. Father's very concerned that you spend as much time with her as possible, to really get to know her."

"And what Father wants," I say with a resigned sigh.

"Exactly," she confirms. "And anyway, Madeline seemed perfectly nice to me, even if she was a little like a deer in headlights at her formal presentation. Amelia thinks she's wonderful."

"Amelia thinks everyone's wonderful," I reply, even though it's one of the things I adore most about my sister.

"Look, we'll all be back for The Games and I'm sure we'll have the opportunity to get to know her better. You and she might be firm friends by then."

I rub my still slightly tender nose. "I'm not convinced."

"Is Father happy with how you're doing?"

"How would I know? He's sporting his resting grump face like it's the new black these days."

She snorts with laughter. "Resting grump face."

"You know I'm right."

"You know he gave you this task because you're his son and heir."

"As he reminds me daily."

"You make it sound like it's a bad thing. It's not. You've

got purpose to your life. You don't know how lucky you are, Alex."

"Come on, Sofe." I don't want to get into this old gripe. A gripe I can do nothing about, at least until I'm King and have some sway with Parliament.

"What do *I* do? What's *my* purpose? According to our parents it's to get married to someone of noble birth, which might even be an arranged marriage, if I don't find someone soon. And when I do get married and have children, we'll all still be in the limelight as members of the royal family but without any actual role. It's so frustrating."

"Tell you what. You can come and cut ribbons for me at all the openings," I say, trying to lighten the mood. "I'll even let you wield the oversized scissors."

"Not helping, Alex." She lets out a sigh and adds, "You're not an extra."

"Is that how you feel?" I ask softly. "Like you're an extra?"

"Isn't Prince Harry's autobiography called *Spare*? Although, unlike Harry, I was born first, and I'm only third in line after Max. Third, Alex! You'd feel the same if you didn't happen to have the biological requirements for the job."

The last thing I want to do is get into the male appendage conversation with my sister.

"You have my word I'll do whatever I can to change that when I eventually ascend to the throne," I say earnestly.

"By then I'll already be married off to some inbred noble with no chin," she scoffs.

I laugh. "Why no chin?"

"Because that's just my luck," she grumps. "But seriously, thanks. You're all right, Alex."

That's quite sentimental coming from her, and I can't

help but be touched. Sofia isn't exactly known for her soft side. I suppose it's because she's the first-born, driven to succeed in whatever she does.

Only the thing she wants to do, she can't.

It must be hard.

I spot Princess Madeline treading toward me. She's wearing an odd combination of a silk dress and a pair of grubby sneakers. She notices me and comes to an immediate stop, turns on her heel, and begins to stomp away in the opposite direction.

I watch her leave, my eyes skimming across her receding figure. She's definitely beautiful, with her small waist that makes the womanly curve of her hips so much more pronounced. Her brunette hair is long and wavy, and when she wears it down like she is today, it frames her beautiful face perfectly.

Utterly against my will, I feel a stirring in my belly. I recognize it in an instant as attraction.

Not helpful.

"Sofe, I've got to go and make friends with the American," I say.

"You'll need to stop calling her that if you have any hopes of making inroads with her, you know."

"Princess Madeline. Is that better?"

"How about just Madeline?"

I think of the nickname I gave her when we first met. *Texas.* She seemed to hate it.

"Madeline. Fine."

"I'm sure you'll weave your magic and she'll be your dear friend in no time. She's probably half in love with you already. Isn't that what happens to women around you? They fall blindingly in love?"

Considering Madeline just spotted me and turned to

walk the other way, I would say that's a highly unlikely outcome.

"I'm not even going to dignify that with a reply."

"Suit yourself, but your reputation precedes you."

"Goodbye, Much Older Sister."

"Goodbye, Prince of Broken Hearts Brother."

I stride after Madeline, my long legs a clear advantage in this cat and mouse chase.

When I reach her, she gives me the side eye.

"What?" she snaps.

"Don't let anyone tell you you've got good manners," I reply with what I hope is a winning smile.

She ignores the jibe. "What do you want, Alexander?"

"To spend some time with you on this lovely day." *Because you're so thoroughly charming*, I want to add.

She comes to a sudden stop, throws her hands on her hips, and glares at me. "Why?"

"Perhaps I can pull you out of your dark mood?"

She pulls her pouty lips into a forced smile and blinks at me. "Who said I'm in a dark mood?"

"Isn't it obvious?"

"You're wrong. I'm in a perfectly good mood."

And I'm a stable boy.

"If you say so."

"I do, actually, as it happens."

"Good for you."

"Oh, it *is* good for me. Better than good because I'm in a great mood."

Does this woman insist on arguing with me about *everything*? Perhaps I should tell her the sky is blue and she could argue that it is in fact yellow? That would be a fun conversation.

I try a different tact. "Look, I know things didn't go so

well with the peafowl yesterday, but I wouldn't worry about it. I'm sure it's happened before."

"It's not the peafowl."

I arch an eyebrow. "It's not? What is it then?"

She folds her arms across her chest. "It's you," she states simply.

"Me?" I ask on a surprised laugh. "What have *I* done?"

"You're following me and you're making me feel uncomfortable. I don't like it."

"I'm not following you, and the last thing I want to do is make you feel uncomfortable."

You're doing that all on your own.

"It sure feels like that to me. Why did you even need to be at that whole meet the peacock thing?"

"I represent my family and country, and as such, I'm invited to events like you meeting the pea*fowl*."

She rolls her eyes at me in irritation.

I press on. "Ledonia and Malveaux have a very special—"

"—relationship," she finishes for me, her jaw tight. "So I've heard."

"Then you'll understand why I was present."

She twists her mouth, clearly not happy about it.

"Look. We didn't get off to the best start with what transpired between us at the ball and then the...err, bird thing yesterday," I say.

"You think?"

"But we're here now and we're going to see a lot of each other over the next few weeks or so, right through to The Games. I suggest we find a way to coexist, if not harmoniously, then at least without acrimony."

She arches her brows. "You like big words, don't you?"

How old is she, eight??

"I'm trying to help here. It would be good if we could get along, don't you think?"

She twists her mouth, her arms still crossed, although not as tightly as they were only moments ago.

Progress.

"So? What do you say, Madeline?"

I can almost see some of the tension leave her shoulders.

"I guess we could try," she concedes.

"See? That wasn't so hard."

"Hmm."

We begin to amble through the gardens in silence together for a while before she says, "You mentioned something called The Games. What is that?"

"They're the annual games between our two countries. It's a long-standing tradition, and they're held in either Malveaux or Ledonia each year. It's your turn this time. There are serious events with professional athletes, and then the more light-hearted ones. My family always attends and we always partici-pate, although we compete in the light-hearted events only."

"Does that mean *I* have to play these games?"

"It would be circumspect of you."

She gives me a look that clearly says *you and your big words*.

"It would be a good idea," I say.

"I know what 'circumspect' means."

I cannot win with this woman.

"I'm sure you do. It's very clear to me that you're bright."

She gives me a sideways glance, as though she doesn't trust the compliment.

"I mean it."

"Sure," she replies uncertainly. "I'm smart. Thanks."

"Of course."

We walk around a thicket of trees and onto the Grand Walk, a stretch of grass that leads up to a neoclassical rotunda atop an incline.

"What do I have to do at these Games? It'd better not be rugby."

"You don't like rugby?"

"I don't know anything about rugby but ask me anything about football."

"By which you mean American football?"

"Of course. Go Texans!" She punches the air.

"Ah."

She bristles. "What does 'ah' mean? Are you looking down your royal nose at me because I don't know what rugby is? Because that's unfair. No one in Texas knows what rugby is."

I press my lips together to stifle a smile, and most definitely don't look down my nose at her, royal or otherwise. "You'll be pleased to know that The Games do not involve rugby."

"What are they then?"

"Traditional games, such as archery, steeple chase, and log throwing, but also less usual sports such as cheese rolling and wife racing."

She scrunches up her nose. "Did you really just say 'wife racing'? That cannot be a thing."

"It most certainly is a thing."

"Tell me it's not men telling their wives to race against one another, because that would be a seriously sexist throwback to…to old-ee world-ee times."

My lips curve into a smile. "Old-ee world-ee times?"

She frowns. "You know that I mean. Old fashioned. From a long time ago."

"When we all lived in caves and hadn't even heard of the wheel?"

I'm teasing her to lighten the mood, and by the quirk of her lips, it looks like it may be working, but then she shakes her head as though she's annoyed with me for doing just that. "You know what I mean."

"It's a lot of fun, actually. Men carry their wives in a running race. The first to cross the line, wins."

She blinks at me in disbelief. "That's insane, you know that?"

"It's actually a traditional game played in northern countries, such as Finland, adopted here many centuries ago when a Finnish prince married into the royal family. Don't tell me you don't want to see your grandfather carrying your grandmother over his shoulder, firefighter style?"

Despite her best efforts not to laugh, she lets out a giggle and it ends in a snort. Her hand flies to her mouth in a vain attempt to stifle it, her eyes wide.

God forbid she allow herself to laugh at one of my jokes.

"I thought so," I reply with satisfaction.

"Won't they get a break for being super old or something?"

"You'll have to wait and see."

"Did they compete last year?"

"They did not."

"So, they won't this year, either."

"If you say so."

We climb the incline of the Grand Walk under the dappled shade of the trees lining each edge.

"Does your family compete in the wife race?" she asks.

"My father is adept at carrying my mother, who I can't say loves the sport."

"Who can blame her? It's not exactly dignified for the wives."

"It's just a bit of fun, although my father does get rather competitive at these events. I only just managed to beat him in the cheese rolling last year, and he was not happy."

The way in which he glared at me, red faced as I briefly celebrated my win has stuck in my mind. Father is not adept at losing—particularly to his son and heir it would seem.

"You'll have to tell me what cheese rolling is now, Alexander."

The fact she's actually used my name is a giant leap forward.

"Call me Alex," I say as we reach the rotunda at the top of the hill.

Her eyes flick briefly to mine before she looks away. "Sure. Alex," she mumbles.

Is it just the warm day, or are her cheeks reddening a touch?

I for one am enjoying this unexpected chemistry between us.

"That wasn't so hard, was it, Texas?" I ask.

Her face is bright from the exercise, and as she bites down on her lower lip it suddenly strikes me how very kissable those lips of hers are.

The atmosphere around us seems to shift.

She holds my gaze for a beat, and my pulse quickens. But no sooner have we shared an unspoken moment, when she pulls her gaze from mine, shrugging.

"It's fine. Whatever," she replies glibly.

I can't help but feel a stab of disappointment.

Strange. What was I hoping for? That she'd tell me she

got me wrong and now sees I'm a great guy, someone she wants to spend time with and get to know better?

Someone she perhaps even wants to…kiss?

No. That's crazy.

The woman's made it clear. She doesn't like me. And anyway, Father told me it's my job to win her over—and feelings like attraction cannot be a part of my plan.

"Shall we head back? I've got an engagement to get to," she says.

"Of course."

We make our way down the hill, the splendor of the palace glowing in the morning sun.

"I didn't explain cheese rolling to you," I say as we reach a bench. "Would you like to sit for a while?"

She eyes the bench as though it could bite her. Or, perhaps, that's what she's worried I'll do.

"Actually, I need to get going."

"Allow me to walk you back to the palace, then."

"Sure. Hit me with the cheese rolling," she says.

"It's just what you imagine it would be: rolling a wheel of cheese."

"That sounds more like a job than a game."

"Well, you do have to roll the cheese on a course down a hill using only a stick as a guide. The first to cross the line at the bottom of the hill wins."

She laughs. It's a pretty tinkling sound that makes me smile.

"And you beat your dad doing that last year?"

"Proudest moment of my life." I pause before I add, "Not his."

"He wasn't ecstatic his son beat him at something publicly? Weird," she jokes.

"Weird," I confirm.

We share a smile. Was that another bonding moment? Could we have come to some kind of truce between us?

By now, we've reached a side entrance to the palace.

"I look forward to seeing you poking a cheese wheel with a stick at The Games, but now I've really got to go."

"Where are you off to?"

"Why? Are you going to try and crash my next thing, too?"

"I didn't crash the peafowl event."

Why can't she get this point? Obstinance, that's why. She's an obstinate woman with thoroughly kissable lips.

She shakes her head at me before she turns towards the door. "See you 'round, *Alex*."

"I'll look forward to it, *Texas*." I watch as she breezes through the door into the palace, satisfied I've begun to melt the iceberg, just as Father instructed.

Chapter 15

Maddie

"Why do I have to change again, Grandmama?" I ask as Alice zips my dress and fusses with a silver belt, fixing me for the fancy lunch.

My grandmama smiles at my reflection, herself wearing a pretty pink dress that complements her skin tone. "Because, my dear, you were already photographed in a similar dress. If you're seen in what seems to be the same dress within a couple of days? Well, people will talk."

"What will they say?" I ask on a laugh. "New Princess

wears the same dress for an entire 12 hours! National scandal! Bring in the military, STAT!"

"You may not understand this yet, my dear, but one way or another you are the country's newest style icon. Think of Kate Middleton, or Grace Kelly, or Princess Diana. Even your old grandmama was a style icon in her day."

"I bet you were a total style icon, Grandmama."

"Oh, I was quite the fashionista," she replies with a grin. "Some said I was the Jackie O of Europe, although I never quite bought into the idea. I was my own person with my own ideas about fashion, even if, between you and me, the idea of being known as the European Jackie O was rather exciting."

"I bet she had nothing on you, Grandmama."

"You were very stylish and beautiful, ma'am," Alice agrees. "You still are."

"Oh, you both flatter me," Grandmama replies, flushed with happiness.

"I need to see this fashionista. I'm going to Google you," I tell her.

"Is that another one of your Texas expressions?" she asks.

"Google. You know, search the Internet? Not Texas, more like global," I explain.

Grandmama looks at me blankly.

How can my grandmama not know about Googling? I mean she's old, sure, but she lives in the world, doesn't she? I open my mouth, ready to try to explain what the Internet is when she nudges me.

"Of course I know what Google is, Maddie dear. I was just playing with you. There's life in this old girl yet, you know."

I giggle. Grandmama's willingness to relate to me and

her desire to know me has made it easy to form a quick bond with her. Her sense of humor helps, too, and I genuinely enjoy spending time with her and Grandpapa, a little family unit I feel very much a part of.

It's something I honestly didn't expect. Weird, I know. I mean, they're my grandparents, so of course they should feel like family. What I didn't expect was to find family in the real sense of the word. A closeness. A bond.

I search on my phone and land on an image of Grandmama in a beehive hairstyle and a slinky 60s dress.

"Oh em gee, Grandmama! You really were the Jackie O of Europe."

"Oh, no," she replies.

I scroll down to see a photo of her dressed in a brightly printed 70s dress that sweeps the floor, her fair hair more relaxed and flowing down her back.

"You were a total fox! Look at this." I turn the phone around for both my grandmama and Alice to see.

"So beautiful," Alice declares.

"That was an evening at the King Edvard Hall where we saw the Malveauxian Royal Orchestra perform. I remember it because I had just learned that I was pregnant with your mother."

"Mom?" I turn back to the image, but of course there's no visible sign. Grandmama's dress is slim-fitting, skimming over her hips. "That's crazy."

"It was a happy evening," she replies, a sad smile on her face.

I look into her eyes. "I miss her so much right now, which sounds nuts because she's been gone a long time. I guess it's being here where she grew up. I've been thinking about her a lot."

"I'm sure you have," Grandmama replies tenderly. "I have, too."

We share a look and for the first time, I wonder whether she's finding a living, breathing reminder of her daughter difficult.

"Alice, can you give us a sec?" I ask, taking the opportunity to get her alone to ask her something that's been on my mind.

She does a little curtsy and leaves the room.

"What is it, dear?" Grandmama asks.

"Can I ask you a question and you answer it honestly?"

"Of course you can." She pats the seat next to her and I sink down into the soft cushion.

"Okay." I toy with my fingers before I launch into it. "Here's the thing. Someone mentioned that I'm only here as a backup in case Nicolas goes through with his abdication. Is that true?"

My grandmama takes a beat, placing one ankle over the other and folding her hands in her lap. "Your uncle has made it clear that he wishes to abdicate. However, he hasn't yet signed the official paperwork. He's taken a leave of absence."

"With all due respect, that's not telling me a whole lot, Grandmama. Give it to me straight: am I the backup princess?"

"I would never call you a backup, my dear Maddie. Not in a million years."

My pulse quickens. "But that's what I am?"

"In all likelihood, Nicolas will abdicate the throne, making you your grandpapa's heir."

Sounds like a backup to me. Dang Alexander for being right!

I pull my lips into a line and nod my head. "Got it."

"But Maddie, please understand the position we're in. With Nicolas telling us his desires we needed to act before Edgar turned, demanding his rightful position. As

Josephine's daughter, like it or not, you are the next in line for the throne. Nicolas told us he was almost certain to sign before he left for his yacht, which is why we sent Vladimir to get you."

I don't think she realizes she's now painted a picture of me as the undisputed backup princess here.

"I get it. It's fine, Grandmama. Really."

Her features crease into a relieved smile. "We are so very happy to have you here, regardless of what Nicolas decides."

I offer her a smile. Truth be told, I'm beginning to enjoy my life here as a princess. Potentially not being the heir to the throne does definitely take the pressure off.

So why do I suddenly feel like a rug's being pulled out from under me?

Grandmama clearly wants a change of subject when she asks, "Do you feel ready for today's luncheon?"

"Sure do. We're meeting the Prime Minister, Margarita Grayson, and her husband, Bill, as well as all the members of the Cabinet before my formal presentation tomorrow at the Houses of Parliament," I tell her, remembering what was in the briefing paper Alice handed to me with my breakfast this morning.

That's the thing I'm learning about being a princess: other people organize you and your day. All you've got to do is turn up and try to act regal—something I might have failed at during the peafowl incident, but something I've begun to feel more and more.

"You sound like you know exactly what you're doing," she says with a proud smile. "I knew you would. I told your grandpapa that any daughter of Josephine's will do a splendid job as a princess of Malveaux."

The memory of my mom tugs on my heart. I'm doing

the things she once did for the country she once called home.

But she gave it all up for love.

I hope I'll never have to make such a decision.

"All I did was memorize the list, Grandmama. Up until this morning, I thought a cabinet was a piece of furniture."

Grandmama lets out a laugh, assuming I'm making a joke. I'm not. When I first read I was meeting the Prime Minister and her Cabinet, I had an image of the Prime Minister in some kind of oversized piece of furniture. I figured it was a weird Malveauxian thing, because let's face it, any country that requires its royals to "meet" peafowl has some pretty weird traditions. Then, Alice explained that the Cabinet is a little bit like the Senate, each person responsible for a portfolio, and the Prime Minister is of course like the President, although they do need the monarch's approval to form a government.

It still scrambles my brain.

I wish I'd paid more attention in world history class.

"When we sit down to eat, I start using the utensils from the outside and work my way in, right?" I ask.

"That's right, dear. I'm sure it's the same as it is in America, only we use both knife and fork as we eat. No shoveling things in with simply a fork," Grandmama replies with a hint of judgment.

I'd be affronted if I hadn't been known to do my fair share of shoveling.

"It seems every movie I've seen about someone suddenly become a royal involves them messing up by using the wrong utensil at the wrong time. It's a total minefield to me."

"I'm certain you'll be absolutely fine," Grandmama replies, clearly not concerned about potential Forkgate. "Alice took you through it?"

"She sure did."

"In that case, I'll leave you in her capable hands to put the finishing touches to your outfit. I'll see you at the luncheon at 1:00 PM."

My nerves put their running shoes on and prepare for a sprint.

She turns to leave and a sudden thought occurs to me. "Prince Alexander isn't coming today, right? This is just me meeting the Prime Minister before my formal parliamentary investiture. It has nothing to do with him or Ledonia."

"Prince Alexander is attending."

I think of the way he looked at me in the garden that time, as though he could so easily kiss me. Then my mind spirals to the fact that he called me an opportunist backup princess that first night we met, and then laughed at me scaring the peafowl.

I wonder which version I'll get today?

I can't deny that I feel something for the guy, even if I absolutely do not want to. Anything more than purely platonic feelings for the guy is not a good development, and something I need to fix, STAT.

I need to keep reminding myself he's not at all my type. Not at all my type. He may be handsome and charming, with a voice like liquid honey, and he may look at me as though he finds me both utterly ridiculous and at the same time extremely intriguing, with those deep brown eyes of his with the gold flecks that catch the light, but...I... I...Wait.

Where was I?

Ugh!

This is so typical of a man like Alexander. He's using his obvious good looks and general hotness to distract and confuse me. Just because half the world's female population is desperately in love with him doesn't mean I plan on joining their ranks anytime soon. Or ever.

"His father, the King, is anxious that Alexander be present at as many events as is appropriate," she says. "He spoke with your grandpapa and me about it while he was here. I think it's very sweet of him to want to ensure you feel part of the special relationship between our two countries."

"But Grandmama, is it appropriate for Alexander to come to something that has nothing to do with him or his country? That's like a Canadian prince coming to meet the president of the US with me. You know, if Canada had a royal family."

"Canada does have a royal family. As part of the Commonwealth, their monarch is King Charles of Britain."

Not getting the point here, Grandmama.

"But Alexander, isn't a part of our family and the government isn't his country's government, so it makes sense that he sit this one out. Right?"

She studies my face for a beat. "Is there something you need to tell me about you and Prince Alexander?"

My grandmama, it would seem, is an astute woman, although it's not what she thinks. But then who would guess the "thing" between us is that I punched him and he's keeping it a secret and now I've begun to wonder what it would be like to kiss the guy?

"There's no 'me and Prince Alexander', that I can assure you," I reply with more force than I feel. "It's just... I guess we're not a fit, you know?"

"A fit?"

"He's not my kind of guy."

He's not my kind of guy? I'm even making myself cringe.

Grandmama pulls her brows together. "Prince Alexander will be King of Ledonia and, if it so transpires, you will be Queen of Malveaux. Our two countries have a long history together over many centuries. You and the prince don't need to be friends, but it would help grease the wheels between our two countries if you were."

"I think the wheels got jammed," I admit.

She looks alarmed. "Oh? I know he has a certain reputation with the ladies, so I sincerely hope—"

I raise my hands quickly, shaking my head. "Oh, no. Nothing like that," I reassure her, and she looks relieved. "It's just I feel judged by him, I guess."

"Judged? That simply won't do. I'll have a word with his father. He keeps a very tight leash on his son, although possibly not tight enough where you're concerned?"

My grandmama telling the King on Alexander is not only so very elementary school, but way too mortifying to even contemplate.

"Please don't do that," I reply in a rush because that idea needs to be squashed right now. "I hardly know the guy. There's a chance I rushed to a conclusion about him. I'm sure he's a really great person and an awesome prince."

I don't mean a word, and anyway, what exactly makes someone an "awesome prince"? A good wave? Great ribbon cutting skills? Looking good in a jacket with a sash?

Okay, yes, he's got that one nailed.

"As long as you're sure?" she asks, her brow creased in concern.

"We'll work it out. No worries."

"And become friends?" she asks hopefully.

I pull my lips into a smile as false as my high school science teacher, Mr. McClusky's teeth. "Friends. You got it."

OF COURSE I have to sit next to Alexander at the luncheon, and of course he looks ridiculously hot in his suit and tie, all dapper and royal looking, not a hair out of place.

It seems wherever I go, Alexander is soon to follow, looking the way he does.

I could have him prosecuted for stalking where I'm from.

Here, it just seems to be royal protocol.

We're seated in a huge formal dining room with super high vaulted ceilings, large windows overlooking the formal gardens and the beautiful peacock fountain, and about 25 people, all dressed in suits, sitting at a long table decorated with the sorts of floral arrangements you see in magazines.

On my left is the Prime Minister, Margarita Grayson, an intelligent woman in her late 40s in a navy pant suit, with a black, bobbed haircut and bangs that make her look like Anna Wintour, only a lot more friendly. No offense to Anna Wintour, but she does seem super scary to me. I've seen *The Devil Wears Prada* three times.

We've chatted about the weather in Malveaux and how it compares to Texas—a lot less humid—as well as how I'm finding Malveaux, and now she's busy talking to Grandpapa.

So, I'm stuck with Alexander, who seems intent on making nice, just as he did in the garden.

I sit and listen to him talking about where his family has palaces, and which one he likes the best and how drafty some of them can be in winter, and all his privilege, privilege, privilege. As I watch him, I remind myself how horrible he is. Simple fact.

But as he asks me about my life in Texas, the way he

listens intently to my replies, picking up on things I say, always with his eyes trained intently on me as though I'm the only person in the room, I begin to forget how much I dislike him.

Dangerous territory.

"You know, Texas, I'm wondering at what point you're going to apologize," he says, catching me completely off guard.

"Apologize? What for? Not having as many palaces as you?"

Ha!

I'll admit, I'm a little pleased with my retort.

"Actually, Malveaux has quite a number of royal residences, one more than Ledonia."

Trust him to know that.

He does that thing where he leans in closer to me and I can't help but catch his scent, which of course, just like him, is a little too compelling for comfort.

"If you just apologized for the cupboard incident, we could call it a truce and move on with our lives," he says, his voice low and intimate.

It does things to my belly that I try to ignore.

I glance around us. Everyone is involved in their own conversations, not listening to Alexander or me. I lift my water glass to my lips and take a sip. "Here isn't the place to talk about that."

Or any place. Ever. It's way too mortifying.

"Why not? No one's listening. They're all talking politics, which frankly, I find rather dull."

I choke on my drink. "But you're going to be King someday. Shouldn't you at least try to talk politics?"

"There's plenty of time for that. My father doesn't retire until he's 65. There's a lot of time before things have to get boring. So, let's have it out. Air the dirty laundry, as they say. That way we can both get through our time together in one piece. And it's Alex, remember?"

He's got a point, but *apologize* to him? Is he drunk?

I try to keep the sting from my voice. "You were horrible to me that night," I say under my breath. "I'm not going to apologize to you when you told me I was milking my new found position in life for all it's worth. Which, by the way, is completely untrue and so very not a part of my character, that it's laughable. The way I see it, *you* should be apologizing to *me*."

"I think you'll find that particular conversation happened well after your fist met my nose, princess."

I know he's right.

I bite down on my lip, my irritation rising, mixed with a healthy spoonful of guilt.

I decide to level with him.

"Look. The thing is, I was in the closet taking a moment to myself when you burst in suddenly, totally freaking me out, and I genuinely thought you'd followed me in there to hurt me. You were muttering to yourself like some kind of crazy person. I saw red."

He takes a beat before he replies. "I understand how you might have felt threatened."

My eyes widen in surprise. "You do?"

"Of course I do. I'm not an ogre."

I see an opportunity to lighten the mood between us. "You mean like Shrek?"

His features relax, his lips curving into a hint of a smile. "Like Shrek."

"I knew it. You drink a potion to make you human every day."

He lets out a low, rumbling laugh that seems to reach

inside and tug on my belly. "Oh, you should see me when I wake up. Not a pretty sight."

I can't help but laugh at the image of the handsome Alexander as a big ole green ogre.

I'm storing that one away.

"Look, I'm going to level with you," he begins. "I went into the cupboard because I was having a…a bad moment, should we say. I needed space, a breather. Just for a while. I had no idea I wasn't alone."

I study his face and find only honesty—and vulnerability. It takes me by surprise. Long gone is the haughty, teasing, sometimes flirty Alex, replaced by this new, real version.

A version I could actually like.

"Were you feeling anxious?" I ask.

"Less anxious and more frustrated, I suppose. People have certain expectations of my character, and sometimes I find that difficult to take."

I pull my brows together. "In English?"

"I used to be someone who enjoyed a good party, someone who found it easy to attract women, which I was happy to do, playing the field and having a good time."

I pretend to be aghast. "No!"

His lips quirk. "I know. It's hard to believe, looking at the shell of a man I am today."

There's no denying it. Prince Alexander of Ledonia is super, sizzling, scorching hot. Only now that I allow myself to know it, I can never *un*-know it.

"You went to the closet to hide from all those expectations that you're a bad boy partying womanizer?" I ask.

"Nicely put."

"I try."

"I was also hiding from the waitress who was hitting on me."

I huff out a laugh and several guests glance our way.

Alexander smiles at them benignly as though to say "nothing to see here" before he returns his attention to me. "I needed some time out. Just a moment. That's why I was looking for my meditation app. People have suggested it, and I thought then was as good a moment as any to give it a try. I've got a bad habit of talking to myself when I think no one else is around."

I feel a flash of unexpected comradery with him. "I do that!" I press my lips together. "I'm sorry I messed that up for you."

"I'm sorry I messed up whatever it was you were doing in the cupboard, too."

We share a look, each of us understanding a little more about the other. It feels nice. New.

New and dangerous.

"One thing," he says.

"What?"

"You're in Malveaux now. It's a cupboard, not a closet."

"I'm still an American." I pause a beat before I say what I should have said all along, but I was so wrapped up in my dislike for him that I didn't. "I am actually sorry I hit you. I shouldn't have, whatever the excuse."

"You've got an impressive right hook. Ever thought about going pro?"

I giggle and it ends in a snort. "Do you think I could make it?"

"Heck, yes. I can see it now: the Mighty Princess Madeline the Mauler, coming soon to a ring near you."

"Maybe you could be my manager?"

He gives a little bow. "Nothing would make me happier."

We share a smile. Somehow, we've come to a truce, a

truce that means I can become friends with Alex, the way Grandmama hopes.

But that's where it needs to end. I absolutely can't go catching feelings for the world's Party Prince.

Even if I wonder whether I already have.

Chapter 16

Maddie

I sit in the backseat of the black palace car and look out the window at the bustling city streets. I'm trying to distract myself from my next engagement, aka my impending doom. It's my first public appearance outside of the palace as princess, and I'm almost as nervous as I was the night of my presentation ball.

So far, no panic attack though.

I'm hoping to keep it that way.

My mind turns to Alex. Talk about a conundrum wrapped up in an enigma and stuffed in the back of your sock drawer.

Today he wasn't what I'd expected at all, not after the ball and the peafowl incident.

He was…nice. Friendly. Totally disarming.

And when he looked at me with those deep, soulful eyes, I got the distinct impression he felt something for me. Something beyond the fact I'm his opposite number on the Malveauxian side of the fence. Something besides just doing his duty befriending the new girl.

It felt romantic. Definitely electric.

But then it's so hard to know with that guy. He's not exactly easy to read. He's rude and then charming. Stand-offish and then open.

Seriously, it's enough to give a girl whiplash.

One thing I know for sure, I don't have time to pull the enigma that is Alex out of the sock drawer to analyze him. I've got a job to do, and I'm starting to freak right out.

I glance out the window at the old stone buildings lining the streets as the car moves through the city on its way to the Tleurbonne Children's Hospital, the location of my first public appearance. I'm happy that it's for one of my newly acquired charities, and the fact it's in support of sick kids means a lot to me.

I just need to make sure I hold it together and we'll be good.

"We're about three minutes away," Vladmir says from the front passenger seat, making the nerves that are already bouncing around my belly like rubber balls pick up their pace.

"Thanks," I reply, trying to sound bright and breezy.

Less than three minutes later, my driver pulls the sleek

black car up to the entrance to the hospital, where a cluster of people are milling around on the front steps. A number of them have camera equipment, and those rubber nerve balls begin to bounce like Olympic high jumpers.

"Are they all here for me?" I ask Vlad.

"Of course, ma'am," he replies. Like Alice, he only calls me Maddie when no one else is around. "You are the new and exciting princess. You can expect a lot of media attention, at least for a while."

Although I've met a bunch of people in my new role already, it's all been within the carefully controlled confines of the palace. There's been no paparazzi and only the official photographers, who everyone seems to trust.

This feels different.

Of course I know Royals get media attention. I haven't been living under a rock. The British Royals are super popular, and the media has been known to hound their princes and princesses. But this is Malveaux. Perhaps they're nicer here? Less persistent?

I clasp my hands in my lap and take a few deep breaths.

I've got this.

Vladimir, good guy that he is, senses my nerves. "I know it seems a touch overwhelming, but I know you will be absolutely fine, ma'am."

"You sure about that?" I eye the growing crowd.

"Of course I am, ma'am."

Me? I'm not so confident.

I've got to remember how to get out of the car elegantly and without showing the world the color of my underwear. Easier said than done, believe me. Then, I've got to walk up the steps without tripping while being photographed by a clutch of photographers, all calling my name. And then, the most nerve-racking of all, I've got to act all put together and princess-y while meeting sick kids who will probably make me cry right there on the spot, ruining my makeup as well as my composure, and I'll end up a streaky, blubbery mess.

Not the way I need this to go.

I glance at the crowd once more. I know I need to give Vlad the word and get out of the car, walk up those steps, smile and wave maybe, and then I'm inside the hospital. But right now, that feels like one of the scariest things I've contemplated in my life.

"I've got this. I've got this," I murmur to myself as a mantra, when there's a sudden frenzy of voices and camera flashes outside the car, grabbing our attention. All the photographers seem to be focusing on one person, who is walking down the steps toward our car with a very familiar gait.

No! It *can't* be him.

Prince Superglue himself.

"What the heck is *he* doing here?" I say against the window. I lift my arm to wipe the fog formed by my breath from the window when my door springs open, the noise from outside suddenly filling the space.

I pull back in shock and gape at him.

Alexander leans inside and says, "Would you mind scooting over please, Texas?"

"What? Why? What are you doing here?"

The flash bulbs are still snapping around us and I can hear people excitedly calling Alexander's name amidst the hubbub.

This is crazy.

"How about you let me get in the car and I can answer any and all questions you may have?"

I glance at Vladimir. He does one of those subtle head nods of his, giving the go ahead to allow Alex in. I slide over the black leather seat and he closes the door behind him, the outside noise dulled once more.

"This is a lot better in here. It's rather busy out there," he says with a smile, as though he hasn't just been yelled at, photographed, and generally pawed at by an excited mob. "Everyone's very eager to meet you, Texas, but I believe you need to get *out* of the car in order to do that. It would be rather crowded if everyone came in here, don't you think?"

"Why are you here?" I ask him again, getting straight to the point. "This is my event. They're here to see me."

"Which is why you're still in the car?"

I bite down on my lip.

"I was waiting inside the hospital, actually. I knew this was your first big public outing, so I didn't want to steal the focus from you. I slipped in a back entrance."

I gesture out the window. "I think you definitely stole the focus."

"They're here for you, Madeline, not me. I simply got caught in their photographic crossfire when I came down the stairs to see if you needed me."

"Why would I need *you*?" I ask, my voice high and shrill.

I know how incredibly rude that sounds, but this is Smug Alexander busting into my car. Smug Alexander who is also Confusing Alexander and Unexpectedly Kind and Sexy Alexander, all at the same time.

He's the last person I want to see right now—and, oddly, the first.

I'm not going to pick that thought apart.

He gestures at the lowered privacy screen between us

and the front seats. "May we?" He gives a hand gesture to show lifting it up.

"Why?" I ask.

"For privacy. Clearly. That's what they're for."

I pause for a beat before I decide to give him the benefit of the doubt. I press the button and the divider lifts into place.

"So? What do you want to say to me that my bodyguard and driver can't hear?"

Despite the fact we're now alone, with no one listening in, he leans closer to me, and just as I did the last time he got this close, I can't help but breathe in his scent. It's a mixture of spice and musk with a distinctive note of Alexander.

"It's just that—and please tell me if I'm on the wrong track with this—I wondered whether you're feeling the same way you did that time we met in the hallway cupboard?" he asks. "If I may be so bold as to inquire."

Is he really raising that whole incident again, even though we've already agreed to put it behind us?

"Because if it is," he continues in a soft voice. "I want to be here for you."

I swallow, totally wrongfooted.

He wants to be here for me?

He seems so genuine, and part of me wants to believe him. Really, really wants to. I can use all the friends I can get in this new life I find myself in. Friends who know how this whole royal gig goes. Friends who've been there.

But this is *Alexander* we're talking about. Alexander, the guy who delighted in my peacock disaster. The guy who told me he thinks I'm cashing in on my new-found fame as Malveaux's backup princess.

The guy who quite clearly thinks I'm ridiculous.

But he's also the guy who's been unexpectedly nice to

me, telling me about The Games and his family, trying to relate to me and make me feel at home.

Dang it! Prince Alexander wasn't supposed to be thoughtful or kind. He was supposed to be a privileged, self-interested, self-satisfied, total jerk of a human being who spent all his time wooing women and living the high life with no interest in real human connection with anyone ever.

He's supposed to be the kind of man I'd never in a million years want to even strike up a friendship with, let alone have real, actual feelings for.

But this is a new version of him. One I did not see coming.

One that touches my heart.

"I have first-hand experience of what it's like to step out into that mob. You're new at this. The least I can do is help you navigate it all. I'm an old hand, you see. Long in the tooth and all that."

I nod, not quite sure how to respond.

"Tell me if I'm wrong, Texas," he continues in his soft, intimate voice that is somehow managing to help calm me. "You never told me why you were hiding in the cupboard, but I think I can work it out. You were overwhelmed, weren't you?"

I bite down on my lip.

Thoughtful, kind, and observant? Who *is* this guy?

He places a hand over mine. "It's a lot. But it's all going to be okay. You'll see."

I look up into his eyes and I find only kindness and concern. The part of me that wants to believe he's here to genuinely help grows and grows until it fills my heart, pushing out my feelings of inadequacy and fear.

Instead, I feel calm. Ready.

Who knew Alexander could do that for me?

The rusty hinges of the gate encircling my heart creak open a fraction.

"Okay," I say, nodding my head like one of those bobblehead dolls, eager to get this over with now that I have Alexander here to encourage me.

"Okay," he echoes.

We smile at one another, and any remnant of my nerves vanish.

"I can wait here for you, if you like, or I can go up the steps with you. Totally your choice."

I glance out at the crowd. There's got to be at least a couple hundred people here, maybe more, from nosy passers-by to photographers and journalists.

I know to be the sort of princess I want to be—poised, together, involved in a whole bunch of worthy causes, able to be an ambassador for Malveaux—I need to get comfortable with crowds, the paparazzi, all of it.

And besides, as far as romantic gestures go—which is what this has definitely begun to feel like—this is easily in the top three I've ever experienced.

Okay, the top one.

I haven't had a huge number of romantic gestures sent my way.

"They already know you're in the car, so it'd be weird if you stayed here."

"There is that," he replies.

"Come with me." I press the button to lower the screen. "Okay, Vlad. I'm ready to get out there. With Alex."

Vlad's eyes flick briefly to Alex. "If you're sure, ma'am?"

"I'm as sure as the bluebonnets in spring," I reply, using one of my dad's favorite expressions.

Both men shoot me a quizzical look.

"It means I'm positive," I explain.

Vlad exits the car and opens the back door. Alexander climbs out and then turns back and offers me his hand like a dashing prince. I do my best imitation of a poised princess myself, swinging both legs stuck together like they're glued out and onto the sidewalk.

The crowd erupts into a frenzy of camera flashes and cheers and people calling our names.

I let go of Alexander's hand and wave at the people. The crowd parts like the Red Sea as we climb the stone hospital steps, side-by-side.

"What is your relationship to the new princess, Alexander?" someone calls out.

"Are you dating?" comes another voice.

"You two look great together, are you a new thing?"

"Don't answer them, Texas," Alexander instructs.

"I wasn't planning on it."

At the top of the steps, Alexander says, "I usually give them a smile and a wave to keep them happy. Do you want to do that?"

"Sure thing."

We turn and wave and smile at everybody, the practiced royal and the newbie. The crowd goes crazy.

Alexander pushes the door open and steps back for me. "After you."

As the door closes behind us, the sounds of the cameras and people dull, and I let out a relieved sigh, suddenly giddy.

"That was actually quite fun," I exclaim.

Alex grins at me. "You did well, Texas."

"I did, didn't I? Thank you."

"All part of the service," he tells me with a wink that makes my belly do a little flip.

"Welcome to the Tleurbonne Children's Hospital," a

woman says, pulling my attention from Alex, and I notice for the first time she's one of several people standing in a line. "I'm Dr. Alison Dalgleish, Chief Medical Officer. We are so thrilled to have you here, Your Royal Highness," she says to me.

I shake her hand and she curtsies. "It's a pleasure to meet you, doctor."

"We were not expecting Your Royal Highness." She curtsies to Alex. "Although with your excellent work with CAYAC, I'm sure you're no stranger to children's hospitals."

What have kayaks got to do with hospitals? Unless Alex goes kayaking and ends up injuring himself? Maybe he's not very good it at?

We're introduced to the rest of the people, and then they lead us down the corridor toward the cancer wing.

"You're going to have to explain to me what kayaks and hospitals have to do with each other," I say to Alex.

"Not a kayak," he replies with a laugh. "C. A. Y. A. C. is an acronym for Children And Young Adults with Cancer."

That makes more sense.

"It's a project I'm involved with back in Ledonia. We fund cancer research specifically for younger people. We're having some promising results, although it's early days of course. We started out in Ledonia, but it's expanded into nine European countries already, including Malveaux, and we're hoping to increase that number each year. The more countries that are involved, the more money we make, which means we can do more."

With every meeting, every conversation, I'm getting to know a different Alex. He's not the shallow-as-a-puddle playboy prince everyone thinks he is. He does kind things like turn up to help me at my first public appearance and spearheading cancer research for young people.

He's not the man I first thought he was.

We reach the oncology ward and immediately we're shown into one of the rooms. It's brightly colored, with murals of farm animals on the walls, the curtains separating the three beds drawn to show the full room.

I step inside, my eyes landing on a young girl with sparse hair, sitting upright in a bed. She can't be much more than eight or nine, and she's wearing a Barbie pink jumpsuit with the word "Princess" in looping gold script across the chest.

She beams at me as we approach.

"Princess Madeline and Prince Alexander, this is Ava. She's been with us for some time," Dr. Dalgleish says.

"Hi, Ava," I say as I crouch down beside her. "It's great to meet you."

She beams at me, her entire face lit up with joy. "You're a princess," she says.

"I think you're the princess. You have it written on your shirt. See?" I gesture at myself. "I don't have that."

She looks down as though not knowing what's emblazoned on her chest. "That's only because I've decided I want to be a princess when I grow up," she says, her tone serious.

"I bet you'd make a wonderful princess," I say, and win another one of her beautiful smiles. "What would you do?"

"Oh, I'd make ice cream free and get rid of vegetables," she replies promptly.

"You've already thought about this?" I ask, and she nods.

Alexander raises his brows. "You'd get rid of vegetables all together?"

"Oh, yes. Especially broccoli. I hate broccoli," she replies.

"You know what, Ava? I'm with you on that. Broccoli is truly horrible," he says, and she lets out a giggle.

It would seem even eight-year-old girls aren't immune to Alexander's charm.

"Do you like being a princess?" Ava asks me.

I think of the changes in my life, the fact I miss Dad and Chloe, and a bunch of things about my life in Houston. I think about my new-found closeness with my grandparents, the way I'm fulfilling a role here that has begun to mean more and more to me. The life I lead is so very different, but it's new and exciting, even if it's scary at times. But I get to visit places like this and help to brighten a little girl's day.

"You know what? I do like it," I reply. I glance at Alexander and notice he's smiling at me. "Do you like being a prince?" I ask him. "Did you know this is Prince Alexander from Ledonia?"

Ava's eyes widen.

"I do like being a prince, but mainly because I don't have to slay any dragons," he replies, and Ava bursts into laughter.

"That's knights, silly," she says.

"Did I get that wrong? Sorry," Alexander replies, all easy charm.

"Prince Alexander *is* silly," I say. "But let's keep that between us, okay?"

She gives a solemn nod. "Okay."

Dr. Dalgleish suggests we say goodbye to Ava, which we do, and she leads us to the next bed, where we meet another girl, named Lola. In contrast with Ava, she's in a navy pajama set, her head completely bald.

"Hello, Lola. It's great to meet you," I say.

"Hey," she says without a smile.

"Lola's having a bit of a down day today," Dr. Dalgleish tells us.

"I'm so sorry to hear that," I say. "Tell me, do you want to be a princess when you grow up, too?"

She shakes her head, her lips twisted. "Nope. I want to be a police officer and catch bad guys or drive cars really fast on a racetrack," she replies with an endearing lisp.

"Lola's one of our tomboys here on the ward," Dr. Dalgleish explains.

"My sister, Amelia, is a tomboy," Alexander says.

"Is she a princess, too?" Lola asks.

"Of course. But between you and me," he says, leaning closer to her and speaking conspiratorially. "She'd much rather wear jeans than a ballgown, and she used to be an excellent tree climber, although she does less of that these days, now that she's a grown up. Do you like to climb trees?"

"I used to," Lola replies, and my heart breaks for this young girl, unable to do what she loves.

"It's one of her goals when she's better," Dr. Dalgleish explains. "All our patients have lists of things they want to do when they leave here. We find it works for them to have something to look forward to."

"How high have you climbed?" Alexander asks.

"So high. Way higher than Stuart. He's my brother," Lola explains.

"Would you say you're the champion tree climber in your family?"

"Definitely. Do you know what else I can do?"

"Tell me."

"I can hold my breath under the water for ages."

"That's impressive, and very useful," Alexander replies.

I watch as he chats with Lola, and then other children

as we make our way around the ward, always with ease. They respond to him as though talking with a fellow child, not a grown up or a prince.

Something moves in my heart.

I feel a connection between us I did not see coming. More than friendship. More than attraction.

And it's both exciting and terrifying.

Chapter 17

Alexander

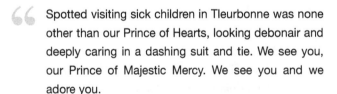 Spotted visiting sick children in Tleurbonne was none other than our Prince of Hearts, looking debonair and deeply caring in a dashing suit and tie. We see you, our Prince of Majestic Mercy. We see you and we adore you.

Princess Madeline was there, too.

#KnightInShiningArmani
#NotJustAPartyPrince

Yours in besotted admiration,

Fabiana Fontaine xx

I arrive at Parliament on my borrowed motorcycle, a little after 9 in the morning. I'm annoyed with myself for being late. Earlier, I'd taken my horse, Guinie, out for a morning ride, visiting an old haunt Prince Nicolas introduced me and my siblings to many years ago, a stunning lake about a 25-minute gallop from the palace.

I had a lot to think about, and riding always helps me clear my head.

The woman I've come to see today is at the very heart of it all.

I know Father wants me to be at all her events. I know he wants me to stick to her like glue. And I've been doing my best to comply with his wishes, to the point where I feel exactly as Madeline described me: like a stalker.

But the truth is, the unthinkable has happened. Something I didn't see coming.

I find myself liking Madeline. As in actually *liking* her. Not just feeling attracted to her, because of course I feel that. She's beautiful and sexy and smart and funny. In a way, attraction was inevitable.

It would also seem I got her so very wrong. She's as much an opportunist as I'm a chef (I'm the first to admit I'm terrible at cooking). She doesn't have a calculating bone in her body. She's genuine, and it seems to me she's here in Malveaux for the best of reasons. She wants to do the right thing by her family and her new-found country. She's someone whose life has been turned upside down by this new role she finds herself in, a role she seems determined to do justice.

I'm so glad I crashed her event at the hospital. In short, I did it because I felt an overwhelming need to help her. To dispel any concerns she may have about her first public appearance. To show her how strong and amazing she really is.

As male and old fashioned as it may sound, I wanted to protect her.

Then, getting to see how she interacted with the children and staff at the hospital showed me so much about who she is. Talking with the children, so warm, so gentle, so natural. Like she was born for the role. Which of course she was. But it seems as though it's her calling, something she was meant to be.

In short, she touched my heart.

I huff a breath.

This is brand new territory for me. I've not once felt the need to do something for a woman I'm not related to. Of course, I would do anything to protect my mother and my sisters. But a woman I've only just met? A woman I was deeply suspicious of from the moment her fist met my nose? The odds were low at best.

And that's what's playing on my mind.

How can I feel that level of emotion toward a woman I'm only just getting to know? It's unfathomable to me.

I know one thing for certain. I'm not going to go falling for this new princess. Heck, I've been involved with women before and never become emotionally involved.

Lots of women: zero emotion.

All I have to do is keep my head and all will be well.

Although there is a small voice in the back of my head telling me *it's already too late*.

By the looks of the dispersing crowd, Madeline has

already entered Parliament for her investiture. I park the motorcycle behind the magnificent Neoclassical building, trailed by Paulo, my security guard, in his car.

Paulo wasn't overly pleased with me for choosing to ride a bike here, evidenced by his scowl. But then I've never met a bodyguard who doesn't sport a frown 99% of the time. And besides, riding a motorcycle through the streets of Tleurbonne is fun.

And I've got a plan in mind for it, too.

"This way," I tell Paulo as I dash around to the front, and rush up the steps, pushing through the heavy wooden doors at the entranceway.

"Prince Alexander!" I hear people call, but I don't pause for photos. I'm on a mission, and I'm late.

I nod in acknowledgment at surprised besuited men and women as I make my way through the tapestry-adorned walls, past the towering columns, across the polished marble floor, toward the Parliament Chamber.

"Your Royal Highness!" an insistent voice calls from behind me as I reach the doors to the Chamber.

I swing around to see a grave looking, stout man in a dark suit, his jowls so soft and droopy they could rival a Basset Hound's.

"Yes?"

He pauses to give a quick bow before he says, "May I escort you to the Distinguished Visitor's Gallery? We prepared it for you when we received notice of your attendance today."

"Actually, I'm looking for Princess Madeline."

"The Princess is in the antechamber, where she's preparing for her speech. You will be more comfortable in the Gallery, sir. I assure you." He gestures down the hall.

I pull my lips into my most charming of smiles. "I'll be

happy to do as you suggest once I've had a quick word with the princess. She's expecting me, you see."

It's a total lie, but he doesn't need to know that.

I know he's going to comply with my wish. It's one of the benefits of being a prince.

"Of course," he concedes after a beat. "If you'll follow me?" He leads us down the hallway to the antechamber, where Vladimir, Madeline's security guard, greets me with a stiff nod.

"Sir, I'll wait here to escort you to the Distinguished Visitor's Gallery once you've had your conversation with the princess," Mr. Bassett Hound says.

"That would be just great," I reply. "Now, the Princess?"

"Certainly, sir," Vladimir replies.

I instruct Paulo to wait for me in the hallway, and Vladimir leads me to an adjoining room where Maddie is seated, her head bent over as she concentrates on reading, her lips moving with each word.

She's in a slim-fitting, demure Malveauxian blue dress that shows off her figure, with a peacock brooch pinned near her shoulder. A nude pair of pumps elongate her slim legs. With her hair curled around her shoulders she looks every inch the princess she is.

"Good morning, Texas," I say, and she looks up at me in surprise before her lips pull into a smile that seems to reach inside of me and tug at my heart.

How's my not *getting emotionally involved going?*

"Alex? What are you doing here?"

"I came to see you, of course." I nod my head at the now closed door. "I don't get the feeling your Vladimir likes me all that much," I say as I sit down on a chair opposite Maddie.

"Who can blame him? You don't exactly have the best reputation with the ladies, you know."

"On the contrary, I have a very good reputation with the ladies, if their enthusiasm is anything to go by."

She snorts with laughter, although I can tell she's nervous about her upcoming speech.

I lean my elbows on my knees. "Are you feeling prepared?"

Her smile drops and she bites down on her lip. "Speaking in public isn't exactly my strength, and even though it's only short, it's in a foreign language. How do you think I'm doing?"

"You'll be fine. I know you will. Look at how you handled the hospital visit. Like a pro."

"That was only because I literally had you hauling me out of the car."

I smile at the memory. Knowing I was able to help her in some small way made me feel pretty dang great. "I could do that for you again today, but I'm not sure how that would look."

She sighs. "I know."

"You can do it. You've had lunch with the Prime Minister and her Cabinet, you've done your first public outing, and you even managed to win this cynic over with your beauty and charm."

"You're a total flatterer, did you know that?"

"I'm only saying it like it is, princess," I reply truthfully and I win a blush from her. "How about you practice on me?"

"Do you speak Malveauxian?"

"Of course I do. It's one of several languages I speak, including Ledonian, of course, as well as French, Spanish, German, and English. How many languages do you speak?"

"Two, if you include Texan."

I laugh. "We can include Texan. So, you've never spoken Malveauxian before?"

"My mom had this thing she'd say to me at night when she tucked me in, and I would say it back to her. It was Malveauxian, and I remember it word for word. *Ti seet sivoltio dreetia, mi sheeri.*"

"You are the light of my life, my darling," I translate for her.

She presses her lips together as though overcome with emotion at the touching memory of a mother she lost far too early.

"Maddie, it's a beautiful saying."

She nods as tears pool in her blue eyes, made all the bluer by the color of her dress.

I leap to my feet and am by her side within a couple of seconds. I place my hand on her arm as I reach into the top pocket of my suit jacket and pull out my pocket square. Father taught me to always have a handkerchief available for a lady in distress, and I laughed at him as some kind of relic from a bygone age. But right now, with Maddie tearing up before her first speech as a princess, I'm glad I can offer her one.

"Thanks," she mutters. She dabs at her eyes with it. With another sniff she pronounces, "You are such an old-fashioned gentleman, did you know that?"

"Not too old fashioned, I hope."

She smiles a watery smile. "No. Just the right amount." She sniffs loudly before she wipes her nose. "I figure you don't want this back right now?"

"As delightful as I'm certain your snot is, thank you, but I'll pass."

She lets out a gurgling laugh. "Who needs a new

princess crying over her dead mom at her welcome to Parliament party?"

"Absolutely no one," I reply, and we share a smile. "Why don't you dazzle me with your speech."

She scrunches up her nose in an adorable way. "I'm not sure."

I sit back in my seat and intertwine my fingers. "I promise I won't bite. Or judge you, for that matter."

She takes in a deep breath and releases it. "Okay. Here goes nothing." Gripping her notes, she stands and launches haltingly into her speech, her Malveauxian heavily accented.

Once she's done, she looks up at me with hope in her eyes. "How'd I do?"

"You did so well, considering you've never spoken Malveauxian before. Honestly."

She grimaces. "That bad?"

She sees right through me.

"Try it again and I'll point out where you said 'peasants' instead of 'parliamentarians.'"

She looks at me aghast. "Oh, no, I didn't!"

"No, but it would have been very funny if you had."

She snorts out a laugh.

She practices again, me correcting her mispronunciation of a couple of words, before there's a light knock on the door and King Harald and Queen Maria enter, wearing ceremonial robes. Malveauxian blue, naturally.

"Alexander," the Queen says as she greets me with a kiss to both cheeks. "I thought you'd be in the Gallery."

"I'm just on my way there now," I assure them. I turn back to Maddie, who seems considerably less nervous than when I entered the room. I take her hand in mine and brush a soft kiss against her skin, her floral scent filling my nose. "Good luck," I murmur. "I'll sit in your line of sight. That way you can focus on me rather than anything else."

She bites down on her lip and it's unclear to me whether it's nerves or something else. "Okay."

"Knock 'em dead, Texas," I whisper, and she grins, her face flushed pink.

Finally allowing a thoroughly agitated Mr. Bassett Hound to show me to the Distinguished Visitor's Gallery, I take my seat just before the trumpet fanfare announces the arrival of the King and Queen. I rise to my feet along with everyone else as the national anthem of Malveaux is played.

As the Prime Minister addresses the audience, I glance around the Chamber. Circular in design, it features tiered leather seating for Parliament Members, which encircles a central speaking area, all sitting under a domed ceiling overhead.

Finally, Maddie arrives, cutting a nervous figure amidst the sea of dark suits. As she approaches the podium, her smile is as shaky as a leaf in a storm, and I know she must be extremely nervous.

"Look at me," I whisper to myself, willing her to do just that. When she scans the Chamber, her eyes land on mine, and I offer her an encouraging smile, mouthing "You've got this."

She flashes me a nervous look before the Speaker of the House introduces her. "Presenting Her Royal Highness, Princess Madeline!"

I say a little prayer this all goes smoothly.

She fumbles with her papers, sending a few fluttering to the ground, and I have to hold myself back from rushing to her aid, frustrated I'm up here in the Gallery and not near her on the floor.

"Good day esteemed... um... Parliamentarians," she

begins in faltering Malveauxian, her voice quivering like a violin string. "I am honored to be officially welcomed as a princess of Malveaux."

I glance around the audience and notice that everyone is hanging on her every word. Are they judging her for her heavily accented speech? For the fact that she's not Malveauxian born and bred? I feel offended on her behalf. But then when she comes to the end of her short speech, telling the assembled guests how excited she is to be a part of their country, everyone bursts into uproarious applause, giving her a standing ovation—not something I've seen often at Parliament, if ever.

I, too, spring to my feet, whistling like a farmer as I applaud. She grins out at everyone and I can see her relief written right across her face. Her eyes find mine once more, and as I give her a salute, my heart fills with pride—and a healthy dollop of relief, I'll admit.

It's in this moment it hits me like a punch to the solar plexus.

I know beyond doubt that this thing between us, however new, is more than me doing Father's bidding. It's real. It makes my heart sing. And I don't think I could stop now for all the tea in Malveaux.

Chapter 18

Maddie

"You were amazing! They loved you," Alex says as we make our way through Parliament House with our respective security guards toward the waiting cars out front.

"I'm just glad it's over."

He chuckles. "You're being too modest. You totally won those old cronies over."

"I did, didn't I?" I reply with a self-effacing laugh.

"You so did. Is it weird that I feel proud of you?" he asks. "Not in a fatherly way, of course."

"You can feel proud of me. I'm proud of me, too."

"I feel like we need to celebrate. Have you had the chance to see much of the city yet?"

"Not really. I did get to see the sea from the car on the way to the palace on my first day here."

He shakes his head. "You're a princess of a country you've barely seen. How about we remedy that?"

"How?" I ask, but instead of answering me with words, he takes my hand in his and leads me down a passageway and out to the back of the building. We're trailed by Vlad, and I can feel his tension rising with each step I take.

"Where are you taking me?"

He opens a door and I step outside into a courtyard.

"I thought you might like to go for a ride," he says, gesturing at a motorcycle.

I eye it. "On *that*?"

"Why not?"

"For starters, I'm in a dress and a pair of heels, not to mention the fact that I can't imagine my grandparents would be too thrilled about it."

"Don't worry about the clothing. I've got you covered on that front. And your grandparents? They'll understand. They were young once."

"I'm not so sure."

"Any other concerns?"

"Vlad will definitely freak."

He turns to Vlad. "Are you okay with me taking the princess on a short tour before we head back to the palace? You can trail behind in the car, of course, like I know Paulo will do. I do promise not to kidnap her." His eyes flash to mine as he adds, "Although I think we could both do with being kidnapped. Don't you?"

I can't help but smile, the elation I feel following the

successful speech morphing into something else. Something I know I shouldn't allow it to morph into.

"I thought as much."

"I'll need to clear it with the palace, sir, although she is expected to greet the press, plus the princess will need the appropriate protective clothing," Vlad replies, somewhat predictably. "Perhaps we can plan such an outing at a future time?"

"No time like the present." Alex opens the seat of the motorcycle and pulls out a pair of my jeans, my favorite tennis shoes, and a couple of leather jackets.

"How did you…?" I ask in astonishment.

"I had your lady's maid get them for me before I left for Parliament, and I grabbed an extra helmet from my mate, Jeremy, too. This is his bike."

"You thought of everything."

He offers me the clothes. "Go get changed."

"Are you sure? Vlad said he needs to get it cleared first."

"Tell me something. Do you ever just decide to do something and then do it? Or are you middle-aged before your time?" His eyes are dancing, and I challenge any woman to have the strength to turn this man down.

I pull my brows together as though contemplating my options when really, my mind is already made up.

"Come on, Texas. Let's go have us some fun."

I make a snap decision. I'm 24, not 54. I need to live a little.

"Clear it with the palace, please, Vlad," I instruct. "It looks like Alex has everything else under control."

"Good choice, princess," Alex says with a wink as he replaces his suit jacket with a leather version.

A few minutes later, I've changed into my jeans and jacket, my long hair falling down my back from under my helmet. Alex is already sitting on the bike, his leather jacket zipped up, with the engine running. He looks about as sexy as I've ever seen him. Temptingly sexy. Dangerously sexy.

I don't allow myself to change my mind.

So what if I'm attracted to Alex. So what if he's not the horrible person I thought he was at first. So what if he's fun and witty and kind and caring and all the things. I can control myself, *and* my feelings. We're just two young people, going for a ride on a motorcycle.

I refuse to think any deeper than that.

I swing my leg over the bike and position myself up against him. He feels warm against me, and my heart rate picks up—and not just from the anticipation of the ride through the city. I haven't been this close to Alex before, my thighs pressed up against his.

It's a lot. A *wonderful* lot.

I clear my throat. "What kind of bike is this?" I ask over the low rumble.

"A big one."

"Do you know anything about bikes, Alex?"

"I know enough." He pulls on his helmet. "Ready?"

"Ready."

Vladimir throws us a warning look.

"Promise to bring her back no worse for wear," Alex says.

"We will tail you," Vladimir assures, to which Alex revs the engine a few times, *Fast & Furious* style, making me giggle.

Vlad does not look amused.

"Hold on, Texas," he instructs and I wrap my arms around his waist, my body pressed against his back.

I'm not going to lie. Holding on to him is spectacularly good, and I quietly congratulate him on coming up with the motorcycle plan.

The engine roars beneath us like a caged beast as we make our way across Parliament's cobbled quadrangle, through the grand gates, past the waiting members of the press and public, eager to catch a glimpse of their new princess.

In our helmets, we're incognito, and the feeling is exhilarating.

Alex weaves the motorcycle through the narrow streets, the bike's low rumble echoing off the old walls. We whiz through the city, lined with old stone buildings and new, little churches and shops. We pass a market, filled with fresh produce and flowers, picture perfect in its quaintness. As we climb the hill, zig-zagging up the steep streets, the fresh and salty sea air fills my nostrils.

Eventually, we wind our way to the summit of the hill, where Alex slows the bike to a stop.

Climbing off, I remove my helmet and run my fingers through my hair. Helmet hair is worse than hat hair, let's face it. I unzip the leather jacket, warm in the summer sun. I look across at Alex and notice him watching me. "What?" I ask, self-consciously.

"Just admiring the view," he says with a grin, and his eyes tell me I don't need to wonder whether he means me or the actual view.

I smile back at him, my pulse beating like a frenzied drum.

The wheels of our respective security guards' cars crunch over the gravel behind us, pulling my attention. It's a strange feeling to have your every move watched, particularly when you're not used to it, and not just by one bodyguard, but by two.

"Come with me." Alex holds out his hand, and I take it in mine, walking to a platform overlooking the city below.

"Is that the palace?" I point at the large structure at the

edge of the city, surrounded by greenery, the parklands stretching all the way to a forest and lake in the distance.

"It is."

"And that's the airport where I flew in, and that's the sea! Oh, I would love to go to the beach someday. That's something we didn't have in Houston. A beach. I always wanted to live by the sea."

"And now you do." His eyes flash to mine and he lets out a laugh.

"What?" I ask, wondering if I have something on my face.

"You're having fun. I like it."

"Isn't that the whole point of this? I'm being impulsive and non-middle-aged." My eyes land on an ice cream truck a hundred meters or so away.

"Does the non-middle-aged princess want an ice cream?"

"That would be a firm yes."

"I'll shout you one."

"You'll do what now?" I ask, confused.

"I'll shout you one. It means I'll buy you an ice cream."

"I didn't think royalty carried cash."

He pulls a card from his top pocket. "No, but we do carry Visa."

We meander side-by-side along the path to where a small crowd is looking out at the view, enjoying ice cream and chatting. A small blond child runs across our path, almost hitting us in his enthusiasm, and Alex wraps his arm around my waist to stop him from careening into me.

I'm not going to lie. It's incredible to be held by him, even if it is just to stop me from falling.

"Thanks," I murmur.

"All part of the service," he replies.

My shoulder nestles perfectly under his arm, as though

we were made to fit, and I notice that he doesn't remove his arm from my waist for a little longer than necessary.

The ice cream van proprietor asks us something in Malveauxian.

Alex translates for me. "What flavor would you prefer, Texas?"

I squint as I try to read the list. "It's all in Malveauxian."

"Funny that. They've got vanilla, of course, as well as double chocolate, pistachio, and lemon."

"That's easy. I would never waste an ice cream on something like pistachio or lemon, and I'm not a vanilla kind of gal. It's double chocolate all the way for me."

"Good choice." He orders two double chocolate cones and hands over his card.

With our ice cream in hand, we find a free picnic table where we sit side-by-side, licking the creamiest of chocolate ice cream and gazing out at the view.

"This is good," I say.

"It is good, but it's not as good as the gelato in Ledonia. That's next level."

"I'll have to try it someday, as long as you've got my favorite."

"Which is?"

"Mint chocolate chip, of course."

"Not chocolate?"

I lick my ice cream once more. "It's a very close second."

"I've got an idea. Let's play a getting to know you game. You can ask whatever you want, but you need to answer honestly," Alex says.

I give him the side eye as I lick my ice cream. "What kind of questions?"

"Anything you like."

"Hmmm. As long as I get to go first."

"By all means. Ask away, Texas."

I may be getting used to that nickname, but it still gives me a small thrill every time he uses it.

I formulate my question as I rotate my ice cream on my tongue. It's the way I've always eaten ice cream in a cone. I notice Alex watching me closely, as though in a trance.

"What?" I ask, suddenly aware how sexy licking an ice cream can actually be when looking out at a stunning view with a hot guy at your side.

He pulls his gaze from me. "Nothing," he replies, but that look in his eyes was definitely not "nothing" and I can't help but feel a little thrill.

"Are you going to ask a question before nightfall?" he teases.

"Of course I am. I was just thinking."

"Is that what you were doing?"

I nudge him with my shoulder.

"What's your dad like?" I ask.

"My dad?"

"Yeah, you know, the tall guy with the prickly moustache. King of Ledonia. You call him 'Dad'? Ringing any bells for you?"

"Actually, I call him Father, at his request. He's not a 'dad' sort of guy."

"Huh. That explains a lot."

"About what?"

"You. Him."

"What do you call your father?"

"Hey! This is my question."

He chortles. "Touché."

"But for your information, I call my dad 'Dad' or 'Daddy', depending on my mood. Not Father."

"From what I've seen, your dad is very much a 'Dad'

kind of man. My father is…exacting. Yes, that's the word I'd use for him. He's exacting in the way he treats me and others, and himself, for that matter. He has high standards, and I need to live up to them."

"Why?"

"Why? What sort of question is that?"

"The sort you're meant to answer. Why do you have to live up to his high expectations?"

"Because I'm his son and heir," he says simply, as though it's completely obvious to anyone.

"Which you look thrilled about, by the way."

He adjusts his expression. "Better?"

I tilt my head to the side as I study his face. "Less honest."

"Okay. Full disclosure?" he asks, and I nod. "He's not the easiest man to have as a father. He's not exactly the warm, cuddly type, and he's never really taken the time to know me as a person. To him, I'm a reflection of him as both my father and my King, which is exactly how he treats me."

My heart hurts for Alex. The relationship he's describing is a million miles from the one I have with my own dad, and it's plain to see he wants so much more from his father.

"That sounds hard. I'm so sorry."

"It's fine. We're dealt the hand we're dealt, and my hand comes with a lot of privilege, as well as some challenges. He's different with my sisters, and he doesn't give two hoots about what my brother, Max, gets up to."

"Why not?"

"Because Max isn't his heir."

"That's terrible. Parents are supposed to love their kids equally, no matter what."

He arches his eyebrows wryly. "Tell that to my father."

"Have you tried telling him how you feel?"

He lets out a bitter laugh. "Of course not."

"I don't know him, and I get that it's complicated because he's also your King. But he's your dad. I'm sure he loves you."

"I don't doubt his love."

"Tell me if I'm stepping out of line here, but you're worth knowing. Take it from someone who decided not to like you from the get-go and then did a 180."

His eyes are soft. "You've done a 180?"

"Oh, yes. Possibly a 181."

"181? That's even better." He furrows his brow. "Or worse? It's not clear."

I nudge him with my shoulder again. "Definitely better."

"I've done a 181 on you, too," he says, his eyes soft, and my stupid heart jumps for joy. "It would seem we both jumped to conclusions about each other."

"At least we've got it straight now."

"Indeed. It's important for our countries' special—"

"—relationship," I finish for him and we share a smile.

"Before you start feeling too sorry for me, my mother is amazing." A smile claims his face, and the pain in my heart is dulled by the obvious love he shares with his mom. "She's warm and kind and a lot of fun. She's also smart as a whip."

"I really liked her when we met at the ball."

"You know, you remind me of her."

My heart skips a beat. An actual beat.

"Is that too cheesy to say?" he asks, looking embarrassed by his admission.

"Not at all," I reply with a giddy laugh. Because that's how I feel around Alex: totally giddy. And hearing I remind him of his mom, a woman he so clearly loves? Well, it doesn't get much better than that, people.

His eyes are soft as they hold my gaze. "Good."

"Yes," I murmur.

A girl could get lost in those deep brown eyes—a girl a lot like me.

"Your ice cream's dripping," he says and I notice a stream of creamy brown liquid running down the cone and onto my fingers.

"Oops!" Quickly, I lick the drips from my fingers and the cone, conscious Alex is watching me once more. I shoot him a sheepish smile. "I think I got it all."

"You, err…yes, I think you did," he replies, his voice gruff.

I flick my gaze to Vlad and Paulo, standing at a distance, keeping a close eye on us. Time to get this conversation back into the PG range.

"Your dad must have some amazing qualities to have a woman like your mom love him," I say, because talking about your parents is about the least sexy thing I can think of.

"It was an arranged marriage."

Wait, what?

"Your parents had an arranged marriage? How old are they? 110?"

He laughs. "Some cultures still have arranged marriages. Look at India. And besides, there are different rules for royalty from everyone else. It's just the way it is."

"The way it is, or the way it was?"

"Is," he says simply.

"Are you telling me that you can't just fall in love with someone and marry them?"

"Of course I can. My parents chose to have an arranged marriage. I certainly won't be doing that."

I size him up. "I'm sure you won't."

"What does that mean?"

"Oh, come on, Alex. You're Prince McHottie. You've got your pick of beautiful women from all over the world. You could get anyone you want, and by the looks of things…" I trail off but we both know where I'm heading with that statement.

"I told you; I've changed."

Has he? I want to believe it. So much.

"As my daddy always says, 'you can say the cow jumped over the moon, but that don't make her an astronaut.'"

His laugh is low. "What have cows and astronauts got to do with the fact that I'm no longer out partying every night, and haven't done so for over a year?"

"Blame Texas. It means saying it doesn't make it true."

"Well, this cow has become a top astronaut on his first mission to Mars." He gestures at himself with his thumb. "A very charming and handsome astronaut, at that."

I snort out a laugh, spraying chocolate ice cream into the air. Immediately, I throw a hand over my mouth, totally mortified.

"So becoming," he says as he offers me a napkin.

I dab at my face. "Sorry about that."

"It's a waste of excellent chocolate ice cream, as far as I can see."

Embarrassed, I ball the napkin in my palm. "You know, Alex, whenever I think of you, I'm going to picture you dressed as a cow in an astronaut suit."

"I would hope you'd think of me in anything but that." He's got a twinkle in his eyes that makes my belly flip, and instantly the photo of him in his trunks, his lean, muscular body and smooth olive skin shown off to total masculine perfection, fills my mind.

Prince Alexander is so very far from being a cow in an astronaut suit.

"I get to ask my question now," he says.

"Fire away."

"What was it like growing up without any siblings?"

I shrug. "Fine, I guess."

He mimics holding a microphone to his mouth. "The subject appears to be unwilling to truly examine her experiences. Further questioning is recommended, and other measures such as ice cream removal may be required."

I hold what's left of my cone protectively against my chest. "You wouldn't."

"I would, but only in the name of science."

"In that case, let me think about it."

"You have three seconds from now."

"Three seconds? Tough crowd." I can't help but smile. "It was great growing up with no siblings because my parents made it great. They loved me and they made sure I knew it. That's not to say I didn't want a brother or a sister, and I was super jealous of my friends who had them. But they always used to complain about how annoying they were, and at the time, I thought it was better to be the one and only. I got to do lots of stuff with my parents, like going bowling, or heading to the shooting range."

"The shooting range?"

I shrug. "It was Texas. What can I say?"

"Fair call."

"Then, when my mom died, it was just Daddy and me. It was...different. Harder, I guess. It got better over time."

Alex reaches for my hand and gives it a squeeze. "I'm so sorry, Maddie. Losing a much-loved parent must be so hard, especially when you were so young."

"It was no picnic," I reply with a laugh that masks my pain. "She died when I was on the precipice of womanhood, as Dad put it. But you know what? My dad's the best. He must have been hurting real bad when she passed, but he never showed it. He'd say things like 'shine bright while you can because life's shorter than a firefly's glow on a July night,' and 'don't sit waiting for the rain to pass because life's about learning to dance in a thunderstorm.'"

"He sounds poetic."

"He's Texan, through and through. Did you meet him while he was here?"

"I did, actually. I asked him how he liked the weather in Malveaux, and he told me to stay away from you."

My mouth drops open. "He did?"

"He did."

"What did you say?"

"I told him I had no intention of going anywhere near you, because at that point you had already punched me in the face and told me exactly what you thought of me. You were the last person I wanted to be near."

"Thanks a lot," I reply with a laugh.

"Come on, admit it. You didn't exactly enjoy my company either."

"I hated you," I say simply. "No offense."

"As long as you don't hate me now."

I bite down on my bottom lip. "I don't hate you, Alex."

"I don't hate you, either," he replies, his voice soft and tender, doing things to my heart.

Tension crackles in the air between us.

Has it suddenly gotten hot out here?

I concentrate on finishing my ice cream before I ask, "What made you decide to put in effort with me? I mean, you could have simply gone back to Ledonia and gotten on with your life, but you hung around, attending all my functions, wearing me down until I stopped hating you."

He pauses for a beat, then splays his hands in front of

himself. "Full disclosure, my father instructed me to get to know you."

My heart drops to the ground.

"Oh."

"That may have been my initial motivation, but I never expected to like you. You were an enigma I wanted to work out."

My face lifts into a smile. "And have you worked me out?"

"Not yet. I think I might need to whisk you away more often for non-middle-aged excursions."

Alex shifts his thigh so it's touching lightly against mine, and my heart begins to thud like a drum.

"I'd like that," I murmur, my gaze automatically dropping to his lips. I find myself thinking about pulling him to me to taste them.

It would be so easy. So easy and so very, very nice.

His eyes are fire, the contact between our thighs hinting at the electricity between us.

He swallows, his Adam's apple dropping before it rises. "Maddie, I—" He begins but then stops himself.

"Yes?" I ask, breathless.

Does he feel it too? This incredible pull between us? A pull that, for me at least, goes beyond simple attraction to so much more. It's a pull I haven't felt before, not with Eric, or even my boyfriend back in college.

I wasn't looking for this. I certainly didn't want it. And yet sitting here with Alex, the beautiful city of Tleurbonne at our feet, I feel it with such an intensity it sucks the air from my lungs.

"Your Royal Highnesses," a booming voice says, bursting our bubble.

With great reluctance, I pull my gaze from Alex.

"What is it, Vlad?" I ask, and I can't keep the tremble from my voice. "Everything okay?"

"The palace is concerned. They would like you to return as soon as possible."

And just like that, whatever was going to happen between us is stopped in its tracks. As Alex whisks me back to the palace, with my arms wrapped firmly around his waist, the wind in my hair, I cannot help the feeling that he and I are on the very precipice of something. Something big.

Only, now that I know the true Alex, I'm not scared anymore.

Chapter 19

Maddie

Alice is putting the finishing touches on my hair to attend today's polo match between Ledonia and Malveaux when there's a knock at the door to my rooms.

"One moment, Maddie," Alice says.

I bounce to my feet. "I'll get it. You've been working all morning. Why don't you take a load off."

"A load off?" she questions.

"Chill out for a bit. Relax. I'll get the door."

"If you say so," she replies uncertainly.

Alice is a hard worker and we're becoming close, but she's still not used to my relaxed, non-elitist vibe. A work in progress for yours truly.

"I do say so," I reply as I pad across the plush carpet of the living room and out into the entryway. Pulling the door open, I'm met with a smiling Alex, and my pulse rate jumps up at the sight of him, right on cue.

Because oh, what a sight he is. He's wearing a red polo shirt complete with the royal Ledonian monogram, tucked into belted white pants and a pair of over-the-knee leather riding boots. His bare arms are tan, the muscles sinewy and strong, and his eyes alight as they land on me, his lips lifting into a smile.

He's so unbelievably sexy and handsome, I'm surprised my knees don't give way.

"Morning, beautiful," he says with his heart-stopping smile.

"Alex. What are you doing here?"

I step out into the hallway and pull the door closed behind me so Alice won't see us. Of course it's completely useless. She has eyes, after all.

"I came to see you," he replies simply.

"I figured that much out for myself."

"I wanted to give you this." He holds out a single white rose with a short stem, wrapped in ribbon.

"A rose?" I like to point out the obvious sometimes, too, it would seem. "It's beautiful." I lift it to my nose and breathe in its scent.

"It's more than just a rose, and I warn you: this part might seem a little cheesy."

"Try me."

"It's a tradition in my country for a soldier to give his chosen one a token of his affection before going into battle. I know I'm not going off to war, but I am competing in the polo match today, and I wanted to give you this rose to let you know I'll be thinking of you."

My chest expands, the grin that's claimed my face threatening to break it in two.

Our moment may have been interrupted by Vlad on top of the hill yesterday, but this has to be ranked as the number one romantic gesture *ever*. So very *knight in shining armor*.

So very Alex.

I toy with the rose. "I love that. Thank you. This is one of the nicest things anyone's done for me."

The nicest and the most romantic.

If I harbored any doubt that Alex feels something for me, too, it's been dispelled by this gesture.

"I'd say you need more people to do nice things for you, but I'd like to be the one to volunteer for the job."

I let out a giddy laugh. "You're at the top of the list. Believe me."

"I'm glad."

I get an idea. "Can you wait right here for a sec?"

"I don't have long. Polo waits for no man, you know."

"Be right back. Promise." I push the door open and slip through my rooms to my bedroom.

Alice glances at me before she busies herself with folding clothes that don't need folding, and I know she's trying to give us some space.

I rush over to the chest of drawers in my bedroom and begin my search. After rummaging through no less than three drawers, I find what I'm looking for and rush back to Alex, who's waiting patiently in the corridor for me.

"It might be a tradition in your country for a man to give his chosen one a gift before he goes to war, aka polo, but I've watched enough movies to know women give their chosen one a token of their affection, too. And on that note, I'd like you to have this." I hold up my key chain in the shape of a cowboy boot, chipped and battered with age, but still 100 percent Texan.

"You're giving me your set of keys?" Alex asks doubtfully.

"Oops." I slide my apartment and car keys off the chain, trying not to chip my nail polish. "Here." I pass him just the cowboy boot. "I've had this since my mom gave it to me for my 9th birthday. That was the last birthday we celebrated together before she passed. I want you to have it for today's match."

He regards the keychain in wonder. "Maddie, this means so much."

"You don't have to wear it or anything, because it isn't exactly part of your polo uniform, but—"

"I'll wear it. I'd be honored to," he replies.

"It won't get in the way? I know nothing about polo."

"It won't." He attaches the key ring to his belt loop. "A touch of Texas from my Texas Princess."

My Texas Princess. Happiness floods every cell in my body.

If you'd told me only a handful of days ago that we would be exchanging meaningful mementos, grinning at one another like love-struck tweens, I would have laughed in your face at the sheer outrageousness of the idea.

Yet here we are, together, my heart full of him, my entire body aching to touch him. To know what it feels like for him to touch me. For him to hold me in his arms.

To kiss.

How bad do I want to kiss this man right now?

So bad.

"They're expecting me for a pre-match meeting and I'm already late. I have to go."

"I'm glad you stopped by."

"I am, too. You know, I purposely chose a white colored rose as it's neutral, so I hope you'll wear it pinned to your dress."

"Spooked peafowl couldn't stop me."

His laugh rumbles in his throat. "See you out there."

"I'd say good luck, but you know you're on the wrong team."

"We'll see about that," he replies with a wink before he turns and leaves.

I close the door behind me and lean against it, breathing in the scent of the rose, my head full of Alex. It's so weird when you decide something about a person, and they show every sign confirming you're one hundred percent right, and then not only do you start to get feelings for them against your better judgment, but they do things that make you completely rethink their character. Things like giving you a single white rose to remind you that you are his chosen one.

His *chosen* one.

Talk about going from hating a guy to... *not* hating him. Not even close.

The very opposite.

AS A TEXAN, watching polo for the first time is completely baffling. Horses dash, mallets swing, people yell. It's like a fancy, chaotic rodeo with dashing men on beautiful horses chasing a tiny ball. It's like hockey, but with horses.

I'm sitting next to Grandpapa, pretending to understand the fast-paced horse ballet, confused by the whole dang thing. Up until today, my entire experience of polo was the Ralph Lauren shirts Eric wore to the office on casual Fridays. It's safe to say the only thing I knew about the game came from the little monogram on the top left of the shirt.

"What a chukka!" the man to my right calls out, Lord Something-I-Can't-Remember, a man with too many teeth for the size of his mouth.

I nod knowledgeably as others agree it was indeed an awesome chukka. Of course I have no idea what a chukka actually is, but everyone around me likes to talk about them, so it's clearly a polo term I need to know.

Seeing the game in action is a whole other thing, particularly as Alex is playing.

Talk about a great way to help me appreciate the game.

He's commanding his horse as though it were an extension of his own body as he whacks his stick at the ball. He's athletic and strong and proficient and ridiculously sexy. He's a born athlete, just to add to his ever-growing list of skills.

And oh, my, is he good to watch. Prince Alexander is one fine specimen of manhood.

An involuntary sigh passes my lips.

As his horse gallops, he takes a swing at the ball, his mallet sending the ball flying. I can barely keep my eyes from him, just like every other woman here.

Why do I have to have gotten feelings for the most eligible bachelor in Europe? Talk about inviting unnecessary competition into my life.

He barrels past us on his glistening horse in a flurry of thundering hooves, the smell of the churned grass filling the air. Each time he leans in for a swing, I find myself leaning forward too, holding my breath and waiting for the *clunk*.

"The prince is in great form today," Grandpapa says.

"He sure is," I murmur as he gallops forward, his mallet poised to strike as he heads confidently to the goal.

I leap to my feet and let out a cheer.

Grandpapa raises a brow at me, and I sit down quickly. *Oops*. Cheering for the wrong team.

My mind wanders to the top of the hill, where Alex took me on the motorcycle. We opened up to one another, and I feel so much closer to him now.

So much so I almost acted on my feelings for him and kissed him. Almost.

Let's just say it was a good thing Vlad interrupted us, or I don't know what would have happened.

Okay, that's a lie. I know *exactly* what would have happened. Alex would have kissed me and I would have kissed him right back, all those pent-up feelings I've been carrying around for him since the day we met would have come bursting out in an explosion of want.

I sigh.

So not a good idea for a whole host of reasons, least of all the fact that he has this reputation that suggests he goes around kissing women in picturesque spots all the time.

The problem is I've grown to know something about myself when it comes to Prince Alexander of Ledonia. And it's a doozy.

I don't want to be simply the next girl in his long line.

I want to be *the* girl.

I know. It's crazy. I've gone from despising the man to realizing I got him wrong to now fantasizing about wanting to be with him. Not just kiss him.

Be.

With.

Him.

I want to be the one he ends up with, the one who means the most to him. The one he's with for the rest of his life. And I want him to be the one who means the most to me.

I blow out a breath.

This is not the way I saw this playing out, but here I am. I'm falling for him, this strong, loyal, loving man who is nothing like I expected.

I'm in deep. Way too deep.

Alex strikes the ball and it sails through the goal as though it's carried on wings. I leap to my feet in a rush of exuberance once more, yelling out, "Go Alex!"

People around me clap politely, still in their seats. Dang it! I've done it again, cheering for the wrong team.

"I'm, err, just supporting my friend," I explain as I sit back down, my heart thudding from not only the excitement of seeing Alex get a goal, but from embarrassment, too.

Grandmama, sitting on the other side of my grandpapa, leans forward. "Your friend, my dear?" she enquires.

"Yeah. Alex and I kind of found a way to get along."

"I didn't know you weren't getting along," Grandpapa says.

"Oh, it was a whole thing," Grandmama says on a smile, using another one of my expressions.

"Well, whatever has gone on before, I'm pleased to hear you and Alexander have begun to form a friendship. It will be very important once you're both ruling monarchs." He realizes what he said, and adds hurriedly, "That is, if it turns out that way, of course."

"Of course," I agree.

Soon after, we're called onto the field to "divot stomp", which turns out to be replacing the turf disturbed by the horses' hooves back where it came from with your foot.

Considering this is a fancy person's sport on both sides of the pond, it seems weird to me that the spectators in their fancy clothes have to do this. But I didn't make the rules.

"Who won?" I ask Grandpapa as I tap a divot back into place.

"No one yet. This is only half time. There are more chukkas to go."

"How long does this game last? All day?" I ask.

"Heavens, no. About two hours in total."

Someone offers me a glass of champagne and I tell them no.

"Oh, but my dear, you must. It's tradition to toast the divots," Grandpapa explains.

Reluctantly, I take one, the cool liquid forming condensation on the glass. I remember Amelia telling me how horrendous the Malveaux champagne is. I'm not exactly pumped to try it now.

"Madeline, after The Games, your grandmama and I are going on a short tour of several European countries, ending in France."

"Cool. How long will you be gone?"

"About 10 days. It will be a good opportunity for you to take the reins for a while. See how it feels."

"Wait. You want me to be like a temporary Queen?"

"Not in title, of course, but in practice. You can meet with the Prime Minister for our regular weekly appointment, as well as oversee the running of the palace."

"Do I have to make any laws or anything?" I ask, only half joking.

He chortles. "Heavens no. Your job is to listen to what the PM says, and only offer your thoughts if completely necessary. Are you ready to try it all out?"

I wait for the expected knot in my belly to form. It doesn't.

Huh.

"You know what, Grandpapa? I think I'd like to give it a shot."

He beams at me. "Wonderful."

"When do you leave?"

"The morning after the ball to celebrate The Games."

There's a flurry of excited chatter and applause, and I look up to see Alexander *sans* horse, treading across the grass, smiling and waving at everyone as flashbulbs pop around us.

He's removed his helmet and his hair is all messed up in that sexy *I just got out of bed* way, his red shirt clinging to his torso as though it was sprayed on, showing every curve of every muscle, from his wide shoulders right down to his slim waist. His once white, but now decidedly dirty, pants are equally snug and with each step he takes in his over-the-knee boots, I can almost feel his muscles rippling.

I'm now officially a fan of men in over-the-knee boots, and that is something I never thought I would say. I mean, didn't Julia Roberts wear those in *Pretty Woman*?

Let me tell you right now, the way Alex wears them is nothing like Julia.

I think I just swooned.

Yup, definitely.

I slide my eyes to the Texas boot attached to his belt loop and bite back a smile.

He comes to a stop when he reaches Grandpapa and me and gives a bow. "Your Majesty, and Princess Madeline."

"No need to be so formal, lad," Grandpapa says as he pumps Alex's hand and pats him on the back enthusiastically. "A fine display of horsemanship, dear boy. A fine display."

"Thank you, sir. Have you been enjoying the game?"

he asks us, his face flushed from the exercise, his eyes alight.

"It's been thoroughly enjoyable, although the wrong team is leading currently," Grandpapa replies.

"That depends entirely on which side you're supporting," Alex replies smoothly. "I assume you're supporting Malveaux, Princess Madeline?"

"Of course I am," I fib, because really, all I've been doing since the game began is watching him.

His lips quirk and I can tell he knows I'm lying. He must have seen me out of my seat, cheering him on.

A member of staff approaches us and gives Grandpapa a signal.

"A toast to the divots," he says as he raises his glass.

"To the divots," everyone echoes, and I'm about to take a sip of my champagne when Alex places his hand on my bare forearm and I nearly jump out of my skin from the contact.

"You'll need a splash of this," he says under his breath as he pours an orange liquid into my glass. "Orange cordial."

"Amelia told me about this."

"It helps, believe me."

I take a sip, our eyes meeting over our respective glasses. It's as though this is an intimate moment between the two of us, where we're not surrounded by people in the middle of a polo field.

"Better?"

"Much better. Thanks."

He gives a little bow and it makes me giggle. "For you, Texas, anything."

A man in a royal uniform blows a trumpet to indicate the next half of the game is about to begin, and Alex excuses himself and strides away.

Is it bad that I watch him leave? It can't be, because no sight like *that* could ever be bad.

We return to our seats and watch the second half, Alex once again proving himself the star on the field, my eyes, once again, incapable of leaving him. When Ledonia is declared the winning team by a small margin, people clap politely, although I know they were backing Malveaux.

"Pity about the result, but we'll have our revenge at the next match," Grandpapa says.

"When is the next match?" I ask, trying not to sound too eager.

"You're a polo convert now, my dear?" Grandmama asks.

In truth, I'm a *watch Alex looking hot on his horse* convert, but I'm not going to tell her that. She told me to become his friend, not develop feelings for the guy.

"You can take that to the bank," I tell her.

She crinkles her forehead. "Take what to which bank?"

"It's another saying from Texas, Grandmama. It means that's the truth," I explain.

"You can take that to the bank," she echoes, looking pleased. "I'll use that one when I'm at morning tea with my ladies-in-waiting tomorrow."

"Knock yourself out," I reply with a laugh, and she shoots me a look of concern.

"How about I just write you a list, Grandmama? That way you can study up and understand every word I say."

"A grand idea."

My grandparents chat to our fellow spectators, introducing me. People smile and curtsy, and I ask them questions and try to be all regal yet approachable.

It's odd, but for the first time since I got to Malveaux, I begin to feel like an actual princess, like I can do this role.

It's a nice feeling.

We make our way over to a marquee on one of the palace lawns. Stepping inside is like stepping into another world. There are tapestries on the walls, chandeliers hanging from the ceiling, with wait staff in their black and white uniforms holding trays of nibbles and drinks as a string quartet plays soft classical music.

It sure isn't like any tent I've been in before.

A waiter offers me another glass of champagne, but I ask him for a Coke instead, which I drink down gratefully after the heat outside.

Grandmama walks me around the marquee, introducing me to people.

When we find ourselves alone, she puts on a casual air and says, "Speaking of which, have you made any decisions you'd like to share?"

I recognize the glimmer of hope in her eyes. It's the one I see every time this topic is raised. The truth is, I'm growing to like not only the princess role, but Malveaux more and more. Sure, the idea of being a princess and heir to the throne totally freaked me out to start with, and having to look and behave like a member of the royal family was more than a little daunting in an unfamiliar country with their own rules and standards. But I'm growing into the idea, and with both Alice's and Vladimir's guidance and the love and support I get from my grandparents, I think I might just have this royal thing down.

My old life in Houston feels like a distant memory, and although I'll always miss Chloe and my dad, here I've begun to feel so much more at home. I fit.

"It's gone from a 50-50 to a 60-40. In favor of staying, that is, in case you were wondering," I add.

Grandmama's face breaks into a smile. "Oh, my dear. I am so very happy to hear that." She pulls me into a hug and I breathe in her perfume. "In fact, I would go so far as to say that's lit."

I press my lips together to keep from laughing. "It's totally lit, Grandmama," I agree.

The polo players join the party, all freshly showered and changed, and although Alex moves around the room, talking with different groups of people, I'm always aware of exactly where he is. It's kind of a hot guy telepathy, as Chloe might put it.

Eventually, I turn around from speaking with one of Grandmama's ladies and come face to face with him. Instantly, my heart bounces into 4th gear as his magnetic pull draws me into his orbit.

"Hey," I murmur, my voice soft and breathy.

"Hey, yourself," he replies with a smile that does nothing for the state of my knees.

"Do you want to get out of here?"

I burst into laughter.

"What?" he asks.

"That is the corniest line ever."

His deep laugh rolls through me, tickling my belly. "I admit there's a hint of corn to it, but I mean it. I've had enough of people for one day."

"I'm people," I tease, feeling suddenly brazen.

I'm flirting. Get used to it.

"No, you're Texas."

I love the way my nickname sounds on his lips.

"You can call me Maddie, too, you know. All my friends do."

"And your enemies?"

"Oh, they call me Maddie, as well."

He lets out another low laugh. "Let's go for a walk down by the pond."

"Are there any peafowl down there?"

"I'll protect you. Promise."

"Deal."

Like the gentleman he is, he places his hand against my lower back and leads me through the crowd and from the marquee. Together, we take a short stroll down to the pond. It's a beautiful setting, with rolling green grass leading to deep blue sparkling water, where swans and ducks glide, the early evening sun casting a warm glow.

"It's so beautiful here," I say, taking it all in.

"It is. We have a pond a little like it at the palace in Villadorata," he says, naming the capital city of Ledonia (thank you once again, Wikipedia). "Although we do have a habit of putting as many fountains as we can manage in our lakes, even in naturally formed ones."

"I bet they look amazing."

"They are, if you like fountains."

I think of the images I saw online of Alex with some women, clearly having a good time, their clothes soaked through as they played in the peacock statue fountain near the formal gardens.

"I hear you're especially fond of fountains," I lead, wondering how he'll react.

He twists his mouth. "That was me a long time ago. I'm not that person anymore."

"You're not that person who climbs into fountains, fully clothed, with a group of beautiful women?" I tease, making light of the fact that his past has been playing on my mind.

Every account of Alex is of a womanizing party boy, intent on having a good time, right up to shots of him with a woman at the Lincoln Memorial on his recent US visit.

But those accounts are in stark contrast to the man I've been getting to know. It's like there are two versions of him —and only one that I could ever like.

A pair of peafowl, a male and a female, wander across our path ahead. They're beautiful and serene, minding their own feathery business.

"I know this is going to come off as a line, and trust me, it isn't one."

I turn to face him. "Try me."

"You're right, I wasn't exactly a serious relationship kind of guy. I liked a good party. I liked to have fun. Looking back, I can see the way I behaved was a reaction to my father's expectation of who I'm meant to be. I didn't want to be like him, all serious and grave and extremely focused on just one thing: being King. I knew I had all that to come and I wanted to enjoy myself before I had to become… him."

"Why do you have to become *him*?"

"Because one day I'll be King."

"You can be whatever kind of king you want to be. Whatever kind of *person* you want to be. It's not like you have to change your personality the day you ascend to the throne. If you want to be the Party King then go for it."

"But that's the thing, Maddie. I don't want to be a party anything. That whole lifestyle, being the most eligible bachelor around, isn't in the least fulfilling. Fun, certainly, but not fulfilling."

"I'm not sure your average male would agree with you. I don't think being adored by hordes of female fans ever gets old for most men."

He pushes a strand of hair from my face, his fingers making my skin tingle. "I'm not most men."

That, you most certainly are not.

"What are you going to do now that you've given up your partying ways? Are you going to take up reading important books about climate change and the state of the economy while wearing slippers and smoking a pipe in your library?"

"Is that my choice? Either be the Party Prince or an old man from a Charles Dickens novel?"

I let out a giggle. "Yup. Choose."

"Well, I'm tired of being seen as a vapid prince with as much depth as a puddle in summer, so I imagine I'll need to be the Dickens character. Although I do have one proviso."

"What's that?"

"No pipe, and maybe I could read less intense books. Thrillers or sci-fi novels suit me a lot better."

"That's two provisos, but I'm in a generous mood because my favorite polo player's team won today. I'll let you have them both."

"That's very generous of you," he replies with a smile that warms me through.

We wander along the banks of the pond, chatting about the polo match until Alex says, "I need to go back to Villadorata tomorrow."

His words hit me with unexpected force.

Alex not being here feels…well, it feels plain wrong.

"I thought you were staying until after The Games."

"I was meant to, but Father needs me to meet with an ambassador, and I have some charity events I want to attend. It's not for long, and I promise I'll be back in time for The Games."

"You wouldn't want to miss the cheese rolling," I say.

"There are a few things here I won't want to miss," he replies, his eyes on mine, and I swear my heart skips a beat. "The cheese rolling is number one on the list, of course." His lips quirk.

"That's only natural. Cheese rolling is a very important sport, I'm told."

He takes my hand in his, the enormity of his hand dwarfing mine. "It's the most important of all the cheese-related sports."

We resume walking along the edge of the pond together, hand in hand. "I didn't know there were that many cheese-related sports."

"Oh, yes. There's cheese rolling, of course, and then there's cheese tossing, cheese tennis, and my personal favorite, cheese bowling, which can get a little messy."

I let out a giggle and it ends in a snort. "I bet you're good at all of them."

"I don't put the hours of practice in that my competitors do."

"Too busy romancing all those women, huh?"

"Well, one woman."

I press my lips together, my heart giving a little squeeze.

"Will you compete?" he asks, and for a moment I wonder if he means compete with other women for his affections. But then I figure out he means the cheese rolling.

"Sure. Why not? I'm ready for it."

"You've been practicing?"

"Less practicing and more…visualizing."

He laughs. "You've been visualizing rolling cheese down a hill?"

"The best form of practice."

"I'm sure it is. You have a friend coming to stay at the palace, correct?"

Happiness bubbles up inside of me. "Chloe. She's my bestie from back home. I'm super excited to see her."

"I look forward to meeting her."

"Oh, she's already half in love with you. She used to show me photos of you when we were in the office. Prince McHottie."

"I'm not a fan of that nickname."

"Really? I think it suits you."

"You do, do you? Do you miss your old life back in Houston?"

"I miss my dad and Chloe, and the Mexican food back home is seriously to die for. But my life there?" I shrug. "Not so much."

His dark eyes capture my gaze. "I don't like you referring to your old life as 'home'. I hope you stay here. I hope this will be your new home."

Oh, be still my beating heart.

"You do?" I ask, breathless.

"Is that selfish of me?"

It's wonderful of you.

"No, it's nice to hear."

His handsome face lights up in a smile, and we stand there at the pond's edge, beaming at one another like shy teenagers on their first ever date.

"I've been thinking about staying," I begin, putting my thoughts into words for the first time. "I know it would make my grandparents so happy, and the country would have an heir who won't destroy the monarchy, if my uncle goes through with the abdication."

"What about what *you* want? Not your family, not Malveaux. You."

I think about my old life back in Houston, about Dad, about Chloe, about my old job at the glazing company. About Eric.

Huh. I haven't thought about him in a while.

It feels like a lifetime ago, another world. A world in which I never really felt as though I fit.

Staying here, perhaps becoming Grandpapa's heir, fulfilling my role as a Princess of Malveaux with everything that means, somehow, despite its newness and how very foreign it feels at times, seems right. It fits.

And Alex? Well, he's a big part of my new world, too.

Bigger than I've even admitted to myself.

I chew on my lip. "I haven't told anybody this. Not a soul."

"Should I be worried?" he asks.

I could not stop the smile from claiming my face for all the terrible tea in Malveaux. "I think I want to stay."

His eyes widen to the size of dinner plates. "You do?"

"I like it here. I like doing what I do. Sure, there are endless lunches and events, with lots of people to schmooze and impress, but I feel like I have a purpose. A calling, even. I can do meaningful work here. Make a difference in people's lives."

"Plus, the wardrobe's good," he teases.

I glance down at my dress. "Remind me to show you my closet. It's amazing. Total perk of the job."

He laughs.

"I know this is going to sound crazy, but in some strange kind of way, I think I was born into this role, only it took 24 years for me to get here. Does that sound weird?"

He holds his hands on either side of my arms and gazes intently into my eyes. It makes my heart go all kinds of crazy. Electricity pulsates between us. It seems as, once again, he's going to kiss me. I know I want him to.

But instead, all he does is reply, "It doesn't sound weird in the least, Texas. To me, it sounds absolutely perfect."

And kiss or no kiss, you can't get much better than perfect.

Chapter 20

Maddie

" As though witnessing Prince Swoon-A-Lot's skill and sheer unbridled masculinity atop his horse wasn't enough to fell us for a week, today is the beginning of The Games, the annual event that pitches the might of Ledonia against Malveaux in a smorgasbord of sports. It has to be one of the most anticipated events of the year, thanks not only to the excitement of the battle of strength in the tug of war, competition in precision and mastery of archery, and the sheer fun of cheese rolling, but because Prince Alexander himself competes. And my, does he compete—and look ruggedly handsome while he's doing it.

I'm just going to take a moment to fan myself.

Go well and do your country proud, our most handsome monarch-in-training. We are with you, body, heart, and soul.

#WeAreTheChampions
#AlexanderForTheWin

Holding a very large fan, your royal correspondent,

Fabiana Fontaine xx

I cannot believe today has finally arrived. I've looked forward to this moment since the day I left Houston. Chloe is about to arrive, and I'm pacing my living room, knowing that she is in the car with Vlad right now, being driven through the streets of Tleurbonne.

I wasn't able to meet her at the airport. I had Princess training with Alice first thing this morning, followed by disgusting Malveauxian tea with Grandmama, at which she demonstrated the traditional tea ceremony that I plan never to use unless I somehow manage to replace that tea with coffee, before Gustav arrived to style me for The Games, which are due to start in less than an hour.

"Your friend should be here any minute, Maddie," Alice says. "I've heard so much about her, I can't wait to meet her."

"You too will be besties in three seconds flat. Chloe's like that."

I glance at my reflection in the mirror and see a poised,

if excited, princess staring back. Long gone are the worn jeans and tennis shoes, makeup free face, and hair in a messy bun. "She is not going to recognize me."

Since I'm officially representing Malveaux today—despite the fact my heart is with a certain member of the Ledonian team—I'm in a blue knee-length dress with cap sleeves and a white boat neck, with matching blue pumps. My hair is styled in a high ponytail, which is more fun to swing from side to side than I care to admit.

I'll be changing for the cheese rolling event, but for now I'm looking regal and poised, ready for the inevitable photographers.

There's a knock at the door and Vladimir pushes it open. "Ms. Chloe Sharansky," he announces and I race over to greet her.

"Chloe!" I drag her inside and crush her to me, hugging her for all I'm worth. "It is so good to see you. I can't believe you're here!"

Her hair is even brighter pink than when I last saw her, and she's dressed head-to-toe in black.

"Well, I am, and you're kind of crushing my wind pipe," she croaks and immediately, I let her go.

"Would you look at you!" she says as she scans me, and I do a twirl for her to take in the full effect of my princess transformation. "My friend Mads, a fully-fledged Princess."

"Oh, Chlo, I have so much to catch you up on."

"Me too. Denise continues to be a prize you-know-what, and there's a new girl in the office who is covering your job, although she's not half as fun as you, and, girl, I so miss you." She pulls me in for another hug.

Vladimir clears his throat.

"What's up, Vlad?" I ask.

"You have only 30 minutes before you're due at the

royal box for the opening ceremony of The Games, ma'am."

Chloe mouths the word "ma'am" at me, her eyes alight.

"Might I suggest Ms. Sharansky shower and change rather quickly?"

"You might suggest that, Vlad, and that would be one great suggestion," I tell him, on a high from seeing the best friend I've missed so fiercely.

Sometime later, Chloe has showered and thrown on the white fluffy robe I gave her to wear.

"I cannot believe you live here. You. Live. *Here*," she says as she looks around my rooms. "That was a double shower. You could have a party in that room."

"I know, right? It's not a bad pad. Now, I have something to show you." I pull the double doors to my walk-in closet open. The lights flick on automatically, illuminating the amazingness of the room, and my best friend gasps in wonderment, just as I did the first time I saw it.

"Shut the front door!" she exclaims. "Is all this yours?"

I nod. "And you get to wear whatever you want today."

"Are you *serious*?" she squeals.

"You betcha, babe."

We spend the next few minutes rifling through my day dresses before Alice hurries us up and Chloe chooses a beige belted dress with puff sleeves and a pleated skirt, which she teams with a pair of multi-colored Doc Marten boots—because she might be wearing a princess dress but she's still Chloe Sharansky, style queen of her own universe.

As Vladimir escorts us to the royal box, Chloe updates me on all the happenings back home. It feels strange to hear about the antics of my old boss, Denise, listen to

Chloe talk about sales targets and marketing plans and all the goings on in the office.

"I get to meet Prince McHottie today, right?" she asks.

"He doesn't like that name, and anyway, he'll be in the Ledonian royal box opposite us."

She beams at me. "Which means I get to gaze at him."

"A cat can look at a queen," I say. She gives me a blank look. "It's one of the weird expressions they have here. It means all people should be treated equally no matter their status," I explain.

"How very democratic of you, *princess*." Her voice oozes irony.

We enter the royal Malveauxian enclosure, where I introduce my grandparents to Chloe. She does an elaborate and awkward looking curtsy, complete with arm flourishes.

"It's wonderful to meet a friend of our granddaughter's," Grandmama says as we take our seats with the best view of The Games possible. "I imagine you have some stories to tell."

"Don't stir the pot, Grandmama," I warn.

"I'll tell you later, Your Queenship," Chloe replies, making my grandmama smile wickedly despite the incorrect title.

"I'll look forward to it."

I look around at the scene. Grandstands line the field, full to the brim with eager spectators, and opposite us is the Ledonian royal enclosure. I spot Queen Astrid and King Harald, along with Alex's sisters, Amelia and Sofia, all dressed in red. I catch Amelia's eye. She waves enthusiastically at me, and I do the same back. I'm excited to get the chance to see her again, and I'd like to know Sofia better, too.

I notice a handsome man to Amelia's right and throw

her a questioning look. She shakes her head and mouths the word, "brother".

I throw my gaze over him. He must be Max, the youngest sibling who's been away at college in England. He's so like Alex, with his dark hair and olive skin and his wide shoulders. He's clean shaven and looks younger, but still with those Ledonian royal family good looks all four of the siblings have been blessed with, slam dunking that genetic lottery.

Chloe nudges me. "Who's that?" she asks, pointing.

"That's the younger brother, Prince Maximilien, aka Max. He's been at college in England, so I haven't met him yet."

"He's almost as yummy as his brother."

It's no contest.

And then I find him. The man I can't stop thinking about.

Alex is dressed in a navy suit with a white shirt that shows off his smooth skin. He smiles across the field at me, his hand raised in a wave. I beam back at him, my heart squeezing.

"That's him, that's him, that's him!" Chloe squeals.

Alex looks from me to her and mouths the word "Chloe?" I nod and her mouth drops open.

"Wait. He knows who I am?" She looks aghast.

"Of course he does. I've told him that you're visiting and you're my bestie."

She blinks at me. "Back up the bus here, sister. Are you guys *friends* or something now? Last I heard you hated the guy."

I shrug, willing the blush that wants to climb my cheeks and announce my feelings to the world to disappear.

Although I usually tell Chloe everything, I haven't shared

certain details about Alex's and my relationship. Details like how I've developed feelings for him, and I think he has for me, too. Knowing that Chloe has had a crush on Alexander made it all feel a little awkward. And then there's the fact that I was so vehement in my dislike of him at the start.

So, for better or for worse, I've got a lot to bring Chloe up to speed on.

"Things change," I say simply, turning away so she won't see the color in my cheeks. "I'll fill you in later, 'kay?"

"Madeline Josephine Turner. Do you have something to tell me? Because if you do, I need *all* the sordid details," she instructs.

"There's nothing sordid about it. It's"—I search my brain for the right word and cycle through a bunch before I land on—"new."

She narrows her eyes at me. "What's new, exactly?"

I glance around to ensure no one is listening. "I like him. Really like him. And I'm pretty sure he likes me."

"What?!" she screeches, and both my grandparents and several of the guests turn to stare.

"Is everything all right, Madeline?" Grandpapa asks in concern.

"Everything's fine," I reassure him, throwing Chloe a warning look.

"This is huge. Huger than huge," she says under her breath. "So, you're a thing?"

"Kind of."

"You either are or you aren't. Have you kissed?"

I press my lips together and shake my head.

"Girl, you have got to kiss that man." She looks over at Alex. "If not for yourself, then for the rest of womankind. Me included."

The thought of kissing Alex has my belly buzzing with a band of excited bees.

"I'll see what I can do," I reply. "I'm sorry I didn't say anything. I wasn't sure how you'd react."

She shakes her head at me. "You are one dark horse, missy."

"So, we're good?"

She gives me a shoulder nudge. "Are you crazy? Of course we're good."

Trumpets sound and Chloe gawks at the five trumpeters in their uniforms, monogrammed flags hanging from their instruments.

"It's just as I imagined," she whispers.

The Games are officially opened by Alex's father, who makes a speech in Ledonian, and neither I nor Chloe understand a single word, before people perform a choreographed dance and acrobatics to music, with both the pheasant, the national bird of Ledonia, and the peacock, on large flags, heralding the start of The Games.

"It's like a miniature version of the Olympics, only with weird events like cheese rolling and wife racing," I explain to Chloe.

"Wife racing?" she guffaws.

"I know, right? But Alex tells me it's actually lots of fun, and his parents enter each year."

"You call Prince McHottie *Alex*?" Chloe asks on a laugh. "What am I thinking? Of course you do."

We watch the archery and anvil throwing, followed by the tree hurling. Soon there's a break, and we are offered refreshments and snacks, all of which Chloe devours, telling me how good all the food is. She even likes the Malveauxian tea, which is unfathomable to me, but then she always was the adventurous one.

"What?" she asks with a mouthful of cake. "Jetlag. I'm carb loading."

"Carb loading for jetlag? That's so not a thing."

As Chloe pushes another pastry into her mouth, Alex arrives in our enclosure. He finds me in the crowd and makes a beeline for me, only stopping briefly to greet my grandparents.

"Alex, hey," I say, my voice breathless because Alex has gone and stolen my breath right from my lungs. He's a total breath stealer.

"Princess Madeline." He lifts my hand and places a gentle kiss on it like he did that day at Parliament. It's as though he's a character from *Bridgerton*, only he's so much better because he's real, he's here—and he only has eyes for me.

"Oh, my," Chloe says through her mouthful of pastry.

Still holding my hand in his, he says softly, "You look beautiful, Texas."

"You don't look so bad yourself," I reply with a shy smile.

Alex turns his attention to Chloe. "And you must be Chloe. It's wonderful to meet you. I know Maddie's been so looking forward to your visit."

Chloe's response is to giggle, her mouth still full of pastry, her face flushing as pink as her hair.

"How are you enjoying The Games so far? Did you see that huge guy who tossed the tree? He was amazing," I say to pull the focus from my friend. She needs to swallow— and maybe even stick her head in a bucket of ice.

"Sigmund von Huffier. We only wish he represented Ledonia," he replies. "He wins every year."

"He's a mountain of a man," I reply.

We chat for a bit longer, Chloe recovering her dignity after a while, and when he excuses himself to change for the upcoming races, I give his arm a quick squeeze. "I'd say good luck rolling that cheese, but you know I'm going to beat you, right?"

"That's fighting talk if ever I've heard it," he replies with a laugh. "See you out there, Right Hook Madeline."

"Right Hook Madeline?" Chloe asks when he's gone. "Is that because of the you-know-what on the you-know-where?"

"You're lucky I speak Chloe, and yes, it was. He's going to be my manager if I ever take boxing up as a profession."

"You two are so dang cute together, it makes me sick. I can't even hate you for stealing my future husband."

"Thanks, Chlo."

"I've got you. And you know I approve of this one, unlike the last guy." She makes a face. "Eric. *Ew.*"

"I can't believe I had a crush on him for all that time. He treated me so badly, like a freaking doormat."

"There was no telling you."

"I know. I was a lost cause. It's weird, but I feel like this whole princess thing has given me more self-confidence, you know? I can't ever imagine allowing someone to treat me like that now."

Chloe pulls me in for a quick hug. "It's about time you figured out how amazing you are."

I grin at her. "Thanks. Hey, I need to go get changed for the cheese rolling thing. Come with me?" I ask.

"I don't spot Alexander's younger brother, so yeah."

We breeze past Grandmama, when she touches me on the arm.

"Madeline, may I have a private word, please?" She looks like she sucked on a lemon.

"That's my cue to leave. Catch you at your fancy apartment, Mads," Chloe says and quickly leaves.

"What's up, Grandmama? Have I done something

wrong? I've been trying so hard to act the way Alice and Vlad have been teaching me."

She says urgently under her breath, "Please don't tell me you've fallen for Prince Alexander's charms."

I blink at her in disbelief. Seriously, is this woman psychic?

"You told me to become friends with him, Grandmama. You told me it was in my best interest. I listened to you, and now we're friends."

I'm trying not to sound defensive, but I know I do.

She arches a brow. "Is that what this is? Friendship? Because it looked to me as though it may be something more. I don't see him kissing any of the other young ladies on the hand, and I've witnessed him doing it with you twice."

"Absolutely," I respond firmly. "Friendship."

Grandmama doesn't need to know that what I've begun to feel for Alex goes way beyond friendship. After all, although I strongly suspect Alex feels the same way, really, there's nothing to tell. We haven't even kissed. We haven't shared our feelings about one another. Nothing.

If you disregard the fact I can't stop thinking about him, then we are nothing but friends.

Although there's a slim chance, I'm taking the easy way out and running with it here.

Grandmama's features relax, dispelling that lemon from her mouth. "I'm glad to hear it, Madeline. Whatever you do, don't let it develop into anything more. With a man like Alexander, anything beyond friendship can lead nowhere you would want it to go."

Alex is right. He continues to be judged as the person he once was.

"Grandmama, Alex has changed. He's not the party-loving guy everyone thinks he is."

"I've been remiss, Madeline," she says, ignoring my defense of him. "I must introduce you to some of the younger male members of the aristocracy here in Malveaux. There are several who would make fine partners for you, I'm quite certain."

I pull my lips into a smile. "Sure. That sounds—" Horrible? Unnecessary? Completely superfluous? "—great."

"There's Lord Radisson's son, Herbert, who I understand is a very fine shot, and Viscount Giorgio's son, Stefan, who has a rather nice stately home in…"

As Grandmama lists the virtues of half the single men of Malveaux, I barely listen. If her only reason for not wanting me to become romantically involved with Alex is that he's a womanizer, then I know I can put her straight simply by showing her how incredible he is—and how he's changed. All I have to do is make her see it.

Chapter 21

Alexander

I make my way to the rooms to change out of my suit and tie before the cheese rolling event, where I find Father, talking on his phone in hushed tones. He notices me as I enter the room and ends the call.

"How did the team do in archery?" he asks.

"They won."

"As they should. We'll be competing in the cheese rolling event shortly. I don't need a repeat of last year," he warns.

I slip my jacket off and hang it over the back of a chair. "You mean when I won?"

His lips form a thin line below his moustache. "It simply will not do for you to publicly humiliate me like that, Alexander. I am King."

"It's just a silly race involving a wheel of cheese, Father. It's not exactly the Olympics."

I know I'm pushing him, but Maddie's words have stayed with me from that day on the hill. I'm worth knowing. I'm not just a reflection of him. I'm Alexander, and I've got a lot to offer the world in my own right.

Which would include me poking fun at my father, it would seem.

"Does it really matter who wins, Father? It's just a bit of fun."

He shoots me a look that makes me feel like I've just committed a heinous crime. "Just a bit of fun? It's about public perception, my boy. The people need to see a strong leader. I am that leader. You'll have your turn in due course when you inherit the throne when I turn 65. Until then, you need to take a back seat. Allow me to shine."

"Who cares about a cheese rolling competition? Cheesemakers maybe, but no one else, Father,"

"I care," he says sternly.

"But—"

"No arguments."

There's a finality to his words, and I know there's no point in continuing the conversation. And anyway, the fact I beat him last year can remain one of my own private— and most definitely favorite—memories.

I bow my head. "Yes, Father."

End of topic.

"How's it going with the American? I saw photos of you at some hospital you visited together."

I smile at the memory. I might have been doing my father's bidding but being there for Maddie when she needed me felt so good. So right.

"It was the Tleurbonne Children's Hospital, her first public appearance outside of the palace. It went extremely well. She's an absolute natural with the patients, a lot like I'm told Princess Diana was, back in the day. We met this one child who—"

He waves his hand in the air to stop me. "I don't need a blow by blow."

Chastised, I clamp my mouth shut. "Of course, Father."

"Are you getting on well?"

"We are." A smile tugs at the edges of my mouth, the way it always does when I think of Maddie. There's something about her that draws me to her, like a magnetic pull. It's not just that she's a beautiful woman, but there's no denying she is. She's got long dark hair that frames her fine features perfectly, highlighting her iridescent blue eyes— and the most kissable of mouths with full, inviting lips.

Yes, those lips.

I admit, I've thought about kissing her. More than once. That day we rode the bike to the top of the hill, I could think of nothing else. I mean, really, what's a guy to do when the woman he can't stop thinking about licks her ice cream in the sexiest way imaginable?

It took all my self-control not to take her in my arms and insist she replace her ice cream with me before I gave her the most long-awaited and anticipated kiss of my whole life.

There have been other moments, moments that would have done for a woman I didn't care for the way I do Maddie. There's no denying I wanted it to happen.

But when it does happen—and I so hope it will happen

—I want it to be perfect. This isn't just some girl with which I'm having a flirtation. This is Madeline. She's special. I want our first kiss to be nothing short of perfect.

"And?" father leads.

"And she's not who I thought she was."

"What does that mean?"

"She's not some gold digger who's cashing in on her newfound fame. That's not her at all. She's genuine, sweet, funny. She's smart, too."

He harrumphs. "Perhaps she's merely a good actress? Have you thought of that? Whatever she is, you're doing good work. Keep it up." He gives me an awkward pat on the shoulder.

Did Father just compliment me?

He looks over my shoulder and says, "Ah, Maximilien."

My brother strides into the room and immediately pulls off his jacket and sits down heavily in a chair next to me, removing his shoes.

"What are you two plotting?" Max asks.

"Nothing," I reply, feeling oddly guilty.

"The cheese event next. Who knows, with practice, you may rival your brother," Father says. "I plan on doing so myself this year."

"Maybe," Max replies.

He and I share a look. With the age gap between us, I for one have never been especially competitive with him, despite the fact our father tries to push us into it.

"What's going on with you and the new princess?" Max asks as he pulls on a pair of shorts.

"We're getting along, that's all," I reply evasively.

"I saw you kiss her hand and look at her like she's a bowl of chocolate eclairs," he replies.

"It's all part of the charm offensive, lad," Father replies. "Your brother needs to impress."

Max pulls his lips into a line. "Lucky him. I don't get to go around kissing new princesses."

I suppress a smile. That's exactly what I hope to do soon myself. Kiss the new princess.

"Get a hurry along, you two. We need to get to the event," Father instructs.

Ten minutes later, we're on a grassy hill where the spectators and competitors alike have congregated, changed and ready for one of the silliest races of The Games. Actually, it's probably the second silliest after wife racing, but I have a plan for that race, and it's one I'm very much looking forward to enacting.

Not for the first time today I think of how Maddie has emboldened me with Father.

The best part of the cheese rolling race is that not only is it in the name of fun, but Sofia, Amelia, and Max are also competing, which makes it a real family "sport"—if rolling a wheel of cheese down a hill can actually be considered a sport.

What's better than that?

Maddie's competing, too. That's what.

She grins at me as she lines up at the top of the hill beside Amelia. If I thought she's looked sexy before, it has nothing on the way she looks right now. Her long hair is caught in a high ponytail, her face alight with the excitement of the game. She's in a Malveauxian blue polo top and a pair of white shorts, which she's teamed with a pair of blue and white striped knee-high socks. She looks like a gorgeous, hot soccer player, and I'm finding it hard to keep my eyes off her.

I move so I'm standing beside her, wanting nothing but to be in her orbit. Max shoots me a knowing look, and I nudge him with my hand.

"Looking good, Texas," I say, when really, I want to tell

her she looks incredible and to forget this whole silly cheese rolling game and instead run away with me and be mine.

One step at a time.

"She looks hot," Amelia says. "Have you done this before, Maddie?"

"Roll some cheese down a hill? Weirdly, no," she replies on a laugh, the tinkling sound pulling my lips into a grin.

"Do you need any tips? Alex is extremely good at this," Amelia replies.

"Of course he is," Sofia says, not one to be outdone by her sister.

"Alex is extremely good at everything," Max moans. He reaches a hand out to shake Maddie's. "I'm Max. I'm the much better looking and significantly more charming younger brother."

I shake my head at him in good humor.

"It's great to meet you, Max," Maddie replies with a broad grin that tugs at my heart as an unfamiliar spike of jealousy pierces my thoughts.

Is it selfish that I want her to only smile like that at me?

I don't care. I want all of her smiles. Every last one.

"Any tips will be greatly appreciated," she replies, her eyes flashing to mine.

"It's not like the famous cheese rolling in Gloucester-shire, England," Sofia explains.

"Is it bad that I didn't know there was cheese rolling in England?" Maddie asks.

Sofia laughs. "Not at all. It's a rather obscure sport."

"But fun," Max says.

"Totally fun," Amelia agrees.

"In England, everyone chases the same wheel of cheese down an extraordinarily steep hill. As you can see, here it's more of a gentle slope, and we all get a wheel of cheese each. No one has ever fallen and broken anything here," Sofia says.

Maddie looks concerned. "That's good to know."

"It's a lot of fun," I reassure her. "Let me explain how it works. You hit your stick against the wheel of cheese as you run after it to keep it on course."

"With this thing?" She holds her stick up. Like all of ours, it's a branch from a tree, stripped of any leaves. "Don't they have specific cheese hitting sticks you can buy at a store? This feels way too DIY."

"Afraid not," I reply.

She examines the stick with her forehead furrowed, and I have to stop myself from reaching out and smoothing the lines, taking away any worry she may have.

"Here. Let me help you. You hold your stick like this," I begin, taking her hand in mine and wrapping it around her stick. The touch of her skin against mine sends a wave of desire through me.

"Okay," she says, her voice suddenly breathy.

"And you simply whack it against the side of the cheese," I explain, as though hitting something with a stick needs explanation—and it certainly doesn't need me to hold her hand in position.

But I find myself not wanting to let go.

"Alex, you're such a flirt," Sofia observes to my right.

"I'm not flirting," I protest, but all of my siblings burst into laughter and I slide my eyes to Maddie's. She smiles back and we share a moment before I reluctantly let go of her hand.

"Thanks," she murmurs.

I wink at her. "Anytime, Texas."

"Your Majesty, Royal Highnesses, ladies and gentlemen. Welcome to this year's cheese rolling event," the emcee begins. "The only rule is sticks must be used, which means no hand can touch the cheese. Instant disqualification! The first over the finish line with their cheese wins."

It's the same speech every year, and it always makes me think of that movie *Fight Club*.

The first rule of cheese rolling is not to talk about cheese rolling. What's the second rule? I look my father's way. *Don't win.*

"On your marks. Get set. Go!" the emcee calls out as a gun is shot and the cheeses surge forward.

Everyone springs into a burst of energy. I glance at Maddie to see her taking off at breakneck speed. Not to be outdone, I race downhill, dodging and leaping, the ground uneven under my feet as I focus only on the bouncing wheel. I nudge it into as straight a line as I can with my stick, aiming for the finish line at the bottom of the hill.

And then disaster hits.

My cheese wheel hits uneven ground, flies up in the air, and slaps down, coming to a sudden stop.

I know the rules. I can't touch it with anything but my stick. So, I wedge underneath it to lever it. But I know with momentum gone, I have little hope of completing the race, let alone winning it.

I look up as a blur of competitors dash past me.

"That's it. Game over," I murmur to myself, wondering how Maddie's doing, when someone hurtles into me, sending us both down the hill in a rolling heap of legs and arms.

"What the…?" I exclaim in shock as we come to a rolling stop. I look down to see Maddie lying on the grass beneath me, a look of dazed surprise on her face.

"Are you hurt?" I ask in a rush of concern.

"I-I don't know. I don't think so."

"Are you sure?" I cup her head in my hands and peer into her eyes.

"I'm sure," she replies as she gazes up at me, her

breathing shallow, her chest rising and falling quickly. If it's from the fall or from her sudden, very close proximity to me, I don't know. What I do know is that I want it to be because of me.

Me and only me.

"I'm sorry, Alex. I was chasing the cheese and it got away from me. I didn't even see you."

"It's fine. All that matters is you're okay."

She smiles and it lights up my life, touching my soul in a way I never knew a simple smile could.

This must be the way people feel when they first lay eyes on their newborn child, or when they gaze at their great love, standing at the altar, committing to a lifetime together.

It's the way I feel with Maddie. And it feels nothing short of incredible.

I'm suddenly aware I have one leg hooked over her, my hands cradling her head, her body angled towards me. As she gazes up at me, I know I want nothing more than to kiss her, to hold her, to tell her how much she's grown to mean to me in such a short time. To tell her that this has all taken me by surprise, and that it feels like it was meant to be.

She and I are meant to be.

Gazing at her, she looks so utterly breathtakingly beautiful, I'm not even sure which way is up and which way is down anymore. All I know is she's the woman who's been filling my thoughts, day and night.

"Get up, fools!" someone yells as they zoom past, and I know it's bossy sister extraordinaire, Sofia.

I feel Maddie's laugh beneath me before I hear it, bubbling up until it bursts out of her. I respond by laughing myself, my whole body convulsing. How ridiculous this whole thing is, us lying on a hill, our bodies entwined, as our respective wheels of cheese lie dormant on the ground, a rash of spectators gawking at us as competitors whizz by.

"I suppose we'd better get up," I suggest, even though it's the last thing I want to do.

"I suppose you're right," she replies in that soft, feminine voice of hers that is sweet, sweet music to my ears.

Reluctantly, I rise to my feet and offer her my hand to pull her up. Her white shorts are covered in dirt, her hair a mess of knots and grass, her face smeared with dirt.

But she's never looked more beautiful than she does right now.

The crowd of spectators burst into cheers, applauding our brush with cheese-related calamity, and we smile and wave at everybody, showing them that we're both okay.

But I know with absolute clarity that I'm way more than okay. I'm on top of the world, because in Maddie I've finally, finally found what I've been searching for.

Chapter 22

Maddie

"Congratulations to King Frederic of Ledonia for once again winning the cheese race," the emcee announces to cheers from the crowd as King Frederic smiles and waves at everyone. "And now it's time for the final event of The Games, a very popular event and one we've all been waiting for: the wife race!"

I've barely recovered from the cheese rolling event. Well, not the cheese rolling exactly, more so the fact that I accidentally collided with Alex and, together, we rolled down the hill, coming to a halt in a deliciously compromising position.

I let out a sigh. Alex and his strong, firm body pressed against mine as he gazes at me with such obvious care in his eyes? I can't help but shiver with desire.

It was romantic and wonderful and all the things I could ever want it to be—despite the fact that I bowled into him, knocking him down like a pin, and I just know I'll have a couple of bruises.

They don't matter at all.

I steal a glance at Alex by my side. His face is flushed from the exercise, his red shirt smeared with dirt and grass stains.

"You're a mess," he says.

"Ditto."

"But you're still beautiful."

My heart squeezes. Is this not the best feeling in the world? An incredibly hot guy, who so many women want, has eyes only for me. Me, the lost girl from Texas, who never felt like she was leading the right life. Me, the Texan backup princess.

"You two are so cute," Chloe comments. "You know, even if you rolled halfway down the hill together instead of actually running the race."

Alex and I share a look and things zing around my body.

"Why didn't you give it a try?" I ask her.

"I'm a lover, not a cheese roller," she replies with a wink.

"Are you going to go through with the plan?" Amelia asks Alex.

"What plan?" I ask.

"Alex wants to do the wife race," Amelia replies.

I pull my eyebrows together. "But you've got to be married, don't you?"

"OH, we're talking about all of us doing it this year, just for a laugh. What do you say, Maddie? Would you like to do the race with Alex? That is if you're quite recovered from your fall before when my brother so gallantly helped you." Amelia shoots me a mischievous grin.

I think of how Grandmama told me not to get romantically involved with Alex. Couldn't us doing the wife race be seen as a public announcement of sorts?

Or am I just overthinking this?

Chloe nudges me with her elbow. "Go on, girl. Do it for me."

"It's the 21st century, Maddie. No one's going to bat an eyelid if you and Alex enter the race without being married. Although, now that I think of it, you two getting married is really quite a marvelous idea," Amelia leads.

I blink at her in shock. First she's trying to get us to crash the wife race, and now she's trying to marry us off? Who knew a princess could be such a matchmaker?

"Calling all husbands to the line who wish to participate in the race," the emcee says, and I watch as Alex's parents step forward among a group of other competitors.

I glance over at my grandparents. "Are you competing?" I mouth and Grandmama shakes her head, looking once more like she's sucked on a super bitter lemon.

She needs to see that Alex has changed. That he's not who she thinks he is. That will pull that lemon from her mouth and replace it with delicious cake. Or you know, whatever it is that puts a smile on Grandmama's face.

"If everyone's assembled, we will begin the race," the emcee states.

"Wait! Prince Alexander wants to enter," Amelia calls out and my heart leaps into my mouth.

Such a matchmaker.

"Is that allowed?" King Frederic asks in a gruff voice.

"I want to enter, too," Amelia says. "And Max and Sofia."

There's a murmur among the crowd when Grandpapa rises to his feet. "We have modern practices here in Malveaux. If the prince, or any of the young unmarried people present would like to compete in the race, I will allow it." He gives a sweep of his hand and the crowd erupts into applause.

King Frederic, on the other hand, looks like angry sparks could fly off of him.

Amelia's face lights up and she punches her hand in the air. "Me! I want to do it! Not with my brother, of course, because that would be too weird, but with someone else." She begins to scan the crowd and I notice several men stepping forward, including a guy who looks like he could be a linebacker for the Houston Texans.

Popular girl.

"I'm going to do it, too," Chloe says as she latches onto a handsome guy in a suit.

This thing is becoming a total free for all.

"Prince Alexander? You can compete with whomever you choose," Grandpapa says and instantly it's like a gaggle of women appear out of nowhere, pressing in around us with eager looks on their faces.

I glance at the women. Next to me they're dressed so very gorgeously, with strappy dresses and high heels, their hair not a mess of grass and mud, their knees not covered in circles of dirt.

Should I give up before the competition for him has already begun?

Alexander and I may have shared a few moments together over the last couple of weeks, and I know I've got feelings for him that keep growing and growing each time we meet. But I could never compete with women like these, all polished and shiny and confident. The very thought he would pick me makes me feel like a sow among the elegant deer.

"Pick me, Prince Alexander!"

"No, pick me!"

"I'm as light as a feather, choose me!"

Alex doesn't seem to hear any of them. Instead, he walks straight over to me, and I look up at him with a combination of disbelief, dread—and desire. Who knew such a combination existed?

He offers me his hand. "Princess Madeline, will you do me the honor?"

Being chosen by Alex over all these other women is like the exact opposite of being chosen last in gym class back in high school. I'm being chosen first by the hottest guy around—and it feels absolutely amazing.

My lips twitch. "You got it."

His face lights up in a smile. "Let's have some fun."

"Absolutely."

He leads me to the starting line and I do my best to ignore the glares from the women not chosen. King Frederic and Queen Astrid greet us, only one of whom smiles —and no prizes for guessing who—along with Amelia and the NFL-looking guy, who quickly removes his jacket and tie in preparation for the race. Max arrives with a pretty woman I met in the royal enclosure, and along comes Chloe and her partner, along with a variety of other couples, all ready to race.

"This is an outrage!" King Frederic declares, but no one's listening to him. We're all too excited about the race.

"I cannot believe you chose Luke Carlisle, Ledonia's top rugby player, Amelia," Max says, standing with a petite and pretty woman. "Hey, Luke. Good to meet you."

"Ditto, Your Royal Highness," the big guy replies.

"And you chose my friend, Collette, who happens to be only 5'1"," Amelia retorts and Max grins.

"I think we're all trying to win this thing," Alex says with a laugh.

"I'm just excited that we can compete," Sofia says, and her three siblings turn to her in surprise.

"You're competing too?" Max asks.

She lifts her chin, a smile playing on her lips. "I am."

A good-looking blond man appears at her side, wearing a red royal Ledonian uniform. He bows at us all, before he removes his jacket to reveal so many muscles, he could be a super hero—minus the cape.

Max lets out a low whistle and Amelia complains, "Not playing fair, sis."

"Don't you know all's fair in love, war, and wife races?" Sofia replies with a grin, and as much as I decided I liked Amelia the moment we met, I decide I like Sofia, too.

"How would you like me to carry you, Texas?" Alex asks with a flirty grin.

The thought of being in his arms once more makes my mouth suddenly dry. "Isn't it supposed to be the fireman's hold? You know, over the shoulder."

"It can be any way you like," he replies, his eyes dancing.

This man.

All competitors ready themselves to pick up their partners and run.

I don't have any time to respond before Alex scoops me up into his arms, one arm supporting my back, the other under my knees so we're looking right at one another.

Just as before, his body is warm and firm pressed against mine.

He waggles his brows at me. "Let's win this thing, Texas."

I kick my sneakers off. "You got it."

"Why did you do that?"

"Less weight."

His laughter makes me rock in his arms, and when the horn blares he takes off, striding forward on powerful legs.

"Hold on tight!" he instructs, and with each step I bounce up and down in his strong arms.

I feel so giddy I let out a squeal of delight.

Looking around at the other competitors, I'm the only partner not in a fireman's hold. Has Alex made an error in judgment, carrying me this way? It must be so much easier to run with someone thrown over your shoulder.

But would I change it?

That would be a rock-hard *no*, just like Alex's torso.

I can feel every taut muscle in his body, every confident step he makes, every breath he takes, and I find myself gazing at him, my heart swelling with my almost overpowering feelings for him.

He clutches me closer, his breath coming hard.

"You're doing amazing!" I encourage.

We're ahead of everyone but Amelia and her rugby guy, who I strongly suspect she chose for his long, powerful legs and sheer animal strength. Props to her.

But I wouldn't trade Alex for the world.

"Need…to…catch…them," he pants as I bounce up and down with every step.

"You got this!" I tell him, despite the fact Amelia and her rugby hero are a good three or four paces ahead of us.

In a few short seconds, and enough jostling to make me regret my lunch, we cross the line, coming in second behind Amelia and Luke. Alex drops me to my feet, places his hands on his knees, and sucks in deep lungfuls of air. He ran, carrying me, over 100 yards, which is no small thing. The guy must be beat.

I place my hand on his back. It's hot and sweaty, his shirt clinging to every muscular sinew as his chest heaves. "You did good, hubby," I tell him.

He looks up at me, his face flushed and sweaty. "Not good enough." He gestures at Amelia and Luke, who barely broke a sweat as they had glided across the finish line, Amelia shouting and waving her hands in the air in glee.

"Come on. He looks like he could wrangle a bull with his bare hands."

Alex wipes his forehead with the bottom edge of his shirt, exposing his taut, tan belly.

It's hard to pull my eyes away.

"Is that something you did a lot back in Texas? Wrangling bulls with your bare hands?"

"Not a lot of bull wrangling going on in Houston, unless you count the rodeo."

"Will you take me to a genuine Texas rodeo someday?"

"I'll see what I can do."

We share a smile.

"How about I start with escorting you to a ball tonight?" he asks.

It's tradition that The Games ends with a ball, complete with dancing and fireworks. Gustav has already helped me pick out my dress, and the thought of going to the ball with Alex at my side fills my heart with happiness.

"Perhaps this ball can dispel the memory of the last," he adds.

"Are you telling me you don't want to meet me in a hallway closet?" I ask, and immediately realized how flirty that sounds. Me and Alex in a hallway closet. My belly goes all kinds of crazy.

"If we did I can guarantee it wouldn't go the way it did the last time," he replies, his voice gravelly and deep, sending a thrill through me.

I would go anywhere with this man, hallway closets included.

"That's good to know. I'll keep it in mind when I'm planning an escape tonight."

His eyes flash, his lips pulled into a tempting smile. How can I feel so much for this man, want him so much, have such depth of emotion and never have actually kissed him? Sure, I had a fat crush on Eric for way too long and nothing ever happened there, but with Alex it's different. It's not just a crush. Far from it. I feel things for him I've never felt for anyone before.

It's not what I ever expected, but it's nothing short of wonderful.

King Frederic boulders over to us. "This race is for married couples only and as such, I have spoken with the official. Anyone who is not married has been disqualified," he says without preamble.

Wait, what? Isn't this just for fun?

I turn to Alex, expecting him to voice my thoughts, instead all he does is pull his lips together and nod.

"You're right, Father. I assume that would make you and Mummy the winners?"

King Frederic pushes out his chest. "It would indeed."

"Congratulations. Well deserved," he replies.

I knit my brows together in confusion. "Didn't my grandpapa say anyone can enter it this year?"

"Maddie," Alex warns.

"The Games have been played between our two countries for over 150 years, Princess Madeline. I understand you're new to all this, but we here in Ledonia and Malveaux have traditions to uphold."

"I get that, but Grandpapa—"

He cuts me off. "Your grandfather forgot himself, my dear."

I glance at Alex, half expecting him to defend me.

Instead, he replies, "King Frederic is right, Maddie. This was all a bit of fun for us, but rules are rules. There's something special about upholding traditions. Don't you think?"

"Traditions. Sure," I mutter.

How can Alex be so self-assured in everything he does right up until his dad comes around? It's like he has a personality change and becomes someone I don't recognize.

The emcee announces that the games have now come to an official close, and I push it to the back of my mind. People can be weird around their parents. It's no big deal. And Alex's dad is the King. That's got to be doubly weird for him.

So, when Alex walks me back to my rooms and asks if he can escort me to the ball this evening, I say yes without hesitation, and am rewarded with one of his intoxicating smiles that leaves me floating on a cloud for the rest of the afternoon.

Chapter 23

Alexander

I arrive at Maddie's rooms at the agreed time to take her to the ball, feeling surprisingly nervous. A new feeling for me, particularly where women are concerned. I'm rarely nervous, and never jealous, but I've been both of those things around Maddie in the time I've known her.

Now that I'm standing here at her door, wearing my Ledonian red jacket over black trousers with a light blue vertical trim, a pair of polished black oxfords on my feet, nerves dart around me like a pinball.

I know Maddie is different, different from all the other women I've dated before. And I admit, there have been a few. But none of them compare to Maddie. Not one. I find myself stuck in a whirlwind of feelings for this woman I've known for only a fortnight—initially during which I actively disliked her. I may have been acting under Father's orders, but what I'm feeling is real.

Being around Maddie is like discovering a secret part of myself I never knew existed, a part of me she's somehow unlocked.

As corny as it may sound, it's as if I've been living in a black and white world, interacting with monochrome people, and then I met her and suddenly everything around me has burst into the clearest, most vivid color.

Man, I sound like some romance novel.

I blame Amelia and all those Christmas romances we watch.

Maddie's door swings open and I'm met with her ever-present bodyguard, Vladimir.

"Good evening, Your Royal Highness," he says with a bow.

"Hello, Vladimir. Is she ready?"

There's a whisper of a smile on his lips. "She is, sir. Please, feel free to have a seat in the living room. I'll tell her you're here."

I wait impatiently, looking through the photographs on the mantle. I pick one up of her with her father on a ride at a theme park, laughing, her eyes bright. Another one is of her with a woman with a shock of pink hair and a *don't mess with me* attitude. Chloe. Then there's one with a woman who has the same eyes as Maddie, a woman I recognize as Princess Josephine, her mother. They look so alike, from their thick hair to their blue eyes. I feel a pang of sorrow for her loss, a young girl losing her mother far too early.

"Prince Alexander," a voice says and I turn to see Chloe. She's wearing a striking fusion of black Victorian elegance and industrial edge, her long pink hair falling in curls down her back. "I mean, Your Royal Highness." She dips into a curtsy. "Or Your Grace? Seriously, they told me what to say, but I think I forgot."

"Alex will do just fine. I take it from your dress you're joining us at the ball this evening?"

"Heck, yes. Would not miss it for all the peacocks in Malveaux."

I smile at her. "I like that."

"No, *you* like Maddie."

It's a statement, not a question, and I'm not going to deny it.

"I do like Maddie. Rather a lot, actually."

Chloe snort laughs. "You sound so upper class. *Rather a lot, actually.*" She puts on what I think is meant to be my accent.

It doesn't hit the mark.

Her features drop and she adds in an undertone, "I want you to know that if you do anything to hurt my girl, I will find you, and I will hurt you."

I press my lips together to stifle a smile. Being threatened by a woman who's a good 10 inches shorter than me is most certainly new, even if she does look uncompromisingly tough in her dress. "I'll bear that in mind," I reply in a serious tone.

"Good. She's special."

"Oh, that I know."

"Hey, Alex," Maddie says and I turn to see her, framed by the doorway.

She is nothing short of breathtaking.

Her ball gown is a vision in Malveauxian blue, with a flowing, floor-length skirt that shimmers like the Adriatic Sea under moonlight. Its fitted bodice, adorned with delicate silver, accentuates her womanly figure. Her hair falls across her shoulders, a tiara atop her head. Although she's only been a princess for a short while, tonight she looks like she was born for the role, a perfect princess on a perfect night.

"Maddie, you look…incredible," I breathe.

"It's not too much?" she asks, self-consciously smoothing down her skirts.

I make my way across the floor and collect her hands in mine. "I guarantee no one at the ball will be able to tear their eyes from the beautiful Malveauxian princess."

Her full lips lift into a smile that tugs at my heart. "I love it, but I do feel a little bit like Princess Barbie going to the ball."

"Princess Barbie has nothing on you, Texas," I murmur and win a fresh smile that tugs at my heartstrings.

"Okay, you two. That's enough sappiness," Chloe quips.

Maddie's beauty had made me temporarily forget there was anyone else in the room.

"How did you enjoy The Games?" I ask, turning to Chloe.

"The cheese rolling looked like it could be a lot of fun, if you know what I mean." She winks at us.

"I think *everyone* knows what you mean, girl," Maddie replies, echoing my very thought.

The memory of the way Maddie felt next to me as we lay on the grass, recovering from our fall, is a feeling I want to recapture as soon as I can. And never let go.

"Thank you for choosing me over all those girls,"

Maddie says. "They sure were eager to get to be carried by you."

How could she think for even one second I would want *anyone* over her?

"It was an easy choice," I reply, stating the simple fact.

It was her. No question.

She lifts her eyes to mine, her face glowing. "Coming in second after a professional rugby player ain't too shabby, either."

"Not too shabby at all," I reply.

I escort both women through the palace to the grand ballroom, where all three of us are announced to the ball guests. I'm so very proud to be at Maddie's side, and every eye in the room is trained on us together.

"This is freakin' insane," Chloe hisses with eyes the size of the grandfather clock in the state room as we make our way down the stairs.

"Just go with it," Maddie instructs, which is good advice. There's not much else one can do at these events.

"Ah, there she is. In one piece after today's activities, I see," King Harald says as he greets Maddie with warm kisses to each cheek.

"Good evening, Your Majesty," I say with a short bow.

He grips my hand and pumps it enthusiastically. "Alexander. It's so good to see you two getting on. It really is a very special relationship we enjoy between our two countries. It's important that continues into the next generation."

I smile at Maddie. "I think we've got that covered, wouldn't you say, princess?"

Her smile is shy and utterly adorable. "I would."

King Harald smiles. "Good, good. Pity about the cheese rolling fall."

"I wouldn't say that," I reply. I catch Maddie's eye and see her blush.

"Your Royal Highnesses, ladies and gentlemen, guests of the palace," a member of the Royal Guard says from the top of the staircase. "I would like to invite King Harald and Queen Maria to the floor for the first dance of the evening."

"That's my cue, I'm afraid," King Harald says. "Time my queen and I showed you young folk how it's done."

"Knock 'em dead, Grandpapa," Maddie says.

The music begins, and King Harald leads his wife to the dance floor. They begin to dance, gazing into one another's eyes. They look every inch the young couple in love, and I'm surprised to feel a knot form in my gut.

This. This is what I want.

Not meaningless flings with gorgeous but vapid women who have no interest in knowing me beyond the fact I'm a prince. I want what King Harald and Queen Maria have. A strong and deep abiding love that lasts a lifetime.

I want what they have, but with Maddie.

The thought startles me, my heart suddenly thudding.

I take a moment, trying to get my head around what my heart is telling me, and my brain fights for all it's worth.

In the red corner, ladies and gentlemen, we have Brain, weighing in at 1.5 kilograms. Logical, pragmatic, Brain has the well-deserved reputation of not diving in head first, of calculating risk, dispensing with messy emotions. Brain reminds me I've only known Maddie for a couple of weeks. I can't possibly have such big feelings for someone so quickly. It doesn't make sense to meet someone and fall for them in an unprecedented way in such a short space of time.

Brain shoots me a knowing look. *Trust me, I should be in charge here* it tells me in no uncertain terms.

In the blue corner we have Heart, weighing in at only about half a kilo. Heart is no match for the much heavier Brain, surely. But pesky Heart will not be silenced. My heart is telling me to go after what I want, to put aside logic and run with my feelings for this beautiful, smart, funny, kind woman at my side.

Now's the time, my heart whispers. *She's The One.*

I glance at Maddie. She's riveted as she watches her grandparents move gracefully around the dance floor. Her eyes are soft, her mouth slightly parted, and I can tell she's moved by them, just as I am.

Is she thinking that she wants what they have, too? Perhaps with me?

That I do not know.

What I do know is the idea of spending my life with Maddie, loving her and cherishing her the way her grandparents love and cherish one another, gives me a deep sense of calm, of knowing. I've been searching and searching for something without even really knowing what it is, and now, I've finally found it.

I'm falling for Maddie.

It looks like Heart has beaten Brain with a decisive knock out.

The King and Queen finish their dance, and others join them on the dance floor.

"Would you do me the honor, Princess Madeline?" I ask. "If that's okay with you, Chloe?"

She waves her hand in the air. "Go for it."

"I would be delighted, Prince Alexander," Maddie replies with a twinkle in her eye.

I lead her to the dance floor, where I can finally pull her close in the way I've wanted to since the moment I laid eyes on her in this dress. I place one hand on the small of her back and hold my other hand out for her to take in hers.

As we begin to move, I go one way and she goes the other. Realizing her mistake, she takes a step toward me and immediately steps on my toes.

"Sorry," she says and she bites down on her lip.

I laugh. "It's fine." I resume the dance only for her to stand on my foot once more, her hip crashing into mine.

"Do you know how to dance, Texas?"

"Of course I do. Just not like this. I've started learning, but I've only done it a couple times," she admits.

"Well, in that case, why don't you let go, and allow me to lead us around the floor?"

"Let go? How far do you want me to take that? Ragdoll level let go?"

"Perhaps not quite that far? I don't want you going limp in my arms. Here, I'll show you." I tighten my hold on her to reassure her I know what I'm doing, and after a couple of missteps, she does as I asked. She lets go—just the right amount, no ragdoll in sight—and we begin to glide around the dance floor as though we're one.

It feels amazing to hold this beautiful woman in my arms, dancing with one another in a romantic setting, the music filling the air. People around us watch and stare, and I can almost feel their minds ticking over.

Is Princess Madeline his newest conquest?

How long will this last? One week or two?

Doesn't the new Princess know his reputation?

I push the thoughts away. All that matters is her and me, here, together on this magical night, my heart full.

Eventually, we break for a late supper, sitting at the tables with their crisp white tablecloths and floral displays, enjoying finger sandwiches, canapés, and fruit and cheese. I watch Maddie as she talks easily with Sofia, Amelia, and

Max, her friend Chloe ever present, delivering witty one-liners.

Maddie is all ease and grace, and a far cry from the frightened woman I met that night in the hallway cupboard.

We've come a long way.

But the night isn't over yet, and I have something planned for the woman of my affections.

"The fireworks are about to begin, I'm told," Max announces. "I suggest we all go to watch them in our usual place."

"Where's your usual place?" Chloe asks.

"Actually, let's not do that this year. Let's all go onto the terrace with everyone else," I suggest, not because I don't want to go to our usual place to watch the fireworks. Well, not with my family, anyway.

Max leans back in his chair, slinging his arm around Sofia's shoulders. "If you want. Makes no difference to me."

Amelia narrows her eyes at me. "Why don't you want us to go to the roof?" she asks under her breath. "Is it because you want to take her there?" She waggles her brows at me and I can't help but beam at her. "I knew it. She's your perfect match."

"How did you…?"

She laughs. "Let's see. You spend most of your time with her, and when you're not with her you've got a goofy grin on your face like you've just won the lottery. Personally, I think you're great together, and I'm so, so happy for you." She gives my hand a squeeze.

"She really is quite something."

"She is. Now, go get your girl."

I don't need to be told twice.

"Make sure everyone goes outside with the rest of the guests. This needs to be perfect," I say.

"You can count on me, brother," she replies with a conspiratorial grin.

Amelia's true to her word, and as everyone steps out onto the terrace to watch the display, I take Maddie by the hand and lead her from the ballroom.

"Where are you taking me?" she asks.

"You'll have to wait and see."

I lead her up the winding staircase until we reach a heavy wooden door that looks like something from a Mediaeval castle. Which of course it is. I tug on the wrought iron handle until the door gives and pull it back to reveal the night sky in all its expansive glory.

"Alex, it's gorgeous!" she exclaims.

Together, we step out onto the roof, lined with the ancient battlements of a time long gone. Stars twinkle above us and the darkened mountains bask in the glow of the sunset's final rays of the day. We make our way over to the edge and look down at the throngs of people below, milling around like little mice dressed in human clothes.

"I used to steal up here with my brother and sisters to watch the fireworks when I was a child. Tonight, I wanted to share this moment with you alone."

Our gazes lock and a zing of anticipation soars through me.

Being here alone, with no photographers or family members or staff or anyone else to interrupt us, is as rare as the diamonds in her tiara, and I intend to use every moment we have together.

My eyes drop from hers to her soft lips and she looks so utterly beautiful in the pale moonlight, I have to stop myself from pulling her into my arms and kissing her right here and now.

It's too soon.

This needs to be nothing short of perfection.

She gives a shiver in the cool night air, so I do what any gentleman would do and remove my jacket to wrap around her shoulders. It almost engulfs her, reminding me how much smaller she is than me, smaller and utterly gorgeous.

"Thanks."

"Anything for you."

"Anything?" she asks, a smile on her lips.

"Anything," I confirm, meaning it one hundred percent.

I wrap an arm around her, her shoulder nestled under my arm. "May I?" I ask, more as an afterthought because this feels so natural. So right.

"I think you already did," she replies lightly, and together we stand at the edge of the roof, gazing out at the night sky.

The first of the fireworks is released with a loud screech and bang, and Maddie jumps, burying herself closer to me. Instinctively, I lean down and kiss her forehead.

We stand and watch the fireworks together, the myriad of colors alight in the night sky, the sound of gasps from people below floating up to us.

"What is it about fireworks that's so—"

"Magical," I finish for her, and she smiles up at me.

Our gazes lock.

Now. Now is the moment.

I reach out and gently cup her face in my hand, tilting it up, my eyes not leaving hers. She moves to face me, and I slide my hand from her jaw until I reach the warm, soft skin of her neck. Tangling my fingers in her hair, she lets out a gasp.

I could not hold myself back from kissing her now if a fleet of horses was dragging me away.

Slowly, savoring every single moment, I lean down and breathe in her scent, a heady mixture of summer and sweetness and her.

"You have enchanted me, body and soul," I murmur, my heart thudding against my ribcage, my breath shallow.

I bend my head and as our lips finally, finally touch, it's as though my entire being is set alight. Words are no longer enough. I need to show her how much I want her. How much she means to me.

Her lips are soft and plump and inviting, and finally pressed against mine, it takes every ounce of my strength not to rush this thing. I want all of her. Now. To possess her, to know she's mine, to show her everything I've been holding inside.

With the strength of forged steel, I force myself to pull back from her lips, only for her to bunch the neck of my shirt in her fist, pulling me back against her lips. It's wonderful and unexpected and if I thought my body was in risk of being on fire before, I'm now ready to combust.

This moment is everything. *Everything.*

It's as though I've been waiting my entire life for this one kiss. Time has slowed. All that exists is her and me in this moment, fireworks flashing around us, our kiss deepening, pulling me closer and closer until I could utterly lose myself in her.

My Maddie.

My beautiful, sweet Texas.

Our dizzying kiss quite literally takes my breath away, and we stand and grin at one another.

"That was—" I begin, not sure how to explain the most incredible kiss of my life.

"It was," she replies, her chest rising and falling with each shallow breath she takes, making me want her more.

I forget my resolve to take this slow. How can I when

the woman I'm falling for looks like she does on this perfect night?

I am but flesh and blood.

I place my hands on her waist and lift her up, pressing her against the battlement. She lets out another gasp, and I trail a line of kisses up her neck and along her jawline, loving the sweet taste of her skin, until I reach her lips. I claim her mouth once again, kissing her until the fireworks come to a stop and my heart feels like it may burst.

"Maddie," I say as I catch my breath.

She smiles at me and I notice the way her eyes are the deepest pools in the evening light, her dark lashes curling up towards her perfectly arched eyebrows. There's a smattering of freckles across her nose, and her lips are full and inviting.

I don't want to forget a single detail. I want to remember her. *All* of her.

Our gaze intensifies as something deep and strong passes between us. It makes my breath catch in my throat and I know this thing is so much bigger than I'd ever anticipated. Big and wonderful and exactly what I've been searching for.

Who knew I'd find it with my Texan Princess?

Chapter 24

Maddie

> It's official: Princess Madeline is the luckiest girl in both Ledonia and Malveaux. This reporter can tell you that although sadly no photos exist, both she and our Prince of Handsomeness took a tumble during the Cheese Rolling, only to land in the most compromising of positions, from which they didn't appear too eager to move. Could there be something more with these two than meets the eye? This reporter needs to know.

#RoyalTumble
#SayItIsntSo

Yours on the very edge of her seat,

Fabiana Fontaine xx

Chloe blinks at me, her jaw dropped open. Sitting in our robes on my oversized bed, we've been sipping our coffee and eating caramel drenched pancakes, downloading last night's events. Apparently, Chloe had fun dancing with a bunch of different guys, from foreign diplomats to members of the Malveauxian aristocracy.

And me? Well, I had eyes for one guy only.

"Wait. You and Alexander *kissed*?" she asks. "When? How? Where?"

I press my lips together to stifle the biggest grin ever. "That's a lot of questions, Chlo."

The kisses I shared with Alex are burned in my memory. The way he looked at me, his incredible scent, the way he touched me, so gentle and hesitant—at least to start with. The way things got so heated between us after that first, tentative kiss, the fire between us, growing and growing until it threatened to engulf us both.

I let out an involuntary sigh.

Finally kissing Alex was everything I hoped it would be. And more. Definitely more.

Truth be told, I've never before experienced this strength of connection with a man. It's fierce, all-consuming, and I simply cannot get enough of him.

"So? Are you going to answer any of my questions, or should I just go by the totally goofy look on your face?"

I give her a sheepish grin.

"That good, huh?" she asks, and I nod. "Tell me everything."

"It was wonderful."

"I want details."

"It was wonderful."

"How was the beard?"

I can almost feel the scratch of his beard against my skin, the way it tickled and teased me.

"Wonderful," I reply simply.

"And his technique? I bet he's not a ram-his-tongue-in-there-with-no-finesse kind of kisser. Am I right?"

"Gross."

"Well?"

"His technique was…wonderful."

She arches her eyebrows. "*Everything* was wonderful?"

I lift a shoulder in a shrug. "There's no other word for it, Chlo. Plain and simple."

She shakes her head, her eyes wide. "You lucky, lucky girl."

I beam at her. She's right. I am a lucky girl. Finally kissing Alex after what had felt like near misses and missed opportunities was more than worth the wait.

"Did you *leave space for God*, as your dad used to tell you?" Chloe gurgles a laugh.

"Not a lot," I admit.

She grins, nodding her head. "I bet you didn't."

"Chlo, it was so romantic. He told me he'd wanted to kiss me before last night, but he wanted it to be perfect, so he waited until after the ball when he knew he could take me to the rooftop to watch the fireworks. And it was perfect. Perfect in every way."

"Nice move, Prince McHottie." She searches my face. "I feel like there's a but coming on."

I scrunch my face. "It's not him. It's Grandmama."

"Please don't tell me you thought about your dad *and* your grandma while kissing Europe's most eligible bachelor?"

I describe the way in which Grandmama warned me off of him.

"I don't get it. What's your grandma's beef with Alex?"

"She thinks he's this horrible ladies' man who'll break my heart."

"To be fair to her…" she leads.

I sit up straighter. "He's not like that anymore. He's changed."

"How can you be sure?"

"He told me."

She rolls her eyes. "Oh, right. Because no guy's ever spun that line to a girl before."

"It's not a line. Trust me. He has changed. He's not the bad boy, heartbreaker, Party Prince he was once. He's kind and he's thoughtful and he's smart, and—"

"Hot."

"Oh, yeah." I grin at her, my belly doing a flip as I take a moment to dwell on just how hot Alex is. "You know I'd never go for a guy like the old Alex."

"Hello? Eric? He's like a poor man's Alexander. The old version of him," she adds before I correct her once more.

In the past, any mention of Eric's name would have had my belly doing somersaults. Not anymore. Eric is nothing in comparison with Alex. Not even close.

"Eric walked all over me, which I let him do. Alex would never do that. Chlo, he's amazing. I've never met anyone like him."

If I had known what she was about to say next, I would not have taken a sip of coffee.

She leans back in her chair, studying me. "Oh, I get it. You're in love with the guy."

"What?" I guffaw, spluttering coffee over my bedding.

"Here." As though she hasn't just said something truly shocking, she casually hands me a cloth napkin, and I wipe my chin with it before blotting the bedding.

"No one said anything about love," I protest.

"Girl, you don't have to. It's written all over your face. You. Love. Alex," she says, accentuating each word. "You're the future Mrs. Madeline Prince McHottie." She giggles at her own joke.

Meanwhile, my jaw slackens.

Do I love Alex?

Sure, I've got some serious feelings for the guy, feelings that go way deeper than simple attraction. Do I blush at the mere mention of his name? Do I think about him day and night? Do I feel incredible in his presence, as though together, we could do anything?

The answer to all my questions is *yes*.

It's true when I say I've never met anyone like him in my life. I find myself thinking about him all the time, wanting to be with him, and then, when we are together, I never want it to end.

Alex has touched my heart in a way no man has before. If that's not love, I don't know what is.

The realization blooms inside like a beautiful rose, warmed by the sun.

I love him. I'm *in* love with him.

I sit with it for a beat. *I love Alex.*

I lift my eyes to Chloe's, my heart expanding in my chest.

She's watching me closely, a look of wonder on her face. "Oh, girl. You are in deep."

I let out a giddy laugh. "I am." My voice cracks and

tears spring to my eyes. I cover my mouth with my hand, in shock.

Chloe raises her own hand in the air as though she's in class. "I get to be your maid of honor."

I let out a surprised laugh. "One step at a time, Chlo. I've just barely figured out I'm in love."

"Ma'am?" Vladimir says after knocking on my bedroom door. "His Royal Highness, Prince Alexander is here. He has requested an audience with you."

Chloe and I share a look before she lets out an excited squeal, clapping her hands together like one of those cymbal-holding monkey toys.

"Chill, okay?" I warn her.

"Totally chill," she confirms, looking anything but. "Don't you want to get dressed first?"

I glance down at my robe. "Dang it!"

I dash to my closet to find something to wear. I throw on the first dress I find—a pale yellow shirt dress with cap sleeves—slide my tennis shoes onto my feet and run a brush through my hair.

"How do I look?" I ask Chloe, excitement pinging around my stomach.

"Like a woman in *lurve*."

"You're cornier than a country song," I say as I head to the door.

"I'm not the one in love," she calls out as I close the door behind me.

Vladimir heralds Alex into the living room. The sight of him makes my heart leap into my throat. He's wearing a white polo shirt tucked into a pair of chinos, with brown leather riding boots with black trim. He looks as good as he did at the polo match, and for a second, I cannot believe that last night I got to kiss this man in the most romantic setting ever.

"Hey, you," I say.

"Hello, Maddie," he replies with a smile that makes my belly flip.

Vladimir closes the door behind him, and Alex and I are left alone.

"We need to talk," he says, and instantly my stomach is in a knot. Did he wake up this morning and realize kissing me last night was a big mistake?

He looks nervous when he says, "Last night was—"

A night that changed my whole world.

"What?" I ask, my heart thudding in my ears.

His shoulders drop. "Look, I'm no good at this."

"Not good at what, exactly?" I ask slowly, wondering if I even want to hear his reply.

He presses his lips together. "I've known women in my life. Some would say too many."

I blink at him. Where is he going with this?

"This is not easy for me."

I brace myself. "Just say it, Alex. Get it over with." My voice is steely.

He shoots me a worried look. "All right. Since you asked, I wanted to let you know that—"

I scrunch my eyes shut. This is going hurt.

"—I've never felt this way about anyone before."

I open my eyes to gawk at him. He's got such a look of vulnerability I want to close the distance between us and wrap my arms around him in reassurance.

The thudding of my heart in my ears is almost too loud to bear. "You haven't?"

The intensity in his eyes as they land on mine tells me that what he felt for me last night was more than just a passing attraction to a member of the opposite sex. It meant something.

Something real.

Something big.

Slowly, he shakes his head. "I want to be a hundred percent honest with you. A part of me thinks this is going way too fast, but the other part of me? That part is telling me to rush straight in with you, boots and all."

He's the one to close the distance between us, and he reaches out and slides his hand into mine. The feeling of his flesh against mine sends a shiver through me.

"What kind of things?" I ask tentatively.

"All of it. Getting to know you better, spending time with you, sharing your world. Showing you mine." He pauses before he adds, "Some more of that spectacular kissing we did last night."

I bite my lip. "Spectacular kissing?"

"Tell me you didn't feel it, too. The thing between us. It's...powerful."

I want to punch the air, perform a series of cartwheels, break into an ecstatic dance routine, all at once. Of course that's probably physically impossible, but wow, do I wish I could do it.

"I feel it, too," I say, a smile claiming my face.

He beams back at me. "Good. Great."

I can hear the nerves in his voice, and it tells me how much he cares for me. A man like Alex isn't tense around women. A man like Alex is self-assured and in control. But around me, it would seem, he's like a nervous teenage boy—and it makes me love him all the more.

"I'm leaving to return to Ledonia with my family later today. If you can, I'd love to spend as much of my remaining time here with you as possible."

"I'd love that."

We're like a couple of goofy kids, holding hands and grinning at one another.

"Good, because I need you to change. I want to show you something, and a dress won't cut it."

Ten minutes later, I've changed, filled Chloe in on our conversation, and I rush to meet Alex outside the palace kitchens.

"Where are we going?" I ask.

"I thought you might like to go and meet Guinevere."

My eyebrows spring up. "Guinevere?"

"You're going to love her. She's very important to me."

Well, this has taken a turn for the concerning. He wants me to meet someone called Guinevere who's very important to him?

We reach the stables, where Alex speaks with a man before leading me through.

"This, my Texan Princess, is Guinevere," he says at one of the stalls, and the stunning chestnut horse Alex rode during the polo match pokes her head out to say hello.

"Oh, *this* Guinevere. The horse," I say in a breathy rush of relief.

Alex pets the horse and fishes some slices of apple from his pocket to feed her. "Hello, Guinie," he coos softly, and seeing him treat her with such love warms my heart. "I've got someone special for you to meet. This is Maddie. Say hello."

"Hi, Guinie," I say as I pet her nose. Her coat is warm and silky under my touch, and I can feel her jaw working as she chews on the apple slices. "What a beautiful girl."

"True," Alex says, his eyes on me, and I wonder whether he means me rather than his horse. "I thought we might take Guinevere out for a ride. Tim has prepared another horse for you."

I blink at him. "You want to go riding?"

A smile teases the edges of his mouth. "I told you I

wanted to show you something, and the best way to get there is on horseback."

"Sure. I mean I haven't ridden for ages, but I'll give it a shot." My bright tone belies my nerves at the thought of climbing on one of these huge beasts, handing over all control.

"But you have ridden before? I thought you said you had."

"Oh, sure. I'll just be a little rusty, that's all."

Truth be told, although I grew up in Texas, I didn't exactly spend my time riding horses on ranches. Houston is very much urban, and I spent considerably more time riding in my car, and even the downtown train, than being on the back of a horse.

Tim appears in the stables, leading a majestic horse with a strikingly contrasting blond mane by its reins.

"Your Royal Highness," Tim says with a bow. "This flaxen chestnut is called Cappuccino. I chose one of our older mares for you. She has an even temperament. I think you'll find her very comfortable to ride."

"She's absolutely gorgeous." I pet her nose, and she eyes me with her big brown eyes. "We're going to get along just fine, you and me. Just fine."

A few minutes later, Tim helps me up onto Cappuccino, and I watch as Alex, skilled horseman that he is, easily slides onto Guinevere.

"Shall we go?" he asks.

"Is now a good time to admit I haven't ridden a horse in a super long time?"

Alex chuckles. "Do you need Tim to lead you for a while to get used to it?"

"Good plan."

Tim takes Cappuccino's reins and we wander around

the yard by the stable until I begin to feel more comfortable.

"How about we start out walking and see how we get on?" Alex suggests.

"Walking, I can do."

Side by side, we meander down one of the long paths on the palace grounds, lined with trees. It's a gorgeous day with the sun overhead, a few wispy clouds scattered across the sky, birds chirping overhead, a light summer breeze cooling us. After a while, we reach an open expanse of grass and Alex suggests we try going a little faster.

"As in run?" I ask, more than a little worried.

"How about we trot?"

"Trot. Sure."

Alex squeezes his legs, leans forward, and Guinevere moves into a trot.

"See? Easy. Now why don't you do that with Cappuccino?" he calls out.

I follow his lead, squeezing my legs and leaning forward, and to my surprise, my horse does exactly what I want her to, although I wonder whether she's simply keeping up with Guinevere.

We ride for some time along the palace path until we reach a wooded area.

"Almost there," Alex says over his shoulder.

"We're going off the path?"

"Through this thicket and out the other side. You okay with that?"

"As long as my buddy Cappuccino is okay, then I'm okay."

But really, it's more the way Alex is taking such good care of me that gives me confidence—although my nice, sedate Cappuccino is part of the equation, too.

We wind our way through the trees until, to my

surprise, we arrive at a serene lake that mirrors the pale blue sky. It's surrounded by lush greenery, with majestic, ancient trees standing sentinel. The air is fresh and filled with the scent of pine and wildflowers, and I breathe everything in.

This place is romantic and gorgeous and literally All. The. Things.

"Beautiful, isn't it?" Alex says.

"It's incredible. How did you even know it existed?"

"Your uncle, Nicolas, used to bring us here when we were children. I rode out here a while ago. It's why I was almost late for your investiture at Parliament, actually. I often think of this place when life gets to be too much. I thought it might resonate with you."

I gaze at the beauty. "It totally resonates."

"Let's allow the horses a drink while we sit and talk."

"Sure." I throw my eyes over him in his white polo shirt exposing his muscular, tan forearms, his hair a little messy from the ride, his handsome face flushed from the exercise.

How did I get so lucky? He's one of the world's most eligible bachelors, and he wants to rush into things with me. Wonderful things.

We climb off our horses—Alex with practiced ease, and me with, shall we say, less practiced ease—and take them to the lake's edge, where they thirstily drink water. It's a warm day and we've been riding for 20 minutes or more. After they've had their fill, we tie them up in the shade, and find a log to sit on in full view of the sparkling lake.

I lean back against Alex's firm chest and he encircles me with his arms. It feels so good, so right, and as I breathe in the fresh pine-scented air, all I can hear is the gentle lapping of the lake's water against its shore, birds singing harmoniously in the trees, and the rustle of leaves, stirred by the soft breeze.

"This is heavenly. Thank you so much for bringing me here. I love it."

He places a soft kiss on the top of my head. "I wanted to share it with you before you found it of your own accord."

"You know, this is the first time I've been on a horse since my mom died? She was an incredible rider. We used to go on these treks together, just her and me. Nothing long. Just an afternoon. It was a lot of fun."

"Do you remember much about her?"

"Some. Not as much as I'd like. I've got pictures and videos of her, of course, and they kind of got merged in my brain with my memories, so much so I don't know if I remember something for real, or if it's just from a picture."

He strokes my arm. "That must be hard."

I turn to look at him, propping myself up with an arm. "Do you remember my mom?"

"She'd already left to marry your dad before I was born, but I do remember meeting her here when I was about 10. I know that because it was right before I was sent to boarding school in England."

"Wait. If you were 10, I would have been eight, which means we would have met. Dad told me I used to play in the formal gardens here with other kids, and I only visited a handful of times before my mom passed."

"So we've known one another since we were children, not since that unfortunate incident in the cupboard?"

"It would seem so."

He leans down and presses a soft kiss to my lips, and it sends a jolt of electricity through me. "I like that."

"Me, too." I nestle against him once more and gaze out at the view.

"I would love it if you would come to visit me at my home in Ledonia. I want to share my world with you, and not just the formal royal stuff, but all the other, everyday stuff."

"The real you."

"Exactly."

"I'd love that. I'm there for the Lunar Ball, of course."

"How could I forget?"

"But I'm only staying the night. I have to come back to Malveaux for some engagements. I'm meeting more of my charities."

"You like that part of the role, don't you?"

"I love it. When we were at the Children's Hospital, I felt like I could bring a little ray of sunshine to their day. It might not be much, but it felt important to me."

He gives me a squeeze. "I love that about you."

Love.

He might not have said those three little words, but hearing the one word fall from his lips has my heart expanding in my chest.

"Remember, I'll see you when you come to the Lunar Ball," he says.

"That's not for two weeks."

"13 days," he replies, and it shows me he's been thinking about us being apart, too.

"Maybe you can come for a proper visit in a month or so?"

The thought of Alex not being here with me sits like a brick in my belly.

"I'd like that."

Alex has been such a big part of my whole experience in Malveaux—some of it terrible, but most of it incredible. The idea of him not being here with me each and every day is one I don't want to have to even contemplate.

He pulls me up onto his lap and I let out a surprised squeal. "A month will be utterly terrible because I won't be able to do this every day." He cups my face in his hands and presses his lips against mine. It's a soft kiss, so very different from last night's passion, but so emotional and meaningful.

"Can I ask you something?" I say.

"Of course you can."

The way Alex reacted to his father after the wife race has been playing on my mind. He accepted what he said without hesitation, not standing up for himself—or for me.

"You know the wife race," I begin.

"I seem to have a vague recollection of it," he teases, his hands running up and down my back.

It's making it hard to concentrate.

"I want to be serious for a second."

"Of course. Be as serious as you want, Texas."

"Why did you back down with your dad so easily?"

"What do you mean?"

"When he got us disqualified because we weren't married, even though grandpapa said it was fine for us to compete? Your sister rightfully won."

He lowers his gaze, his body tensing.

"I don't mean to pry or anything, it's just that you're this super strong and confident guy and then when your dad is around, you change," I say in a rush, questioning whether I should even be saying anything. "You said he was exacting, your word. I get that. He's tough. But you are a grown man. You should be able to stand up for yourself if you want to."

He pulls his lips into a line. "It's not that straight-forward."

"Why not?"

"I don't have the same relationship with my father as you do with yours. He's a very different sort of man."

"I know. He's 'exacting', not the warm cuddly type. I

get it. But that doesn't mean you can't be who you want to be around him."

He arches an eyebrow at me. "You're my therapist now, are you?"

"I just care about you, and I didn't like the way things went between you two after the wife race."

"What could I have done? Told him no, that Amelia and her rugby player won fair and square?"

"Well, yes."

"That would go down like a lead balloon."

"And then what would happen?"

"He'd be angry with me, just like he was when I won the cheese rolling event last year."

"Did you survive?"

He pulls his brows together. "What do you mean?"

"Did you survive standing up to him last year?"

"He wasn't happy. I see what you're doing, but you don't know him the way I do. He's uncompromising and tough. That's just the way he is."

Although I'm glad I brought it up, it's clearly falling on deaf ears. And perhaps it's really none of my business anyway. After all, king Frederick has been Alex's dad his whole life. I'm a newbie.

"Okay. Sorry I brought it up."

He lifts his features into a smile. "I like that you care."

"I do." I cup his face in my hand and brush my lips softly against his. "I do care. When do we have to leave?" I ask, not wanting him to go.

"Soon."

My heart drops. I don't want this to end. Ever.

"Oh."

"Look, I know you'll need to be here in Malveaux for Christmas with your grandparents, and I know it's a long way off, but would you like to come for a visit around that time of year? Ledonia is magical at Christmas. And that's coming from a guy."

The thought of spending Christmas with Alex and his family fills my heart with warmth. "Maybe Christmas Eve, and I could leave in time to get back here to celebrate with my grandparents?"

"I'd love that."

There's that word again.

"I need to warn you, my mother is a total Christmas-er."

"That is so not a word."

"It is if I say it is. I'm going to be King someday, you know," he teases.

"Tell me about your mom and Christmas."

"Well, she decorates everywhere, and I do mean *every*where. Some people limit themselves to a single tree, a wreath at the front door, and perhaps some extra decorations on the mantlepiece. That's far too restrained for my mother. She has a tree in every room, including our bedrooms, twinkling lights wrapping every regular tree and fence, garlands draped on the staircases, as well as a life-size nativity scene."

"It sounds magical."

"It is until she pulls out that year's Christmas jumpers, which she insists we all wear from Christmas Eve until midnight on Christmas Day."

I bite back a smile. "I bet you look very fetching in a Christmas sweater."

"You'll just have to wait and see when you spend Christmas with us this year."

"It's decided then."

We share a smile and I feel the strength of the connection that we've built between us over these short couple of weeks. It's strong, so much stronger than I would ever have imagined. But there's something about Alex, something real. Something I never expected to find. The last thing I want to do is let it go.

He leans his forehead against mine, our breath mingling. "I care so much for you, Maddie. More than I have about anyone before," he says, his voice low and soft.

"Really?" I ask, my heart pounding like the rhythmic baseline at a club.

The crack in those rusted-over hinges of my heart has been thrown wide open by this man.

His eyes are darker than usual, filled with intensity that has my breath catching in my throat. "The truth is I'm falling for you, my beautiful Texas Princess."

His words are sweet, sweet music to my ears.

"I'm falling for you, too," I murmur, my throat suddenly dry.

I'm in deep.

He pulls me into a dizzying kiss, and I span my palms across his firm back, my heart exploding with my feelings for this man. This man I misjudged.

This man I'm falling for with every passing day.

"I've never felt like this before," he admits.

"Me neither," I reply, grinning at him. "I think I like it."

He laughs, low and sexy. "I think I like it, too." He kisses me once more before he pulls back and says, "By no means allow the feelings I've just confessed for you to be in any way an influence on how you answer this."

"Answer what?"

"Have you decided whether you're going to stay in Malveaux?"

"Ah."

The Big Question, an answer to which my grandparents, and the whole country, are eager to know. An answer to which I've been eager to reach.

The truth is, I have reached an answer.

Telling Alex will make it a grand total of two of us knowing, him and me.

"I've been working through that question since the day I arrived. Being here, being a princess, is a big change for me. I wanted to spend some time figuring out what's right for me as well as what's right for my grandparents. Staying here could mean agreeing to becoming Queen someday."

"Could?"

"My uncle hasn't officially abdicated yet. I am what you said I was: a backup princess."

His eyes darken. "You're no one's backup, Texas."

This man.

"What conclusion have you come to, if any?" he leads and I notice the eagerness in his eyes.

I clear the emotion from my throat. "I think I want to stay, whether I'm the next Queen or not."

His face lights up. "Think?"

"Okay, I *know*," I reply with a giddy laugh.

"You won't be heading back to your old life in Texas?"

I press my lips together as I shake my head. "I like it here. I like *me* here."

He grabs a hold of me, making me squeal, pulling me up against him as he presses an urgent kiss to my lips. "You have no idea how happy that makes me," he murmurs between kisses.

"Me, too," I reply.

I'm staying in Malveaux. Someday, I could be Queen.

And I'm falling for a prince.

Talk about my world being turned upside down in the most wonderful, unexpected way.

"Have you told your grandparents?"

I shake my head. "You're the first person I've told."

His lips pull into a smile. "I like that you told me first."

"I needed to test the idea out on someone before I told my grandparents," I tease. "You were an easy target."

"Is that so?" He plants another kiss on my lips.

"I plan on telling them when they're back from France next week, so you need to keep it to yourself. I figured it was best face-to-face."

"Mum's the word. What made you decide to stay?"

"I know it's weird, but I feel like I belong here. Like this was where I was always meant to be. It's as though my old life was a holding pattern for this, my real life. Does that sound crazy?"

"Not at all. It sounds like you've found your calling."

"You know I was freaking out when I visited the hospital that day, but doing that kind of thing, showing compassion for people, using my influence to help them in whatever small way I can? That has meaning for me, and it sure as heck has more meaning than filling in endless spreadsheets for a glazing company."

"There are some real benefits to this life. You can bring not only a new perspective to the role, but experiences from your former life also. I suspect you will make an incredible queen someday."

I beam at him, my heart swelling. "Thank you."

"I mean it. I'm not just saying this because of how I feel about you. You're a good person, Maddie, and you take your new role seriously. I cannot believe I was once suspicious of your intentions. You're the very opposite of someone hungry for fame."

"It's about time you noticed that," I reply on a light laugh.

"Oh, I noticed." He glances at his watch. "I hate to tell you, but we need to go."

I glance around at the beauty of this place. "Bummer."

Alex jumps off the log, offers me his hand, and we make our way back to the horses.

We ride back to the palace with not only a plan for our future, but a life-altering decision about mine. A decision I know is the right call, for me and for my family. And now that I've told Alex, I need to share the news with my grandparents—and the world.

It's a brave, exciting, and wonderful world for Madeline Josephine Turner from Houston, TX, and I cannot wait for it to begin.

Chapter 25

Alexander

" Hearts are breaking across the continent as photographs of our dashing prince and his newest conquest, none other than the newly minted Princess Madeline, emerge showing a couple quite possibly in love. Photos of the two dancing at the ball to mark the end of The Games show neither the Princess nor the Prince could keep their eyes from one another. Do we hear wedding bells in the not-too-distant future?

This reader is holding her breath and hoping for the best.

#IsHeOffTheMarket
#PassTheKleenex

Yours in the very deepest of shock,

Fabiana Fontaine xx

It's an odd thing when it finally happens. One minute I'm simply going about my business, living my life the way I always have, and the next I find myself falling for someone so spectacularly perfect for me it feels as though I've been waiting for her my whole life.

Perhaps I have? Perhaps she's why I wasted so much of my time on frivolous things, on surface level relationships with women who ultimately didn't even come close to touching my heart?

I'll never know. What I do know is Maddie means everything to me, and now that I have her in my life, I never want to let her go.

"How short are we from our goal?" I ask Mia Moreno, the C.A.Y.A.C. finance manager, seated to my left in the conference room of our downtown Villadorata offices.

"Put it this way, sir, we're going to need you to weave some more of your royal magic at the next charity event to get people to dig deeper into their pockets," she replies. She presses a button on her laptop and the large screen on the wall shows a graph of where our financials are currently, and where they need to be in order to raise the necessary funds to expand our research as we hope to do.

"As you can see, it's a big number," Mia says.

"We have confidence we can achieve it, however," adds the CEO, Lorenzo Amato, a man with an excellent reputation for getting things done, that we brought into the organization only 12 months prior, who so far, has proven his weight in gold.

"I'll do whatever you tell me," I say.

Lorenzo smiles. "We hoped you'd say that because we've got a few ideas."

We spend the next hour strategizing different fundraising ideas, and me agreeing to approach a number of people in my network. One of the things about being a prince is you get to meet a lot of interesting and talented people. Tapping a few on the shoulder to help in the name of charity is something I'm more than happy to do.

Once I say goodbye to Mia, Lorenzo, and their team, with a plan firmly in place, my phone lights up with a message from Maddie. Since I've been back in Ledonia, it's the main way we talk during the day, and I look forward to seeing her beautiful face in the evening when we finally get the chance for a private video chat.

I read the message.

> I met the Prime Minister today on my own. I rock!

I smile as I tap out my reply.

> You totally rock. I've noticed that. What did you talk about?

> She did most of the talking, which is fine because I don't know a whole lot about Malveauxian politics. Or American politics, for that matter. But I'm learning.

> That's because politics are completely dull.

> You're going to make such a good king some day 😉

> Rude.

> Tell me you've suddenly become interested in politics and I'll change my mind about you.

> I thought you already had changed your mind about me, in the best way possible.

> You know what? I've been thinking about it since you've been gone, and I think I was right about you in the first place.

I let out a laugh as I stand on the footpath by the car, and my driver, Craig, shoots me a quizzical look before he rearranges his features into appearing impassive.

"Just catching up on my messages," I explain.

"Of course, sir. Back to the palace?" He opens the door and I slip inside.

"Actually, I need to make a stop on the way. Can you take me to Via Mazzi?"

"Of course."

I get comfortable and tap out a reply.

> How about we meet in that cupboard when I'm back next month? We could rewrite history together.

> More kissing, less punching?

Desire grips my belly. What I wouldn't do to have her here with me in the back of this car, her soft, plump lips ready and waiting to be claimed by mine.

> Definitely more kissing. It's my favorite thing to do with you.

> I noticed that. It's so weird to be here without you or my grandparents. I really miss you.

> Not as much as I miss you.

> See? That's what I love about you the most: you're not the least bit competitive.

I smile to myself at her use of that four-letter word. Although we've shared that we're falling for one another, for me, I know I'm heading towards love as fast as a bullet train. No one has filled my mind the way she does, every night and every day. No one has made me feel like this, as though I could take on the world itself and win.

If that's not love, I don't know what is.

My phone pings with another message from Maddie.

> It was actually so interesting meeting with the PM. The government is building affordable and sustainable housing, and I've agreed to open the project for Grandpapa in a couple months' time.

> You'll be wielding a large pair of scissors?

> The largest I can find 😅

> I like the way you're passionate about things. It's very sexy, Texas.

It's hard not to be. Margarita is such an inspirational woman. Did you know she grew up in a government house with a single mom? She put herself through college and got a scholarship for a master's program before she entered politics? Totally self-made.

She does sound inspirational. I'm glad you admire her.

Totally. I got all this handed to me on a platter whereas she had to work for what she has.

I know where your vote is sitting in the next general election.

Royal, remember? Can't vote. How did the C.A.Y.A.C. meeting go?

We brainstormed a bunch of fundraising ideas and I'm approaching some musicians to put on a concert.

Anyone I know?

That depends. Have you heard of Taylor Swift?

Are you serious??!!

I'm more hopeful than anything. But wouldn't it be amazing? We have a new research project we need to fund. We're all so hopeful it will give us the breakthrough we're looking for.

I hope so, too. If you do get Tay Tay, I could be your date. Actually, I'd be your date to see anyone perform.

But then everyone would be looking at your beauty.

Flatterer.

Just saying it the way it is.

"What number on Via Mazzi are you looking for, sir?" Craig asks.

"I'm not sure." I peer out the window and spot the shop I'm looking for. "Actually, right here, if you don't mind."

"Of course, sir," he replies as he pulls the vehicle over.

I must go. I've got important things to do.

Go. Do your important things, and make sure you look hot while doing them.

Always 😉 Talk tonight?

I've got a dinner with the King and Queen of Sweden.

Look who's all important now. Afterwards?

I wouldn't miss it xoxo

xoxoxoxoxoxoxoxo

Overachiever.

xoxoxoxoxoxoxoxoxoxoxoxoxoxoxoxoxoxo and more when I see you when you finally come to visit me here.

I'm counting the days. Literally. (it's 11, btw) xoxo

I climb out of the car with the biggest, goofiest grin on my face. In 11 days, Maddie will be here and I'll get to show her my country and Villadorata and the palace and everything. Because I want nothing more than to share absolutely everything in my life with her.

The teenage girl behind the counter blinks at me in recognition. "How-how can I help you?" she asks.

"Good afternoon. Do you by any chance have mint chocolate chip gelato?"

"We do, Your Royal Highness," she replies.

"Do you ship to Malveaux?"

"You want to ship an ice cream to Malveaux?" she asks in disbelief.

"More like a tub. One this size." I point at the large tubs of ice cream under the protective Perspex cover.

"A whole tub? I'm sure we could, for you, sir."

I smile to myself as I imagine Maddie's face as she opens the gift to find her favorite ice cream. "Thank you. I'll give you the address."

Chapter 26

Maddie

One thing I've learned when you're a member of a royal family is you can't just rock up to your grandparents and tell them you've got news, even when you know that news will be music to their ears. That would be way too straightforward. You need to get in touch with their people to request an audience, find a time that suits both your calendars, made all the more complicated when your grandparents have been away for 10 days, and then you probably only get about 30 minutes to actually meet.

So, when Vladimir informs me both of my grandparents are available to see me this afternoon, the day they arrived back from France, I almost faint from shock.

Today, I get to make my grandparents ecstatically happy.

I said a sad goodbye to Chloe last week, promising to keep her up to date with all my goings on, and now I'm sitting with Grandmama and Grandpapa in their private drawing room, the afternoon sun shining through the large windows on the floor, the room decorated just as all the rooms in the palace are decorated: ornate, old fashioned, and super expensive.

But there's a distinct atmosphere in the room, one I haven't experienced with my grandparents before.

"You seem very bright and chipper today, Madeline," Grandpapa observes.

"I do?" I ask, feeling inexplicably guilty.

"There's nothing wrong with being bright and chipper, I was simply wondering whether there was any particular reason?" he asks.

Oh, there's more than one reason. There's my decision to stay, which I'm about to share with them and totally make their day, and then there's the man I haven't been able to get out of my mind.

Alex.

We've been messaging every day since he left, video chatting at night, and a few days ago he sent me a tub of the most incredible tasting mint chocolate chip gelato I've ever had in my entire life. It was so cute of him to remember it was my favorite, something I told him that day he took me to see the view on the motorcycle.

The distance has shown me that what I feel for him is real, and even though I haven't seen him in real life for almost two weeks now, I find I'm falling for him more and more each day.

And in a few short days, I'm going to see him again when I travel to Ledonia for the first time to attend the Lunar Ball.

"While you were away, I went riding to this beautiful lake not too far from here," I tell them, the memory fresh in my mind.

"Lake Glinthorpe. It is a lovely lake," Grandmama comments. "Did you go with Chloe?"

"No, I went with someone else actually. I went with Prince Alexander."

I watch my grandparents for their reaction. They share a look, both of them looking like I've told them I visited the lake with a bunch of gang bangers to play with guns.

Grandmama's already given me two messages about Alex: she told me to befriend him and warned me off of him romantically. I followed through on one of those messages, so the way I see it, she's got to be at least half way happy with me.

"Alexander's a jolly good horseman, I'll give him that. Did you find it hard to keep up?" Grandpapa asks.

"We went slow." I flick my gaze to my grandmama. Her features appear frozen. "You okay there, Grandmama?"

"Quite, dear." She places her cup carefully on its saucer. "You two seem to have become friendly."

I can't help but grin. "Just doing what you told me."

Except the kissing part.

"You know, Maddie, we're so very glad you called and asked to meet with us today," Grandpapa says in a measured tone. "You're making such wonderful progress here. You have taken on your new role with such courage and dedication."

"Courage and dedication?" I ask, genuinely pleased he sees me that way. I would have said I'd taken on my new role more with paralyzing fear and mistakes. But maybe that's just me?

"Absolutely. Your grandpapa is right, my dear. You are doing your mother proud," Grandmama replies and I lift my eyes to the oil painting of my mother, hung above the fireplace. She's wearing a white gown, her hair pinned up, looking out at us with a whimsical smile on her face. It's such a likeness, it almost takes my breath away.

"I really am trying my best, and I wanted to talk to you about something. It's a decision I've made."

"Oh?" Grandmama says.

They both look at me with hope in their eyes, and I feel a surge of joy, knowing that what I'm about to tell them will make them both so happy.

"I've been thinking about it, and I've decided that I want to make my life here in Malveaux," I say.

They look between each other.

"Does that mean...?" Grandpapa leads.

I grin at them, that surge of joy washing right over me until I'm drenched. "If you need me, I want to be your heir."

"Oh, my dear!" Grandmama exclaims, her hand over her heart. "That is wonderful news. Wonderful!"

Grandpapa jumps to his feet. Well, as far as a 70-some-thing-year-old can jump. "Oh, Madeline. I am so happy to hear this. Thank you."

"I'm pretty happy to tell you, too. I feel good about it."

He grips my hands, his skin rough and dry against mine. "You've made me the happiest man in Europe. Truly."

Grandmama joins us, and together we share a hug, our little family joined together in shared delight.

This decision feels good. It feels right. I'd always felt like I hadn't fit into my life back in Houston. Like I belonged somewhere else. Now I've found where I belong, and it's in Malveaux, with my grandparents. Of course I miss my dad, as well as my friends, and I definitely miss the tacos from Manuel's.

But this is where I'm meant to be. This is where I belong. And to know that I'm not only making my grandparents incredibly happy, but I'm perhaps even saving the Malveauxian monarchy from total destruction at my great uncle's hands? Well, that's the icing on the already 10-foot cake.

"Oh, Maddie, my dear. To think, the monarchy is now assured."

"It is, my darling. It is," Grandpapa confirms.

"Someday, you may be Queen Madeline," Grandmama exclaims, her eyes getting misty. "Oh, I do so like the sound of that."

"As nice as that sounds, I hope it's a long way away before I'm Queen," I say, my throat tight.

My grandparents share a look, the open, excited smiles of only a moment ago replaced with something pinched, worried. Fear grips my belly. Is Grandpapa sick?

"What's going on?" I ask.

"Shall we sit?" Grandmama suggests.

This has gone from super happy to super scary in about three seconds flat.

I sit with a healthy dose of trepidation. "Should I be worried?"

"No, no," Grandpapa assures. "As you know, the Kingdom of Malveaux has always passed the crown down to the heir at the time of the monarch's death."

I do not like the direction this conversation is taking.

"Are you okay, Grandpapa?" I ask, my heart beginning

to thud.

My mind takes over with possibilities. None of them good.

I've only just gotten to know Grandpapa and now he's what? Dying?

I can't lose him. Not so soon. Not for a long time.

"I'm slowing down, my dear. It's not that I'm ill or dying or anything quite so dramatic."

"Oh, thank goodness," I reply in a rush, relief sweeping through me.

"It's just that this job, as historical and as noble and important as it is, does take quite a toll. I'll be 76 at my next birthday, which I know is young for many people, but for me it's…well, my role has worn me out a little."

"You're tired of the job, not anything else, right?" I'm implying that I hope he's not tired of life, but I don't want to be quite so blatant.

"Yes, my dear. No one tells you when you ascend to the throne just how all-encompassing it becomes. I've loved it, and it's been my pleasure to perform my kingly duties, but I feel I would like to formally relinquish my monarchical authority."

I look at him blankly. "You're going to do what now?"

Grandmama laughs. "Speak in simpler terms, my darling."

"I want to retire," Grandpapa says.

"Can you retire from being king? I thought it was a whole life thing here in Malveaux."

"It is, however one can choose to step down should one want to," he clarifies. "I would like to be able to sit on the proverbial front porch and watch the world go by for a while. I'd like to slow down and smell the roses, possibly wander around like the peafowl."

Grandmama gives his hand a little squeeze, and I'm

struck afresh by the love they share.

"Your grandpapa has put his all into the role of King," Grandmama says. "He would like a change. We both would."

"It's been very stressful wondering whether Nicolas will actually abdicate," Grandpapa says. "Knowing you want to take on the role in case he does is very reassuring for this old man."

"You're not old, Grandpapa. You're simply mature."

His face creases into a smile. "You're very sweet, Maddie. The country is falling in love with you."

I press my lips together. The country isn't the only one falling in love.

"When are you thinking of stepping down? I mean, I'm good with becoming Queen someday if that's how this works out, but is there any need to rush this thing?"

My grandpapa laughs, and it strikes me it's not a sound I'm all that familiar with. Perhaps the weight of being King feels as though it's beginning to lift for him? "Let's sit down together and work out a plan."

"Sure. Have you heard from my uncle? Do you know what his plans are?"

He lowers his head. "We have not."

When the heck will this man reappear and tell us what his final decision is?

"My sense is that we need to give the people at least a year's notice, possibly longer," Grandpapa says.

"A year?" I let out a breath. "I thought you were going to say next week. A year I can do."

He beams at me. "A year it is then, my dear. A year it is."

"Now, my dear. There's another topic we need to address," Grandmama begins, and I already know where she's heading.

Alex.

"I know, and I want to reassure you on that front," I say to preempt them.

Grandmama's eyebrows raise to her hairline. "Reassure us? Does that mean you and Alexander are *not* involved in a romantic liaison?"

"Look, I get it. Really, I do. We all know Alex had a certain reputation a while back. But that's the old Alex. I promise you, he's changed," I protest. I can't help the smile from claiming my face as I think of what he means to me. "He's so much more than some good-time guy. You have to trust me when I tell you my heart is completely safe with him."

My grandparents exchange a look.

"Your…heart?" Grandmama questions.

Grandpapa lets out a breath. "This is more serious than we thought."

"But you see, that's the point. It is serious. *He's* serious. About me. And I'm serious about him."

My grandparents look like I've told them *I'm* going to abdicate.

I lean my elbows on my knees. "You're worried that he's going to break my heart. I know that's what everyone thinks. If only you knew the Alex I know, you'd see what a truly wonderful person he is."

Grandmama's voice trembles when she asks, "Are you in love with him?"

I swallow, my mouth suddenly dry. "I know I'm heading that way. He's the most amazing man I've ever known."

Grandmama lets out a whimper, her hand flying to her mouth.

"Seriously, why is this such a big deal?" I ask.

"Does he return this affection?" Grandpapa asks.

"He does."

Grandpapa mutters something in Malveauxian I don't understand, and Grandmama looks like she might faint. Actually faint.

"Are you okay, Grandmama?" I ask, springing to my feet.

Surely the fact that I have strong feelings for Alex, a man who is important to my new country, with whom we have a long and important history, is a good thing?

"What can I do?" I think fast. "Smelling salts? Isn't that what people have in the movies when they faint? I can go get you some." If only I knew what they were and where to find them.

She waves away my concern.

"I think you should sit back down again, Madeline," Grandpapa says, his tone grave.

I do as I'm told, something in his tone gripping my belly.

"We thought it was just a passing fancy and that it would run its course. But it seems that isn't the case," Grandpapa says.

My eyes dart between them. "What could be more perfect than me being romantically involved with a prince of the country we have a 'special relationship' with? I-I thought you'd be happy about it."

"Happy?" Grandmama questions, her tone sharp. "How could we be happy about you having an affair with Alexander?" she asks, dismissing my very real and wonderful feelings for Alex with an ugly word.

I cross my arms over my body, concern twisting my belly. "It's not an affair. It's more than that. I don't get it. What have I done wrong?"

Grandpapa raises his chin. "Of course you don't understand. How could you? You haven't studied the history of our two countries. You don't know what came before."

I scrunch my brows together. Is now the time to mention Wikipedia?

"What does the way I feel about Alex have to do with history?"

"Everything we do involves history," he replies.

"With all due respect, you're going to have to stop talking in riddles so I can understand."

Grandpapa is the one to reply. "Our two countries have an extremely important relationship, without which neither of the monarchies would have survived."

The "special relationship". Heard it before.

"We are progressive here in Malveaux, the laws of the land allowing succession to pass from parent to child regardless of their gender. Ledonia is not."

"Alex told me about that. It's kind of archaic that only sons can inherit the throne."

He continues. "Alexander is King Frederic's heir. He will inherit the throne when his father turns 65, which is a matter of only seven years away."

So far, they're not telling me anything I don't already know.

Grandmama steeples her fingers. "Do you know what happens if a Crown Princess of Malveaux were to marry a Crown Prince of Ledonia?"

Wait, what? Marriage? No one said anything about marriage.

"Let's not jump the gun here, okay? We've barely admitted we're into each other. We've only known each other for a matter of weeks."

Despite my protest, an image of Alex and I together, married, fills my mind. He's holding me in his arms, gazing at with me with such love in his eyes it causes my breath to hitch, and I know. I just know.

Alex *is* the man I want to marry.

I want to be with him forever, to build a life with him, to have a family and share all that life can offer.

A deep sense of calm engulfs me. Calm and pure joy.

It's him. It's Alex.

My grandmama whimpers once more, telling me my thoughts are written right across my face in Vegas-sized lights. "Oh, my darling. It's worse than we'd feared."

"It's a good thing, Grandmama. I've never felt like this about anyone before in my life."

Grandpapa clears his throat. "I'll put it plainly for you. Because of the Ledonian law of ascension, if you marry Alexander, you'll have to give up your claim as heir to the Malveauxian throne."

I gawk at him in astonishment. "I would?"

"Marrying Alexander spells the end to your life as a member of our royal family. If Nicolas signs the abdication papers—" he breaks off.

"Is he likely to sign them?" I ask, my voice meek with shock.

"We don't know," he admits. "What we do know is without you, the Crown may end up being passed to Edgar, which will mean the end of the monarchy of this country."

Grandmama lets out another whimper.

I want to be with Alex, but I want my new life in Malveaux, too. But also, I would hurt my grandparents if I chose him over being in line for the throne. But not choosing Alex will hurt him—and it'll hurt me.

My head pounds with the choice I know I'll have to make.

But how can I ever, ever choose?

Chapter 27

Alexander

I dive into the outdoor pool, relishing the cool after my ride through the parklands. I've been back at the palace in Ledonia's capital of Villadorata for a couple of days and my head is full of Maddie. Maddie and the fact that she's falling for me. Maddie and the fact that she's decided to stay in Malveaux.

How lucky can a prince get?

Incredibly lucky, as it turns out.

With steady strokes, I glide through the water, turning

to breathe in a pattern I've used since childhood. *Stroke, stroke, stroke, breath, stroke, stroke, stroke, breath.* Our parents saw the ability to swim as extremely important, and I've never lost the feeling being in the water gives me each time I dive in. It's a combination of a sense of calm, mixed with power, and right now I need it to help me get rid of some of the adrenaline from my system.

Today is the day I see Maddie again after two weeks away from her.

Although we've been messaging one another since I left Malveaux, I've missed her terribly. There's a gaping hole in my heart that only she can fill.

I've tried to focus on other things, to get my work done, but she's invaded my every thought, and I've literally been counting the hours until I can see her again. To touch her again. To kiss her again.

Because kissing my Texas Princess is easily my new favorite thing to do.

I reach the end of the pool and take a tumble turn, using my legs against the wall to power myself back through the water. Stroke after stroke I swim, length after length, and with every stroke, every breath, I'm thinking of her.

Eventually, I reach the end of my set and clasp the edge of the pool, gulping in air.

"You showing off again?" a voice says, and I pull my goggles off to see Sofia standing at the water's edge in a one-piece swimsuit, her hair swept up into a swim cap.

"It's what I do," I tell her with my tongue metaphorically in my cheek as I catch my breath.

"Race you to the end?" she asks.

"That's not fair. You haven't swum a hundred lengths already."

"A hundred lengths? Pull the other one, Alex."

"Okay, not a hundred, but more than you."

"Chicken." She throws me a smile before she puts her goggles in place and dives elegantly into the pool.

"Oh, you've *got* to be joking," I grumble as I slide my goggles back on and throw myself into another length.

I may be exhausted, but I can't let my bossy older sister get away with beating me, now, can I?

But beat me she does—only because she dived in and got a head start—and she's still gloating when we grab our towels and sit on a couple of the pool loungers in the sun.

"Face it, Alex, you're not as young as you once were," she says as she leans back, a smirk on her pretty face, her long hair released from her swim cap.

"I'm younger than you!"

"Yes, but some of us age better than others, don't we? I haven't spent my 20s partying."

I shake my head. "If you say so. But you can hardly say that was a fair competition. Now, if you want a real race—"

"No, thank you," she replies, interrupting me. "I've proven my point."

"If your point is that you can only beat me when you have an incredibly unfair advantage, then yes, you're right. You have."

She lifts her sunglasses and smirks at me before she settles back into her lounger. Beating me fairly does not appear to be a high priority to her.

"I've made a decision," she says after we've been relaxing in silence, me catching my breath after my workout, and her? Well, one length hardly constitutes a work out. She's simply relaxing.

"Are you going to share your decision?"

"I'm getting married."

I bolt upright in my seat. "What?!" I guffaw.

"You heard me."

"But Sofe, you're not even seeing anyone. Are you?"

She shifts in her seat. "Father's arranging it."

It's not often my older sister leaves me speechless, but she's certainly managed it today.

She peers at me over her sunglasses. "Well? Aren't you going to say something?"

"I…I'm not sure what to say, exactly. Why, is probably a good place to start."

"Because it's been a long time since I met anyone even vaguely interesting, and I'm 27. Our parents will arrange a marriage for me when I turn 28, anyway. That's the way it goes for us Ledonian princesses, you know."

"You don't have to give in like that, though. This is the 21st Century. Women are allowed to be single, you know."

"I don't want to be single. I want to be married."

"To a chinless wonder?" I ask, recalling an earlier conversation with her on the topic of arranged marriages.

"He might have a chin, perhaps even a lovely square one."

I arch my brows at her. "What about love?"

"Oh, love isn't all it's cracked up to be, as far as I can see."

My heart softens. Sofia had her heart broken some years ago, and I'm not sure she's ever fully recovered.

"Sofe—"

She shoots me a warning look. "Don't. I'm over him. It was a long time ago. All I want now is to marry a nice man with whom I can spend my life and have children with. If I fall in love with him, then wonderful."

"And if not?"

"Then I'll be absolutely fine," she says with determination in her voice.

I swing my legs over the side of the lounger to face her.

"Don't do it. I'll set you up with some of my friends, put you on every dating app. Anything to stop this madness."

"Alex, I know your friends, and a princess on a dating app? Are you mad? The thing is, we can't all afford the luxury of finding The One, can we?"

Maddie fills my thoughts and I find myself smiling, despite this nuclear bomb Sofia's just detonated about her own life.

"Oh, my gosh." She looks like she's doing her best imitation of a fish. "The stories are true. You and Maddie are involved in some sort of mad affair. I thought the media was just making a mountain out of a mole hill."

We haven't officially come out as a couple, but I'm not going to deny my feelings for Maddie. Not to my sister, anyway. The media is another matter altogether, but then they're right about one thing: I'm very much off the market, as they put it in that trending hashtag of theirs. I'm Team Maddie all the way. And it feels amazing.

"Sofe, it really is the most wonderful thing."

"What is?"

"When you find you're falling for someone."

She pushes her sunglasses on top of her head. "You're falling for her? As in you *love* her?"

I smile, enjoying her shock. "That's right, Sofe. I can shock you, too. At long last, your brother has fallen in love."

"Are you serious? You're in *love* with her?"

"Is it so hard to believe?"

"It is, actually. You're you. None of us ever thought you'd actually fall in love."

"That's because I hadn't met Maddie."

She shakes her head, her eyes as wide as a pool ball. "Tell me everything."

"It's really a very simple story. We met, and after

initially despising one another, we realized we actually did quite like each other. We were spending quite a lot of time together, you see, and one thing led to another, and we fell in love."

"I can't believe it."

"Does that mean you're happy for me?"

"Of course I am." She leaps to her feet and pulls me up into a hug. "I'm really happy for you. I'm just surprised, that's all. I didn't know you'd hung up your party shoes."

"Oh, I did. A long time ago, only the media decided they didn't like the new version of me, so they made it seem as though I was seducing every woman I met."

She gives a wry smile. "Sounds exhausting. And now you've gone and fallen in love with the American Princess."

Warmth fills my heart. "I have."

Maddie is everything I want. Of course she's utterly beautiful, with her long dark hair, sparkling, expressive blue eyes, her perfect nose and full, kissable lips. Oh, those lips.

But she's so much more than just her looks. She's a good person, her heart in very much the right place. She cares. She's kind. What's more, she's got a real spark to her, a spark that lights up the room and makes my heart beat faster.

"Does she love you back?"

I can't stop a huge grin from claiming my face. "She does."

Sofia puts her hand over her heart. "Oh, Alex! You really are a dark horse, aren't you? Here we all were thinking we'd got you pegged and you've gone off and fallen in love with the new princess of Malveaux. I suppose you're going to tell me you're going to ask her to marry you, next." She rolls her eyes.

It's a strange thing when it finally happens. If anyone had suggested I marry any of the women I've dated before,

I would have flat out laughed in their face. But with Maddie, it's different. They say when you know, you know, and not a truer word can be said. With Maddie, I know. It's as simple as that. I want to spend the rest of my life with her. I want her to be my wife.

"You've gone all smiley again," she says. "You *are* going to propose!"

"Not yet, but someday. There's no rush. I've only known her less than three weeks."

"But that's obviously long enough to fall in love." Sofia touches the tips of her fingers to her lips, her eyes glistening with tears. "Alex, I'm so happy for you. For both of you." She hugs me again before we sit back down on our loungers.

"Wait a sec. Does she know about our law?"

I lean back in my lounger and get comfortable. "You may need to be more specific. We have rather a lot of laws here in Ledonia."

"You know, the law about who the heir to our throne marries."

"There isn't a law. I can marry whomever I like, unless I decide to have my marriage arranged, which it seems some of us are happy to do."

She doesn't react. "I'm pretty sure the law says if you and Maddie get married, she'll have to give up her throne."

My heart skips a beat. "What?"

"I can't remember what it's called. Some law that was made a gazillion years ago of course, like a lot of the ridiculous laws around here."

I knit my brows together. "Are you sure?"

She waves her hand in the air as though what she's just told me means nothing, when in reality it means everything. Maddie has found a real purpose in her role as princess, and I know how much becoming Queen someday means to her. Although we've never spoken about marriage, I for one am certain that it's where we're heading. Marriage is the next logical step when you fall as deeply in love as we have, a step I hope to take with her before too long.

But for her to marry me, she would have to give up her Kingdom?

It seems simply too farfetched, like the plot to some royal movie.

"Are you sure you're not just making this up?" I ask, forcing lightness into my tone.

"Of course I'm not, but you'll have to check with Father."

I'm on my feet before she even finishes her sentence.

Chapter 28

Maddie

I wait in the gardens of the royal palace in Villadorata. It's adorned with fairy lights strung from tree to tree, under which a fountain glows in the soft light. The full moon is out in all its glory, casting ethereal shadows across the scene. Vladimir's ever watchful eye is scanning the scene as I await my introduction to the Court of Ledonia.

Tonight is the Lunar Ball to celebrate the first full moon of Fall. Although the palace is stunning, the gardens beautiful, and everyone is in whimsical costumes, it's impossible for me to take it all in.

My mind is elsewhere.

Since the day my grandparents told me I would have to give up my position in line to the throne to marry Alex, it's all I've been able to think about. Through my visit to a homeless shelter, a dinner with the French Prime Minister and his wife, and my journey here this afternoon to Villadorata, the capital city of Ledonia, it's been eating away at me.

I know I need to talk to Alex about it, but this is definitely the sort of thing I've got to do in person. I can't exactly call him and say, *hey, you know how we've kissed a few times now and told each other we've got feelings for each other? Well, I'm jumping 723 steps ahead to us falling in love and getting married, and I've got something I need to tell you.*

Nope. No way.

I mean, what guy wants to hear *that* from someone he's barely even begun to date?

So, tonight it is, the first time I've seen Alex since my conversation with my grandparents.

Nervous? Me?

My stomach's doing more flips than a rodeo clown.

My delicate, translucent fairy wings sit high on my back, my strapless ivory floor-length gown's light layers whimsical. I'm Drew Barrymore in *Ever After*, telling myself to *just breathe*. Only I don't have an evil stepmother about to tear my wings from my dress. Instead, I've got the weight of an impossible decision, choosing between my family, my new country, and *him*.

The man I love.

"Ready, miss?" Vladimir asks in an echo of my first royal event, back when I was a nervous little mouse being presented to Malveaux as a princess for the first time.

Oh, how times have changed.

I might not be that frightened little mouse anymore, but this is not how I pictured tonight.

I bite down on my lip. My mind is spinning. Tonight I should be dancing on Cloud 9, full of joy and giddiness, in love for the first time in my life, and with the most wonderful of men.

I'm not.

I'm torn, my heart cracking in two.

I suck in a breath and force my shoulders to drop.

I've got this.

Saying it in my head doesn't make me feel like I do.

I pull my lips into a line and nod.

It's time.

Vladimir offers me his hand as the gates are pulled open, and I step out as my name is announced.

"Princess Madeline of Malveaux," the herald announces, and just as they did at my presentation in Malveaux, every set of eyes at the Lunar Ball turns to look at me, standing high up on the stone steps, feeling absolutely alone.

I force a smile, telling myself this will be over soon.

Just breathe.

Then I spot him.

Alex.

My heart throbs with unspoken words. Words of love.

He's wearing a tailored jacket in a deep red wine color, with golden embroidered details on the cuffs and chest, matched with a crisp, coordinating vest and pants.

He looks like Simon, the Duke of Hastings from *Bridgerton*, only with a set of small wings attached to his back to fit the ball's "enchanted" theme.

With soft music floating through the air, I take the steps

down to the grass. He holds out his hand, the look in his eyes telling me exactly how he feels about me. "My Texas Princess," he says with a smile that's so full of love, my heart begins to bang like it's in an 80s rock band, laying down a rousing tune.

"Alex," I murmur.

He lifts my hand to his lips, his kiss soft on my skin. "You make an absolutely breath-taking fairy."

"Ditto," I reply with a short-lived smile. "Alex, we need to talk."

He raises his brows, a smile playing on his lips. "Ah, the words every man wants to hear when he's got a pair of fairy wings attached to his back."

"I'm serious."

His features drop. "I know we do."

"You do?" I ask in surprise.

A hush falls over the crowd and Alex peers over my shoulder.

"He's *here*?"

"What? Who?" I swivel around to see and it's as though a lightning bolt has etched a shocking image directly into my brain.

No! It can't be!

Can it?

It's someone I haven't laid eyes on since I was a child. Someone for whom I owe the very existence of my new life to.

Prince Nicolas.

He briefly greets his parents and the King and Queen of Ledonia, before he walks over to Alex and me. With a broad smile on his face, he offers us a bow. "Ah, my niece, Maddie, the most beautiful fairy of them all."

"Uncle Nicolas?" I ask as I take him in. Like Alex, he's

wearing a suit with a pair of wings, although his is pale blue, reminding me of those terrible tuxes guys at my high school wore ironically to Prom. Although taller, he reminds me so much of my mom, particularly the set of his blue eyes, and the way his lips form a smile.

I catch my breath.

"The very same," he replies with a warm smile that tugs at my heartstrings, reminding me of simpler times when Mom was still here and I didn't have an impossible decision to make.

But perhaps Nicolas's reappearance will give me an answer?

"Nicolas. It's good to see you," Alex says, pumping his hand. "Good and unexpected, I might say."

"I thought it was about time I made an appearance. Don't you?"

He can say that again.

"But what are you doing here?" I ask, still trying to wrap my head around his sudden appearance. Despite not having laid eyes on him, he's loomed so large in my life.

"I do so love this ball. I've come every year since I can remember," he replies, without replying at all.

"But—" I begin.

What does it mean that my uncle has turned up out of the blue? Is he here to claim his throne? Is he here to formally abdicate?

And what does it mean for *me*?

"Are you all right, Maddie?" Alex asks quietly, and I nod, although throwing the Nicolas, puppet master himself, into the already complicated mix, I feel pretty dang far from all right.

"Ah, a drink," Uncle Nicolas says as a server arrives with a silver tray filled with glasses of champagne. He takes one and hands it to me. "One for you, Maddie."

"It's French, so it's fine," Alex assures me.

"No need for cordial?" I ask, trying out a smile while my brain is abuzz.

He gives me a reassuring smile. "None."

I thank my uncle and take a sip, the bubbles tickling my nose. It's certainly not the terrible stuff we make in Malveaux, and I resolve to help the champagne makers improve their product in whatever way I can if I become Queen.

But…is that even a possibility now? And if it is, how the heck do I feel about it?

The soft background music is replaced by the sound of bagpipes.

"Ah, the ball is about to officially begin," Nicolas says with approval. "I do so love this part. Did you know, Madeline, that Ledonia has a bagpipe tradition because Queen Jane, a Scottish princess who married into the royal family over 400 years ago, brought the pipes with her?"

I look at him blankly. "No, I…no," I mutter.

Of course I don't know that. I barely know my own name right now, thanks to my thoughts twisting and turning like leaves caught in a tornado.

We watch the small figure of the piper, lit up by a single spotlight in the middle distance. He's dressed in full Scottish regalia as he stands on a grassy knoll. The melody is haunting and reverberates with a rich, deep tone, swirling around us.

Its poignancy tugs at my heartstrings, emotion welling up inside of me.

Tonight is a *lot*.

Alex reaches for my hand and I flash him a grateful look.

"It'll all be all right," he tells me.

Oh, just wait until I tell him what's going on.

The piper finishes his tune, and the emcee announces the first dance of the evening.

Nicolas offers me his hand. "Shall we? It seems rather appropriate, don't you think? And besides, it'll give us a chance to speak."

I glance at Alex, and he smiles at me.

"I'll talk to you afterwards," he says and I nod.

Uncle Nicolas leads me onto the dance floor, and I can feel every eye at the ball trained on us. As the music begins to play, he places one hand on my waist and takes my hand in his, and we begin to move slowly around. I for one am thankful that with such an audience, I'd paid attention in my dance lessons, but my uncle leads me with confidence, so all I have to do is let go and move with him.

"I owe you an apology," he says.

"Because my life got turned upside down when you left?" I ask, tongue in cheek—with a sting.

"For exactly that. I should have reached out to you about what my leaving could mean for you, and for that I'm truly sorry."

I can see honesty in his eyes. "Thanks," I murmur.

He twirls me around and then pulls me back into his arms.

"I imagine you want to know why I'm here."

"The thought had crossed my mind." I add hurriedly, "Not that it's not nice to see you, of course, Uncle Nicolas."

He smiles, and it reminds me of the way Mom's face would light up when she smiled. "You make a beautiful princess. I've enjoyed watching your transformation over the last few weeks."

"It's been a lot."

He chuckles. "I imagine it has. My parents think you're wonderful."

"*They're* wonderful," I reply with vehemence. "So welcoming and kind."

But we can't keep talking around the topic. I need to know.

"Uncle Nicolas...are you *back* back? As in, you're not abdicating?"

Part of me wants him to say yes, that he's back, it's all been a horrible mistake because he's thought about it and he wants to be King. It would mean I could be with Alex and this whole gut-wrenching conundrum will be resolved.

But the other part wants him to tell me he's leaving, and the Crown is mine.

He surprises me by asking, "What do *you* want, Maddie?"

It's a question with which I've been grappling for two days now.

He spins me around once more, and when he places his hand on my back, I feel my old friend anxiety spring to life.

"I...I," I begin, but I can't find the words to explain that I want two things, and that they're in total conflict with one another.

He looks into my eyes, his brows pulled together. "That's unfair of me to ask. Perhaps I should tell you my decision instead?"

All I can manage is a nod, because let's face it, me and words are clearly in a fight right now.

"I signed the abdication papers this afternoon."

I come to a crashing halt and stand and stare at him. "You're going through with it?" I ask as my heart thrashes against my chest like it's trying to escape.

So, that's it then. I'm the sole heir. My grandparents' only hope.

"I've seen the way you've conducted yourself. Maddie,

you were born for this role. You do it so naturally, and so much better than I ever could. You might not know it now, but—"

"I know," I say, interrupting. If there's one thing I'm sure of in all this mess, it's that I'm living the life I was always meant to live.

His lips lift into a smile. "You're going to make a wonderful Queen someday."

I open my mouth to speak, but no words come out. We're obviously still in a fight.

By now the dance floor is filled with couples.

"Why did you decide to abdicate?" I ask.

"The truth is I lost my spark for the role. I knew I couldn't do it justice, not like my parents did. Then there was a particularly savage article in the Royal Malveauxian paper, that said because I suffered from bouts of depression, I was unfit to rule."

"That's terrible," I say, aghast.

"It is, but it gave me an out, an out I leapt on. You see, I've never really felt as though this should be my life. I know that sounds so terribly odd, but it's the way I feel."

I smile, knowing precisely what he means.

"Is your new life a better fit for you?" I ask.

"It's only just beginning. A work in progress, if you will. But the outlook seems positive."

The song finishes, and he bows his head. "Thank you for the dance, Princess Madeline. And for everything."

I watch as though in a daze as he places a kiss on my cheek, and then turns to greet other guests, as if he didn't just spark a wildfire in my life.

So, that's it. I'm to be Queen. There's no other option.

Suddenly desperate to get out of here, I weave my way through the dancers, a swirl of wings and otherworldly costumes.

It's then that I come face to face with Alex, and everything feels totally overwhelming and all I can think of is *escape*.

"I need to get out of here," I say.

He takes my hand in his. "Come with me." He leads me through the throngs of guests, behind one of the tall hedges lit up in fairy lights. There we find a statue of two lovers entwined in a kiss, lit in a soft glow, the sound of the music dulled. It's an utterly romantic spot, one I would love to spend time in with Alex under normal circumstances.

But tonight is the very opposite of normal.

Without even uttering a word, he pulls me against him and presses an urgent kiss to my lips. "I've missed you so much," he breathes before he kisses me once more. It's dizzying and passionate and makes the lid that's barely holding my emotions threaten to pop right off.

"I've missed you, too," I reply.

He wraps his big arms around me and holds me close against his chest. It's exactly what I need right now, and I hang on, soaking up every drop of reassurance.

"Everything is going to be all right," he murmurs against my ear once more.

His warm breath tickles the skin of my neck, and all I want to do is stay in his arms forever—and for his words to be true.

But the heavy brick I've been carrying around fills my belly.

"Alex, I need to tell you something," I say, pulling back to look up into his eyes. "Nicolas has abdicated."

His eyes widen. "He's finally done it?"

I bite down on my lip and nod.

"So, you're going to be Queen."

"I—" I steel myself before I say, "Alex, I need to tell you something else. Something to do with us."

"I know," he replies, his voice tender.

I crinkle my brow. "You know?"

"Sofia told me about it today at the pool, and then I confirmed it with Father. You have a terrible decision to make. A future with me, or your Crown."

My throat tightens as my eyes fill with tears. "Then how can you say everything will be okay? I love you but I can't be with you if I'm to be Queen, and you know how much that means to me. To my family. I can't let them down, but I don't want to lose you, either."

The lid on my emotions falls to the ground. Tears spring to my eyes and begin to spill down my cheeks, my throat tight and hot.

"You love me?" His voice comes out in a whisper, and I nod as I bite down on my lip.

His face creases into a heart-stopping smile. "I love you, too," he says, his eyes like fire in the evening light. Softly, he wipes my tears away with his fingertips. "Which is why I know we can find a way, Maddie, just as your parents did."

"But...but my mom gave all this up for love." I gesture around me. "I don't know if I can do that, even though I know I love you so much."

His smile reaches into my heart and tugs on it. He places a hand softly on my cheek. "One thing I promise you, Texas, I don't want to wait any longer for the rest of my life to begin, and I want that life to be with you."

I want to ask him how, to reiterate what an impossible position I'm in, but all I can do is gaze back at him, this man I love.

This man who's changed my world forever.

He pushes my hair behind my ear, his eyes soft. "Today, after Sofia told me, I made a decision of my own."

I try to swallow down the lump in my throat, my heart banging to the beat of a frenetic drum. "What did you decide?"

"I decided that you are the queen of my heart, and I want you to have the world, my most beautiful, sweetest Maddie. You deserve it, all of it."

What does he mean? Does he mean he's decided to step back and allow me to take the throne? But I don't want that. I want *him*.

"You once told me I was two different people: one around my father, and one around everyone else. Maddie, those words have stayed with me."

"I shouldn't have said anything. It was none of my business."

"I'm glad you did. They made me look at myself and what sort of relationship I have with him. I don't expect the closeness you have with your dad. That's not who he is. But I can be myself around him, tell him what I want, what I need. I can ask for his respect."

My heart bursts with pride. "You're amazing, you know that?"

"Not as amazing as you. I talked to him about it today, before the ball."

"How did it go?"

"I told him I've fallen in love with you and that one day, I intend to ask you to marry me."

I suck in a breath. He's going to ask me to marry him?

My heart squeezes. "You did?"

"You must know the depth of my feelings for you. How can I even think of a life without you?"

I'm lightheaded with happiness, the love I feel for this man filling every cell in my body—until my predicament pulls me back to my senses with a sickening thud.

"If we marry, I can't be heir," I tell him, fresh tears springing to my eyes.

His lips lift into a smile, at total odds with the turmoil raging in my heart. "It doesn't need to be that way. I told father that if we are to marry, I'll step down as his heir."

"You said *what?*" I ask, my voice almost a whisper.

He smiles at me as though this is the easiest choice he's ever made in his life. "Maddie, I would give up everything to be with you, to make you happy. To love you."

"But…but your Crown. Your father. Your country. All this."

"I've never sought the limelight. I've never really wanted to be king. You know me and politics."

"But that's not enough for you to give it all up, is it?"

"All my life I've searched for meaning, and I've only found it in your eyes. In your love. Maddie, you've offered me what I want and need, and I won't give that up for anything, not even the chance to be King, and certainly not to please my father."

I gawk at him, my heart going all kinds of crazy. "You'd do that for me?"

"I already have. And besides, I've got three siblings, one of whom is rather excited about what this whole turn of events could mean."

I know he's talking about his older sister, Sofia. He's told me she's always wanted to be their father's heir, despite Max being the next in line after Alex, and feels the Ledonian law of succession is outdated and wrong.

He leans down and presses his lips against mine with the softest, most emotional of kisses. "You can be Queen of Malveaux, and we can be together."

"Oh, Alex. I love you so much."

My heart fills with the depth of his love, with the depth of his sacrifice.

I never dreamt I would fall in love with such a worthy man. But now that I've found him, and he's moved Heaven and Earth to be with me, I know one thing for absolute certain.

I will never let go.

Epilogue

Alex

" It's Christmastime in Ledonia and after months of reports of the country's hottest couple together, from the slopes of the Pyrenees to the beaches of Spain, our Prince of Sheer Sexiness has been spotted walking hand-in-hand through the snow in Villadorata with his princess. Although it pains this reporter to even type these words, rumor has it we may hear wedding bells in their future, officially making

Princess Madeline the luckiest woman on the face of the planet.

#ICalledItFirst
#SomeGirlsGetAllTheLuck

Yours in jealousy,

Fabiana Fontaine xx

The air shimmers with the magic of Christmas as the snow falls gently outside. Towering above us in the toasty living room, warmed by the open fire, the grand tree twinkles with a thousand lights, its branches adorned with glistening baubles and gold ribbons. The scent of pine mingles with the subtle fragrance of cinnamon, the smell of Christmas in Ledonia.

The past few months with Maddie have been nothing short of amazing. After that night at the Lunar Ball, we've spent a lot of time together, getting to know one another better and better. With her kindness, sincerity, and heart—not to mention her crazy hot sexiness—she really is the perfect woman for me. And from what she says and the way I sometimes catch her looking at me, I'm the perfect man for her.

Who knew our love story would start with a punch to the nose? Maddie calls it our "meet ugly", a play on the American phrase "meet cute".

I call it destiny.

Sitting on the sofa, I swing a possessive arm around the

woman I love. Maddie looks up at me, and we share a smile.

We've had dinner with my parents, who have already retired for the evening, leaving just us 20-somethings to enjoy a hot chocolate in front of the fire in our matching, intensely embarrassing Christmas jumpers.

This year we've all got a garish Santa sitting proud in the center of the jumper, with textured Christmas trees in red and green adorning the arms. Hands-down, it could win any ugly jumper contest, but I admit, there's something wonderful about Maddie wearing the same jumper, all of us equally dorky.

"This is so exciting. Alex has never brought a girl home, especially not for Christmas," Amelia says as she sits back in her seat in front of the fire.

"It's certainly a first. He must be deadly serious about you, Maddie," Sofia says.

"Are you deadly serious about me?" Maddie whispers, and I plant a kiss on her cheek by way of my answer.

Max lets out a laugh and we all turn to look at him. "What?" he asks.

"You can't just let out a random laugh out of nowhere and not explain why," I reply.

"Not unless you've totally lost your marbles, that is," Amelia adds.

"It's the two of you," he says, gesturing at Maddie and me. "You're so"—he searches for the word— "soppy."

It's our turn to laugh.

"Love does that to you, little brother," I reply with a happy smirk. "You'll find out one day."

"Ugh," Max complains as he pats Calypso at his side, one of our Welsh Springer Spaniels. "So cheesy."

"We might be cheesier than a chili con queso at a

Houston restaurant," Maddie replies. "But we like it that way."

"Oh, yeah. The cheesier the better." I tighten my arm around her shoulders.

"Mummy already loves you, Maddie," Amelia says. "Father? Well, he'll come 'round."

Truth be told, I'm not sure Father ever will come around. Not entirely. The day of the Lunar Ball when I told him I was removing myself from the line of succession in order to be with the woman I love, he told me it was the worst day of his life and that he would never recover from my disloyalty. It was dramatic, but then he wouldn't be Father if it wasn't.

Since standing up to him and telling him what I wanted, I've discovered a new-found sense of strength. I may be his son, but I am also a man, and putting Maddie's needs first, diving into loving her, has been the most rewarding decision of my life.

We've made small inroads in our relationship, and I for one am trying to chip away at his granite exterior. However he's treated me in the past, he's my father, and we love one another, even if he finds it hard to show.

It's very much a work in progress.

Father and I agreed that we wouldn't share the news with the media until Maddie and I are engaged—him in the hope that our love would fizzle and die, and me in the knowledge that it never will.

Which brings me to tonight.

I give Sofia the signal, and she shoots me a knowing smile before she stretches her arms in the air, letting out a loud yawn. "I'm shattered. Time for bed, everyone."

"You can't tell us when to go to bed," Amelia complains.

"I think you'll find I can," she replies, gesturing with her head at the door. "You too, Max. Let's go."

Subtle? Not particularly. Or at all.

Amelia is about to complain until she spies the look on my face, which tells her all she needs to know. "You know what? You're right, Sofe. We've got a big day tomorrow, and now that I think about it, I am rather tired. Come on, Max." She prods our youngest sibling with the toe of her shoe.

"Don't kick me," he complains.

"For someone who's about to graduate from Cambridge in the New Year, you're still such a baby," Amelia complains.

"Max," Sofia says in her uncompromising older sister tone.

"All right." He ruffles Calypso's fur a final time before he pushes himself to his feet. "You two coming?"

"I think we'll stay here for a bit," I reply, my nerves suddenly ratcheting up a notch.

Max's eyes dart between Maddie and me. "Oh, I get it. More soppiness."

I press my lips together to bite back a smile. "Something like that."

"I do not need to be here for that," Max replies as Sofia hurries him from the room.

She looks back, giving me the thumbs up, before she closes the door behind her, leaving Maddie and I alone.

"What was that about?" Maddie asks.

"My family being my family."

"I love your family."

"I know you do."

"Now, tell me all about this soppiness you've got planned," she says, placing her hand on my chest and smiling up at me.

344

"It involves us standing up for starters," I say as I rise to my feet and offer her my hand.

"Okay."

I slip my hand in hers and lead her over to the Christmas tree.

"Look. There are a couple of new ornaments," I say, my nerves and excitement duking it out.

She throws me a confused look. "Good to know."

I point out the decorations in question.

"The Texas boot?" she asks, her face lit up in a smile.

"A little worse for wear following my polo matches, but it felt appropriate to hang it here in your honor."

She places a soft kiss on my lips. "That's so sweet."

"I want you to feel a part of my family."

"I already do."

"There's another new one." I point at a leather and gold bound booklet, about the size of her palm. "Open it," I instruct. "I think it says something inside."

She opens and peers at the words. "Oh. It's in Ledonian."

"Can you read it?"

She crinkles her brow, and even though I didn't think it possible, I love her even more. "It says, '*Ali mi sposaria porotil mano de Texas.*' I'm sorry, my Ledonian isn't very good yet."

As she tries to work it out, I drop to one knee and fish a small black velvet box from my pocket, my nerves suddenly disappearing as I gaze up at her. What's there to be nervous about when you already know something deep in your bones?

"Do you know what that means?" she asks, and as she turns her attention from the ornament to me, her mouth forms an 'o'.

I reach for her hand and take it in mine. "It says, will you marry me, my Texas Princess?"

She sucks in a breath, her free hand flying to her chest. "Oh, Alex! Yes, I will marry you. A thousand, million, trillion times, yes!"

Her response is electrifying me, my joy exploding like fireworks.

"I spoke with your grandparents and they gave their consent."

Her eyes widen. "They knew about this? They didn't let on."

"I swore them to secrecy." Gently, with shaking hands, I slide my grandmother's diamond engagement ring onto her finger.

"Oh, Alex. It's beautiful," she gushes as she admires the round diamond, encircled with rows of smaller diamonds. It catches the light as she moves her hand.

I spring to my feet and collect her in my arms. "You're beautiful, inside and out. I cannot imagine loving you more than I do this day, but I promise I'll keep loving you forever."

She slides her hand behind my neck and pulls me to her lips, kissing me with such depth of emotion I swear I actually can feel her love.

"I love you, Alex. I can't wait to be your wife," she says before she claims my mouth with hers once more.

I lift her up and she lets out a squeal before she wraps her legs around me, peppering me with kisses. I hold her close, relishing everything this woman in my arms is to me.

We started out hating one another at first punch, but she's grown to be the single most important part of my world, and I cannot wait to spend the rest of my life with her, the woman I love.

THE END

Acknowledgments

I have wanted to write a royal romcom for many years, and finally getting to do it was everything I hoped it would be. What little girl doesn't dream of becoming a princess? In this book, I wanted to tap into that fantasy, plucking a regular American girl from her not-so-special life, and dropping her straight into a Royal European court—in a land where I get to make up the rules. Cue evil laughter.

To complete this childhood fantasy, of course I needed to have a dashing prince, only a grown up version of him: someone with a past, with his own needs and desires, aka not just a dashing prince in a pair of tights and a fancy top.

So, I created my total fish out of water princess and my dashing, reformed bad boy prince, threw them together, made them dislike one another from the get go, and then we weaved a love story around them, right up to their fairy tale HEA. It was all so royally satisfying, and the little girl in me loved every minute of it.

Now, onto the acknowledgments. I want to give a big shout out to all my loyal readers. You know I wouldn't be doing this without you, and I so value each and every one of you. This is my 26th book, which feels a little amazing to me, but I know I've got at least another 26 books in me, and I hope you'll stick around for this crazy ride, laughing, crying, and swooning right there with me as I continue to share my stories with the world.

I've been relying on my incredible critique partner, Jackie Rutherford, for many years now. In fact, I don't know where I'd be without her in my writing life. She's not only an amazing writer herself, who gives me invaluable feedback on my work, but she's a good friend. I feel so very lucky to have her in my life on both counts.

This time, I had my wonderful assistant, Cathy Jeppsen, read the book before it went out to beta readers. As an avid romcom reader, she gave me invaluable advice and encouragement. Thank you so much, Cathy. Let's do this again!

I also want to thank the members of my advanced reader Super Team who stepped in to help me out with proofreading this book. You ladies did an amazing job, picking up all those pesky typos that somehow got through my editing process, and I want to thank you all so very much for your eagle eyes and willingness to help me out of a tight spot.

Dylan from Simply Dylan designs made the figures on the cover once more. When she sent me Prince Alexander for the first time, I was in Las Vegas at a writers' conference, and I literally jumped up and down on the spot in excitement. The perfect balance of privilege, good looks, and arrogance: my Prince Alex. Of course, being a writers' conference, I didn't get any odd looks. We writers understand the importance of a great book cover. Thank you, Dylan, you always does a great job for me, and it's a breeze working with you.

Thank you, readers. I so hope you loved Maddie and Alex's book.

Kate xoxo

About the Author

Kate O'Keeffe is a *USA TODAY* bestselling and award-winning author who writes exactly what she loves to read: laugh-out-loud romantic comedies with swoon-worthy heroes and gorgeous feel-good happily ever afters. She lives and loves in beautiful Hawke's Bay, New Zealand with her family.

When she's not penning her latest story, Kate can be found hiking up hills (slowly), traveling to different countries around the globe, and eating chocolate. A lot of it.

Also by Kate O'Keeffe

Royally Kissed series:
The Backup Princess

Sisters & Sweethearts Series:
Faking It With the Grump
Faking It With My Best Friend
Faking It With the Guy Next Door

It's Complicated Series:
Never Fall for Your Back-Up Guy
Never Fall for Your Enemy
Never Fall for Your Fake Fiancé
Never Fall for Your One that Got Away

Love Manor Romantic Comedy Series:
Dating Mr. Darcy
Marrying Mr. Darcy
Falling for Another Darcy
Falling for Mr. Bingley (spin-off novella)

Friends & Forevers Series:
No More Bad Dates
No More Terrible Dates
No More Horrible Dates

Flirting with Forever Series:

One Last First Date

Two Last First Dates

Three Last First Dates

Four Last First Dates

Wellywood Romantic Comedy Series:

Styling Wellywood

Miss Perfect Meets Her Match

Falling for Grace

Standalone title:

One Way Ticket

Writing as Lacey Sinclair:

Manhattan Cinderella

The Right Guy

Made in United States
Troutdale, OR
03/12/2024

18405198R00217